THE MOST BEAUTIFUL ROT

BY OCEAN CAPEWELL

P.O. Box 22274
Oakland, CA 94607

Cover art by the lovely & talented Jenifer Cooney.

Capewell, Ocean, 1982-

The Most Beautiful Rot / Ocean Capewell

ISBN: 978-0-9850385-4-0

1. Lesbians--Fiction 2. Bisexual women--Fiction.
3. Punk Culture--United States 4. Housing, Cooperative--United States--Fiction
5. Subculture--United States--Fiction
1. Title

Printed on recycled paper at 1984 Printing,
Oakland, CA

First printing January 2014

TABLE OF CONTENTS

PART ONE: TABITHA

CHAPTER ONE

The house was full of rotting food, but we couldn't help it. It was America's fault for wasting so much, for un-creatively throwing it all away. We were the bottom feeders, the scavengers, the magicians that turned their garbage into gold. The dumpsters in our city had all magically morphed into incinerators or trash compactors. But the ones out in the suburbs were hardly more than unauthorized food banks. The house was full of rotting food, and tonight we were going to go out and get more.

I flooded into the car with my three housemates: Jasmine, with the knuckle tattoos and disarming smile; Lydia, the tough femme with the vintage dresses and cat-eye glasses; and Xandria, our semi-reformed crusty with a truly raucous and glorious laugh. We sat on the duct-taped seats as Lydia turned the ignition key and the car sputtered to life. She pulled out of the spot like a pro, and we were on our way.

"Yo, the funniest thing happened at work today," I said. "Violet came to visit me, and I gave her some free coffee, and we were standing around talking, but then it got busy, so I, like, had to abandon her for a minute. And this totally crazy old guy comes up to her and starts talking to her. He's wearing this really dirty suit jacket with a fake flower in the front pocket--"

"God, your girlfriend attracts all the nutjobs," Lydia interjected.

"Yeah, I know. Anyway, he goes up to her and says, 'You ain't from this city, huh?' and she says no and asks him how he can tell. And he like, cups his hands around his ears, and then he did this"—I bent my finger and ran it over the curve of my head, to suggest a band—"And Violet is like, 'You can see my *aura*?' and he's like, 'No! No! Your goddamn earmuffs! Nobody in this city wears earmuffs, except for you!' And then he stomps away."

Lydia said, "Well, he's wrong! I wear earmuffs, and I'm from here! I got these *amazing* heart-shaped ones that match my red coat perfectly at Village Thrift a month ago. The next time you see him, just send him down to me and I'll straighten him out." Lydia worked super-long hours at some troubled-teen social service agency downtown, but somehow found the energy to compile zany outfits and dig through trash all night.

"Whoa," Xandria said, "does he have curly hair?" I nodded. "Broken glasses?" I nodded again. "I think I know that guy." Xandria knew all the wingnuts. She'd lost a bunch of teeth early in life, and had gotten a swirly, intricate tattoo that stretched across her left temple, snuck over to her forehead, then spiraled down into the depths of her cheek. She'd gotten it when she was nineteen and fucked up on something. The tattoo, her gappy smile and her bad attitude had made her not able to work a regular job, so she worked odd jobs sometimes—pissing on a Craigslist businessman's face, helping the carnies raise the tent when the circus came to town, or picking blueberries during harvest season. But her main job was sitting with a cardboard sign and coin-filled hat downtown, with all the other wingnuts. She knew them well.

"Yeah!" I said. "He's got those really thick glasses that make his eyes all big, with the duct tape on one side..."

"Yeah, that's him. I know that guy. He's not so bad."

"I hope we get some kale tonight," said Jasmine, who was fond of randomly changing the subject. "My body is totally craving leafy green nutrients."

"Kale is pretty good, but you know how you have to pull the stems out? Because they're, like, too tough to chew?" Lydia said.

"Kale chewing gum," Jasmine said, almost dreamily.

"I hate that. It always makes me feel like I'm wasting so much."

"Um, well, I guess we can try and think of something to do with them," I said.

Dead silence for a second, and then Jasmine said, "I can put them on my head like antennas, and pretend that I'm an ant!"

"I could make an anti-christmas wreath with them," Lydia ruminated, flicking her turn signal.

"I could make a diorama of a clear-cut forest, and use them as trees. I'll carve a logger out of a moldy potato," Jasmine pondered.

"Just throw them in the fuckin' compost pile. Who cares?" Xandria said, and somehow that comment struck us all silent. Not necessarily in a bad way. Maybe the conversation had just rolled to its natural end. Or maybe it was the landscape that was making us quiet. We'd left the big buildings of our city behind, and had temporarily traded them in for boxier, shorter ones. The signs, lit up against the road, made it look like we could be anywhere.

I could be back in Ohio, with a carload of friends I had nothing in common with, just driving and driving with nowhere to go. But somehow I'd jumped out of the path of that train. Now, once my friends and I pulled our prize from the dumpsters we could go back home to the city, and these endless chain stores would just be a memory. Or not even a memory, a background dreariness that was instantly forgotten. The streetlights flashed across everyone's faces, touching Lydia and Xandria in the front seat first, and then radiating to Jasmine and me in the backseat. I was bathed in light for just a second, because we were going fast. Light and dark and light again.

The cheesy commercial hip-hop station was on and I was feeling okay, dancing ever so slightly, almost against my will. Lydia and Xandria started talking again, but I couldn't quite follow; Lydia's sharp voice and hitting-the-steering-wheel punctuation; Xandria's quiet, guttural additions. I didn't need to know what they were saying. I could have stayed like that forever, surrounded by the sound of their voices. I almost didn't care if we ever got anywhere.

But eventually, the dumpster we'd come for appeared on the horizon. So we pulled door-handles or climbed over seats, and there we were. We were the only people in the parking lot, so huge it was almost a parking prairie, and there was that quiet excitement around us that only grows underneath the orange glow of streetlights.

All of us had roles that we normally filled on secret missions like this, and tonight was no exception. Jasmine leaned against the car, looking out for the cops. This role was small, but important. Xandria had gone to jail when she was younger, for doing exactly what we were doing now. She was there for three weeks for not having the money to pay her fine, or maybe just refusing to. Or maybe nobody cared enough to bail her out. I couldn't remember. She didn't talk about it much, but when she did, her stories were so calm, so even, her voice not betraying anything. Still, she had a haunted quality to her, and it only got spookier when she talked about jail.

Xandria stood next to the dumpster, so she could run everything back to the car. Lydia stood by the open trunk, ready to load everything in as quickly as possible. And I climbed over the top of the dumpster. I always jumped right in, without even looking. I knew if I hesitated, I'd get scared. I'd think about what I was doing, all the things that could go wrong. And the most exciting moment was when you're in the air, when you haven't landed yet, when you have no idea what's going to be underneath you. Usually it's sharp cardboard, the edges poking you without obtaining proper consent. Usually it's rotting tuna salad leaking out of a hole in the bag and spraying all over your vegan ass. But sometimes, it was crates of perfect bell peppers, so beautiful it hurt to look. It was gallons of juice that expired tomorrow, but tonight they were delicious and they were free.

I landed on my feet, tumbling forward a little. My knee hit something hard, and I pretended it didn't hurt. Gotta keep moving. Slogged over to a trash bag and touched it gingerly, only to discover that it was squishy and wet. I picked up another one and felt some round, hard globes. I poked a hole in the bag's thin membrane and used two fingers to widen it, and then stuck my hand in and felt around—oranges, or grapefruits, maybe. I squeezed about five or six, and only two felt rotten, so I heaved it over my head to Xandria. It was a precarious balance between not bruising any more fruit and not wasting any time. I turned back to the shin-deep mound and unflinchingly put my hand inside another bag. My hands got all wet and sticky and cold. I shuddered, but didn't think too hard about what I was touching. I was getting used to shaking coffee grounds off the cuffs of my pants, used to my shoes getting so slick with grease I could skate across parking lots. I had to keep going.

Growing up, I'd choked on white bread and fluorescent macaroni and boiled hot dogs. My mom grew chubby on mayonnaise and beer, my brother ate corn chips and popsicles and was thin as a bone. No wonder they were crazy. They were crazy, but I wasn't. I made it out of there, and I know that if they could see me now, they would hang their heads in shame for me. They didn't understand that I was superhuman, that trash could make me grow. They didn't understand that I built my own family; that I found them in little scraps and put them together to make something beautiful. They were not there to see us, drunk at two a.m. on wine and pie, dancing in the kitchen; smashing old TVs at the dump; telling the hardest stories and then getting into gleeful rotting tomato fights. They would have wondered how we could live with the stains on our walls. But the stains made me remember that night. They made me proud that we all had so much passion fermenting inside of us that it bubbled over; that there was no other way to show it but to take a tomato and hurl. The splatter, the soft juice, the satisfying thud.

And who was it hurting, really? The tomatoes were slimy and inedible. We didn't pay for them. The landlord lived all the way in the suburbs and was too scared of our neighborhood to come poking around our house. He would never see the walls until it was time for us to move, and the way things were going I never wanted to move. But if that day did come, we could scrub it off, we could paint it over, we could make it seem like nothing had ever happened.

But that day was not here yet, so we left the stains where they were. Because something *had* happened, and we didn't want to pretend that it hadn't. And yeah, sometimes I did look at the walls, with the smashed-up fruitflies stuck to the stains, the pale gross splashes everywhere, and think: *What a dump*. But that feeling would pass soon enough, and the stains would reclaim their status as story-telling old crones.

I had just heaved the final bag of veggies over my head to Xandria. She ran it over to Lydia, and they began re-distributing all the vegetables into other bags and boxes, because the trunk was too full for another bag. Jasmine went to help them, pulling out a few pieces that were obviously too rotten to eat and tossing them back into the dumpster. Vegetables whizzed past my head, so close I could feel the slight breeze they made as they cut through the air, hoping that I wouldn't get hit in the face. I placed my hands on the edge, stepped up on the little handle inside that always made such a handy jumping-off point, and swung one leg over, prepared myself for the impact of boots against concrete.

No matter how many times I climb out of dumpsters, I always hesitate on the lip. Going in I am all footloose and fancy free; coming back out is another story. One leg in, one leg out; trying to figure out the exact angle to jump down. Do I slide? Do I leap? What if I don't swing my leg over high enough and I fall off and bang my tailbone? What if I fuck myself up? I can't fuck myself up. I have to do this right. The concrete below won't forgive me. It doesn't care that I don't have health insurance or that I can't go to work if I break my ankle. Concrete means business, and nowhere is that more obvious than the top of a dumpster.

From my vantage point on top I could see that a car was coming right for us, peeling through the parking lot. Oh shit, the headlights. Headlights mean trouble. I saw Xandria's back tense up and thought of the policeman's boots on it. I thought of Xandria, in general. I saw her shoulders lock and her eyes narrow, ready to fight anyone, anything. I saw her hands shaking, not so ready to fight after all.

The mysterious car screeched to a halt about ten feet away from the dumpster. A short white guy opened the door and popped his head out, his face contorted. "What the fuck are you girls doing?" Who was he? Disgruntled manager? Volunteer busybody? No-life Ned? His back was to my friends, so he was choosing me as our spokesperson. The trunk was slammed shut and they were coming towards me.

"I--uh--I--we're just hungry. And you guys, um, throw out so much...food..." I said, looking down at him, at my left foot hanging in the air, directly above the endless expanse of parking lot. My friends, but also his car. Beyond them was the road, not so busy at this hour, but still providing a distraction. My right foot was suspended above the dumpster. Smelly, dark, but I could hide, maybe.

"Hungry, huh? Aww, that's *sooo sad!*" he yelled, in a mock-caring voice. He was still in the car, still buckled in, on the ground that seemed so far away. Shiny silver beer cans made a frat-boy pyramid on the floor next to him. His hair was clean and pre-shaped, but he hadn't shaved in a few days. He was wearing a jacket with a few buttons undone, showing off a faded shirt. "Why don't you get a goddamn job?" he slurred.

"I have a job," I said. Maybe not the zingiest comeback, but it's not like I'm on the debate team, you know? And it's true, I do. Coffee slinger at the train station, 5am to noon. But that doesn't pay enough for things like fresh vegetables. Why was I telling him, anyway? It's not like he cared.

I felt something on my left calf. I was so jumpy, I nearly fell backwards into the mounds of garbage. It was Lydia's hand, reaching up for mine. "Here, get down," she said. I leaned down, grasped her hand and swung my right leg over, jumped and absorbed the shock with my ankles. She bent backwards slightly but didn't fall, didn't let me fall. She motioned for me to follow her to the car, and I did so numbly, but didn't get inside. I kept one hand on the door handle, not taking my eyes off him.

"Hey," Jasmine growled. "Don't fucking talk to her like that!" He started laughing, this pure disgusted laugh of entitlement, as if the idea of talking to me like a human being was so preposterous that he just had to laugh. I've heard that laugh before. It makes my skin crawl. It reminds me, every time I hear it, that I am absolutely nothing in this world, no matter how hard I work, how smart I am, how much I fight. I have a lot of reminders of this, lots of downward glances and barely-concealed flinches, but none so sharp as the laughter of this drunk sweatpant-ed man.

I didn't do anything about it. I couldn't. But in my self-induced paralysis, my eyes could still move and I saw Jasmine purposefully striding towards him. I saw a tiny glint in her right hand and I thought, *oh, shit.*

"Yeah, yeah," he snapped, not noticing Jasmine, his eyes still on me. "Just run away, with all your little friends. That's really great of ya."

I wondered if Jasmine had been arrested too, if she'd been beaten by the cops or sent to jail or something. Almost everyone I knew had stories like that; it was just a matter of whether or not they'd gotten around to telling me yet. I did know that she always carried a knife with her, tucked inside her right boot. I had held it once and shivered with the weight of it in my hand. "It's powerful, right?" she had said, exposing her yellowing snaggly teeth in a hard smile. I nodded, holding onto it for a few seconds longer than I should have, reluctant to hand it back to her when it fit in my palm so well.

And now that knife was playing a starring role in this evening's drama. It was powerful, as much so in her hand as it was in mine. I did not breathe as I watched her advance on him. I wanted to say *no, don't.* But at the same time, just for a second, I wanted her to do it. Just so he could never laugh at anyone like that ever again.

But she did not approach the driver's side door, where he was still snickering to himself. She went for the passenger-side rear wheel, and in one beautiful motion, she stabbed his tire. Once the knife was in, she moved it in a circular motion, like she was coring an apple. Her hands were quick and sure and I was positive this wasn't the first time she'd done this, but I wasn't planning on asking too many questions. A huge *whoosh* came out and the tire began to deflate. And then Jasmine ran. We all got in the car in record time, and once we were in, I looked back to see the guy, his door still open, his head turned towards the rapidly deflating tire, yelling, *You think you're so fucking tough, huh? You ain't shit! You ain't shit!* His face was all contorted and he was pointing violently.

Lydia turned the ignition key. The car coughed, but it didn't let us down. As it accelerated shyly, I was quiet again. We all were. I could hear myself breathing, I could feel my heart panicking in my chest. *He was just some stupid guy. And he's gone now,* I told myself. Lydia had cracked the window and was smoking a cigarette, looking pissed off, flicking the ash roughly with her thumb. Xandria was in front of me in the passenger seat, rolling a cigarette on her lap. I saw her arm on the door. Her seat belt was off and her white-girl dreadlocks were blowing slightly in the breeze from the window. I couldn't see her face, but I wanted to.

I turned to Jasmine and looked at her as if she were some text I was trying to memorize: the slight sweat that had spread across her brow, nearly hidden beneath her black stocking cap. She was breathing hard, too, and looked vaguely on the brink of barfing or fainting.

She had taken that paralyzing laugh and broken its spell. How could I thank her for that? She had been sick for a while, so sick that she didn't work at all anymore. I thought of how much energy she must have used up stabbing the tire, how I saw her muscles strain as she pulled it through the thick rubber. She looked totally exhausted, resting her head against the back of the seat. She would probably have to lie down and stare at the wall for hours, like she always did when she exerted herself too much. And she knew that would happen once she pulled the knife out, but she did it anyway. No, really, how could I thank her?

I opened my mouth a few times and then I shut it. I think I might have squeaked once or twice. I was just trying not to cry. Or I was trying to get my breathing back to normal. Weren't they the same thing? It was all so logical, like math: calm breathing equals no crying. So simple. But I didn't have an equals sign. I didn't know how to make it true.

Jasmine looked up, and her eyes met mine. I almost looked away, but didn't. She just nodded in a curt, butch way and said, "We've gotta look out for each other, you know?" I nodded back, super-hard. Fuck those people with my last name, who lived in that little house, who called themselves my family. They scared me into corners, they told me I couldn't, they said I was crazy. They never made me feel like this.

"Yeah, fuck yeah," Xandria said from the front seat. Lydia nodded her assent. It didn't matter that I'd just met all of them a few months ago: I was worthy of a tire-stabbing now, and nothing could have made me more proud. No roses or candy or trinkets could make me feel as loved as that thin blade slicing through rubber, as the stream of air that poured out. I knew what it cost. I knew what it was worth.

"Yeah," I said to Jasmine. "Yeah, we do." We gave each other hard smiles, but inside my heart was jumping around. I met Lydia's eyes in the rear-view mirror. Xandria turned around and looked at us both. The radio sang, *I consider her my blood, and it ain't come no thicker.* We looked at each other, all of us, and we *knew.* We just fucking knew.

CHAPTER TWO

A year before the tire-stabbing, I'd been holed up in a wood-paneled bedroom in Ohio, blasting the local loud-guitar radio station and smoking cigarette after cigarette. I'd leave my room whenever my mom's boyfriend wasn't awake and watching TV. Usually I'd just tiptoe past him as he was snoozing on the couch. I'd wince at the slightest noise, worried that my mom's boyfriend would wake up and yell at me to go to bed. He'd usually stir and snuffle in his sleep and then settle down, and slowly, painfully, on the shitty computer my mom got from the Rent-A-Center, I'd load my email, my heart fluttering, hoping I would have heard from her, hoping she wasn't too busy with finals or roommates or whatever.

I had no idea, yet, that Xandria or Lydia or Jasmine existed. I'd never heard of Asterisk Street or the house that would be my home. I did know about the city they lived in, because my internet girlfriend lived there. Yes, my internet girlfriend. Don't judge me unless you've been a queer teen in rural nowhere, okay? It fucking sucks. All my friends were wallet-chain-wearing dudebros. We'd get high at lunch and talk about bands. Sometimes we'd hang out on the weekend and throw eggs at the jocks' cars or go to the shooting range. We'd drive for hours and hours, the radio loud enough to cover up the fact that we didn't really have anything to say. We only liked each other because we hated everyone else, and we hated everyone else because they hated us.

The only person who I could really talk to was this girl on the internet. I would write her e-mails about my boring days, and what I was thinking about, and everything that ever had happened to me. She would write to me about being in college and feeling lost, her roommate drama, and what she was thinking and everything that had ever happened to her. I only knew her as pixels on a screen, and then handwriting on a mix CD, and then a hesitant voice on the phone. I was willing to ignore the bubbliness of her handwriting and the cliches she spouted in her emails, because she was the only thing I had that was even sort of real.

I worked at the drugstore, saving up money to go visit her after I graduated from high school. I gave my two weeks' notice on graduation day, spent what was supposedly the highlight of my young life behind a cash register, selling film to my classmates' parents. And the day after my job was over, I got on the bus. My plan was to stay with her for a week. If she was as good as I thought she was, I just wouldn't go back home. I was young! I was in love! My mom thought I was meeting a boy! I pulled into this city with only a few hundred carefully-saved bucks, and a suitcase with a few clothes and books and drawings, to meet SkaterGrl69. That screen name alone should have been a red flag, but like I said, I was young and desperate.

The first week was exciting. Within six hours of getting off the bus, I lost my virginity and she finally found out what it's like to have sex with a woman. Fortunately, she'd been kicked out of the dorms by then, so we had a whole crappy apartment to fuck in. She held me one morning, four days in, and said, "I don't want you to go home," and I said, "I don't want to go home!" and it felt so magical that I called my mom to tell her I was staying for longer, that I wasn't sure when I'd be back. I got her voice mail, and she didn't return my call. When my mom finally did call me back, over a week later, it was to ask if she could sell my guitar so her boyfriend could get a new tattoo. So I started to think that I had no home in Ohio anyway, that this girl was my new home.

But too not long after that, I realized that this girl's favorite catchphrases made me clench my teeth, made me grind them. She lived on cheap beef products that made the house stink, she didn't apologize when her cat peed all over my suitcase, she didn't have any political convictions besides "Republicans suck!" and she'd met all her friends hanging out in front of Hot Topic. Her home was decorated in cheesy pin-up girl pictures and glowing, grinning black-light skulls that she bought at flea markets. But it was still better than Ohio--anything was better than Ohio--so I stayed. For four months.

Four months of greasy Chinese take-out and rented movies; of staying up all night either fucking or crying, of being hungry when I didn't have a job and exhausted when I did. Of passive-aggressiveness and silence, of slowdancing naked in the shower. Four months of sitting in front of the TV with nothing to say. Of awkward nights digging my fingernails into the damp label of a 40 while all her friends cackled at something I didn't think was funny at all. Of her blasting the crappy alterna-hits radio station and vacuuming while I was trying to sleep in on my one day off. Of making her come harder than anyone had ever made her come before, looking at the trembling mess of a girl beside me in bed, thinking *I did this,* and feeling so proud. And how she'd cling to me afterward, like I knew some sort of magical secret and she was terrified to let me slip away. Four months of fishing out that crumpled round-trip bus ticket from the bottom of my backpack and wondering if I should get a refund, or if I should use it.

By the time she finally dumped me, I still didn't want to leave. I guess I could have gone back home and gotten into fights with my mom's boyfriend as she rolled her eyes and puffed her cigarette. I'd be calling him a racist motherfucker, he'd be calling me a liberal commie dyke, and my mom would be raising the volume on the TV like we weren't even there. I could go back to my job at the drugstore. I could go back to the shooting range with my friends, who in a few years would probably be getting into shouting matches with stepdaughters of their own. I could do all this, but why? The only reason I could come up with was I'd have enough money to start smoking again. But even though I twitched for cigarettes, it hardly seemed worth it.

No, I was living here now. I'd found a sweet bike in the trash. I had a job. I had a library card. I'd joined a group called Food Not Bon-Bons that fed homeless people with food that grocery stores would have just thrown away. I had friends, I had people who'd go on bike rides with me in the park or awkwardly nod their head with me at shows.

My ex-girlfriend let me sleep on her couch while I looked for a place. Or, more accurately, she let me lie awake on her couch. I wasn't sleeping but instead listening to her annoying sex noises, induced by some moped-riding dude she'd met at the flea market, buying yet another tacky sweatshop black-light skull to add to her enormous collection. Those same noises had sounded really hot when they were in my ear, but from the vantage point of the couch they were earsplitting. Why was she so whiny just before she came? Ugh. They didn't stop until around 4am, which is half an hour before I got up for work.

So I went to the library every day after work and looked for a roommate on CraigsList. I was crazed from not sleeping, so I moved into a practically-unheated basement with a sullen goth boy whose last roommate went crazy and had to move back in with her parents. Another red flag, but I hadn't lost my desperation just yet.

It was nice having my own bedroom and nice not fighting with someone all the time, but the apartment was so dark and so quiet. My roommate never spoke to me except for things like, "Rent's due." "Bills are due." "You wanna get some paper towels?" "You know how to plunge a toilet?" I spent most of my free time reading at the local radical bookstore. It was called Runaway Train Books and it had lots of good shit, employees that didn't yell at you if you just hung out and never bought anything, fair trade coffee and a cute bespectacled dyke owner.

It also had a colorful and informative community bulletin board, and one day a flyer caught my eye: *Roommate wanted for queer-positive, fat-positive, pro-sassiness house on the west side of town. Cheap rent. NO DUDEBROS PLEASE.* I tore a number off, shaking slightly. Only 21 words, but it felt like a tunnel to somewhere better.

I'd slid a quarter out of my jeans and called the number from the payphone across the street. A woman picked up the phone and said "Hello?" with a voice that I could wrap around me like a shawl.

"Hi," I said. "Um, my name is Tabitha, and I just saw your flier at the bookstore. And, um, I need a place to live. I'm, like, queer and kinda fat. I don't know if I'm sassy, but I guess I can try..."

"Ha. That's cute."

"Um, how can you tell?" and her laugh, like bathwater. I wondered if she could also tell that I was a broke-ass nineteen-year-old shivering in a hoodie, spending the last money she had for the day on this phone call. I hoped not. We made plans for me to come over later that evening to look at the room and I hung up.

I rode my squeaky bike over to the house as the sun was setting. I had written the address on my hand--637 Asterisk Street. The house was a dilapidated wood-frame. The front porch was gigantic, but as I stepped on it, I saw that one end of the porch had completely caved in, and there was a hole that was nearly six feet wide. An ashy, weather-beaten couch greeted me, snuggled next to an enormous coffee can full of spent cigarette butts. I pressed the doorbell nervously, as though a dagger would spring out from underneath and gouge my hand.

Jasmine opened the door. I didn't know she was Jasmine, of course. She was just some tall androgynous dyke, with black nerd-glasses and wild wavy hair that looked like it was about to claw its way off her head. Her face said *I could kick the shit out of you if I wanted,* but then it broke into a huge smile, like she recognized me from somewhere. "Are you Tabitha?"

"Yes," I said. She motioned for me to come in, and locked the door behind me with a click, and led me into an overstuffed living room. A short, chubby girl with intensely fascinating glasses sat on the faded blue loveseat, clutching a steaming mug of coffee that read "#1 GRANDPA". A taller, thinner girl sat on the floor, shining some filthy boots with an even filthier rag. Her coffee mug had a gorgeous, leafless tree etched into the side of it. Her face had a not-so-gorgeous black spiral etched into the side of it. They both nodded a hello at me, and then Jasmine motioned to me to follow her through the house. "If you move in here, you'll be moving into Teta's room, so I guess I'll show that to you first." We walked through a room full of boxes of produce, disembodied mannequins, bike rims, newspapers and plywood, and then climbed up a huge wooden staircase.

We crossed the threshold of a room in various states of packedness, with neat piles of books and clothes. The artwork on the wall was mostly of the woodcut-raised-fist variety. The window was huge, and covered by a crooked, home-sewn curtain with spiderwebs printed on it. I pushed it aside and looked out onto the rooftops in the neighborhood. The sun was just sinking beneath the tops of the slummy three-story apartment buildings, casting an eerie light on the cement. I was taken aback for a moment. That stupid basement had nearly made me forget what the sunset looked like.

"Why is she moving out?" I asked, not wanting a repeat of my current hell.

"Oh, I guess she's tired of this city, and she just broke up with her boyfriend, so she's going to live on this crazy subsistence farm in Manitoba."

"Whoa," I said. I couldn't imagine ever being that cool.

"Yeah, it sucks that she's leaving, but she's really stagnating in this city. And she's been, like, really obsessed with permaculture and off-the-grid living so this'll be good for her. I think she's probably leaving her bed behind, if you want it. And her dresser. And I think she's selling or giving away a lot of her stuff, because she's, like, getting a ride with my friend Kendra on this bus that she converted to biodiesel. She's going all around America and Canada in it, giving workshops about how to convert your engine to run on vegetable oil. And I guess Teta is going to hop on board for a few weeks until they get to this farm, because they, like, have a workshop all set up there, and I guess she'll stay and everyone else is going to keep on going. And Teta's a mechanic and Kendra isn't and you really need to bring a mechanic with you if you go on a cross-country veggie oil tour, because that's hell on your engine. But, um, the point is that she doesn't have a lot of space on the bus for things, so she'll be getting rid of a lot of them." We stepped out of the room into the hallway.

"You can look at our rooms, too, if you want. This is Lydia's, she's the girl with the glasses," and the ornately-knobbed door swung open to an immaculate temple of curious trinkets. Knitted cupcakes perched on vintage chairs that were just mismatched enough to suggest that they were from the garbage while at the same time being just nice enough to suggest that they were purchased. A gigantic Frida Kahlo print was hanging next to the elaborate mirror. Pale pink mosquito netting floated above the multi-pillowed queen-sized bed in glorious bunches. Photobooth pictures bloomed from the wall in perfectly spaced formations, and the whole room had a sense of sanctuary.

Next, we shuffled into a room that was really a glorified closet, with a bare futon on the floor, an army bag with clothes spilling out, a few worn-looking pictures taped to the wall, a broken snare drum full of socks and underwear, a teetering tower of box wine in one corner, and one wall covered with pictures of maps that seemed to have been lifted from National Geographic. "This is Xandria's room. She's the other girl. She gets the Facial Tattoo Discount Suite. She can't get a job, so she lives in the storage room for fifty bucks a month."

"Oh, uh, cool."

"Yeah, she is cool. She moved in because she's one of Teta's projects." She gave me a knowing look, and I returned it, even though I didn't actually know. "We were both classmates at Crusty Punk Finishing

School. But Xandria's got an advanced degree in that shit, you know what I'm saying?"

"Did you drop out?" I offered, with a tentative little grin.

"Yeah, I guess you could say that." Jasmine opened the door to her room, showing me model dinosaurs stomping through a pile of cut-up pictures of political figures. There were plastic planets hanging from the ceiling. There was a tower of books stacked high next to the bed. "Or I guess it's more like I couldn't thrive in that climate, you know? So I had to build my own greenhouse."

We continued tromping down the hall. The bathroom had interesting-looking magazines and pamphlets piled high next to the toilet bowl, inside a wooden crate with a peeling label. Then back downstairs—the kitchen sink was lousy with dishes, but the refrigerator was full of good photographs, and Lydia poured me a cup of coffee from a battered white coffeemaker, with a grimy sticker proclaiming DEATH BEFORE DECAF. "You drink it black, right?" I said a shy, nervous *yeah*. "I don't know how, but I could tell." She handed it to me and I placed it between my two hands, looking up at her gratefully, like a real gift. She met my eyes, not looking away until after I did. I sat down at the kitchen table, on a wobbly too-tall stool, and took a tiny first sip. My tongue was not burned, but bathed in its soothing warmth. Xandria shuffled in, and we all sat around the table, looking at each other.

"Well, Tabitha," Lydia began, in a very even, negotiation-friendly voice, "I'm going to tell you a little about the house. Rent for Teta's room is $340 a month, and bills usually are about forty bucks each, more in the winter."

"Okay," I said.

"And," Lydia continued, "this isn't really a punk house. We're just a bunch of ladies who hate american culture and like hanging out with other ladies."

"Except for Punky Brewster over here," said Jasmine, punching Xandria lightly in the shoulder. "She punks the whole goddamn house up."

"Hey, fuck you!" Xandria said, laughing.

"So, like, if you're looking for a punk house, this isn't really it."

"Oh, no, that's fine," I said. "I'm not a punk. I'm just a kid." That answer seemed to satisfy them.

"I guess we should tell you a little bit about ourselves. But first, we wanna hear more about you." Lydia said.

"Oh, uh, sure. I'm Tabitha....I'm nineteen.....um, I'm from Ohio, I live in a really depressing basement with a goth dude"--this elicited a round of sympathetic looks, which gave me courage-- "and, uh, before that I lived with my girlfriend, but she, like, dumped me, which really sucked. So I'm hoping, like, third time's the charm?" I gave them all a hopeful smile.

"What do you do with yourself?" Lydia asked.

"Um, well, ever since I moved here, I started doing Food Not Bon-Bons, and I'm learning how to cook and stuff, and I'm like, really into it. And I ride my bike around, and I read a lot. Oh, and I work at the coffee stand at the train station. Um, what about you guys?"

"You have a job? That's good," said Lydia, shooting a pointed look at Xandria. "My name is Lydia, I grew up in this city. I just finished school with a Master's degree in social work and now I'm a caseworker at this troubled-teen center downtown. God, I feel like I'm writing an OKCupid profile...I like crafts, garlic, and social change!" She said this a little too perkily, like she was a game show host, and then laughed at herself. "Um, I'm a youngest sibling..."

"And it shows!" Jasmine said.

"...And, um, I'm a Leo, which means I'm chatty and fun but if you fuck with me I'll rip your face off! What's your sign?"

"God, don't scare her," the facially-tattooed girl said.

"Oh, she won't be scared off easily. She looks like she's been through something already," Lydia regarded my face intently, as if looking for directions on a map. "But you're still sweet. You haven't gotten crazy yet. That's a good combination. You should try and stay that way." I smiled. The tattooed girl was right; I was a little unnerved. But I could tell the house held something good, so I tried to not let the fear show in my face.

"Uh, I'm a Capricorn," I stammered. "But I don't really believe in that stuff..."

"Capricorns *never* do," she smiled. "It's too impractical. Too much trust in the unknown."

"God, now you've *really* scared her," said Jasmine. So much for not letting on. "Anyway..." and she looked at the facially-tattooed girl.

"I'm Xandria," Xandria said. "I've lived here since I was nineteen. This city, not this house. I ran away from lockup when I was fifteen, and I had a bunch of crazy years, and I got on a freight train when I was really fucked up about something, and I thought I was going to Cleveland, but I wound up here instead. And I was still fucked-up when I got off, and the sun was coming up and I saw this wall in this abandoned building and someone had spray-painted STAY on it, and it felt like a sign, so I stayed." She cleared her throat.

Jasmine and Lydia looked like they'd heard this story a hundred times, but also like it still held some meaning for them. "That was a long time ago. I'm twenty-two now. I'm not on drugs anymore, but I still love my booze!" At this, she waved her beer in the air for emphasis. Jasmine and Lydia rolled their eyes at each other slightly, and the energy got a little more tense. "I think I saw you at Food Not Bon-Bons before, which is cool, especially because we were talking about moving it into this house."

"Oh *God*," Lydia sighed.

"But we're all still having the debate of the century about it," Jasmine said. "I am Switzerland. I can see both sides."

"Oh, pick a goddamn side already," Lydia yelled, and they all giggled in a tense way.

"I don't want to beat that poor dead horse, so I'll just introduce myself. I am Jasmine. I'm 25 and the old bag of the household. I'm a poet, which is kind of embarrassing—I mean, I'm not like one of those goth fourteen-year-olds..."

"She's a *good* poet!" Lydia interjected. "Really, really good."

"But, I mean, even *that's* embarrassing. I can't go around saying I'm a good poet. That's like going around bragging that I'm a really good masturbator or something. I used to be a dishwasher, too, but then I got... sick. I've been sick for a few months now. I don't really know with what. Anyway, lately I've been just kinda hanging out. I have a lot of stories, I've done a lot of stuff with my life. I'll tell you about it sometime, if you move in. I, like, talk a lot--"

"No shit!" said Xandria, releasing a spectacular cackle that was not encumbered by a full row of teeth.

"Oh, shut up! Oh, no, don't shut up. She's right. I plead guilty; I am a talker. A chit-chatter. It's true, it's true, it's all true--oh, *God*--" and with that Jasmine mock fainted on the counter with a forearm draped artfully across her face.

"Yeah, so," Lydia said, "this is what living here is like. Do you think you can put up with it?"

I thought of going back to that basement where the beige and the silence advanced like twin monsters. "Oh, *definitely*," I said, in the tone of voice I'd have used if she'd offered me water in the middle of the desert. "Definitely."

I left the shitty cold basement by telling the goth boy, "I'm moving out." He shrugged and went to his computer to post a new roommate ad on CraigsList. I got a few boxes from the drugstore dumpster down the street and packed them with everything I had, which wasn't much. Lydia picked me up, put my boxes in her trunk and backseat, while I rode to the house on my bike.

And so I moved in with these supposed strangers; strangers who knocked the breath out of me with hugs, who danced maniacally at the corner store and made the neighbors laugh, who woke my brain up like blood pumping through veins. I had a little room that was all mine. I burrowed underneath blankets; I stacked up books from the library about everything I ever wanted to know started on the floor, but soon it was a stack that dwarfed my bed. Compost, permaculture, Stonewall, wiring, insurrection, welding, anti-racism, small engine repair. I read about all that stuff at the radical bookstore when I lived in the goth basement, but it all seemed so impossible. It seemed like I was never going to have any space to apply it to anything in my life. But here, there was a backyard with a little earthy corner perfect for a compost pile. Xandria knew how to weld. And a favorite house pastime was getting drunk and speaking passionately of revolution. I didn't have much to say, but I absorbed it all, and I felt the electricity of their words zap through my body. I felt like I had finally found the path. It almost didn't matter where it was heading.

My name was scrawled on masking tape on the mail-cubby all the way to the left. And I never got any mail, but it was nice to know that someone could send me a letter if they wanted to, and that there would be a special place for me to get it. Sometimes when I walked downstairs in the morning, I let my hand trail longingly on the wall, as though I were touching the skin of a lover.

I walked by Jasmine's room one night, on my way to bed, and saw that her walls were plain white, as always. When I got out of bed at 4:30 the next morning, I found her in the center of a firestorm of purple, all over the walls. It wasn't calm, temperate purple, applied with a roller. It was swirls and pops, it was different shades that bounced all around. It was the kind of purple that was entertainment in and of itself, where you could look at it and remember things; where looking became an experience. "Wow," I breathed, poking my head in. "That's really, um, cool! But aren't you, like, worried about the landlord?"

"No!" she said, so fierce I thought she was yelling at me for a second. "The landlord doesn't care about us. Why should we care about the landlord?" So simple, but it had never really occurred to me. I glanced around at the holey sheetrock, the drafty windows. I thought of the six-foot hole in the front porch that was clearly never getting fixed. I thought of how we never saw our landlord; hidden away at a suburban address. "Besides, what's he gonna do? Steal our security deposit. Big deal. Nobody gets their security deposit back anyway. And at least I won't have to wake up to white anymore." I smiled at her and waved goodbye, but she was already painting again.

Every time I walked by Jasmine's room and saw that splash of color, a little voice whispered to me *you can do this, too*. It was like I had been trapped my whole life in a sterile chain bookstore full of books about people who bought things on credit cards and made their nailpolish match their convertibles, and the girls are all skinny when you flip on the T.V., even the queer ones, they don't look like anybody I know or anybody I care about. And finding this house was finding that one book, tucked away, on the 90% off rack, that said something real to me, something that I could take as a little bit of armor for the rest of the world, something that made my fingernails rake the pages in anticipation.

In the basement I bought a plant, but it died. I made color copies of paintings in art books from the library, but the colors were swallowed up by the unrelenting beige-ness. It was so cold in that apartment, and I didn't have anyone to share that cold with. The goth boy kept the thermostat low, fifty-five degrees, and mysteriously was still able to wander the house wearing his tank-top and mesh shirt. But ever since I moved into this house, I was around people who had the right idea about cold.

One day, I was miserably shivering in the living room, reading a book but losing my place because my gloves were too thick to turn pages with any sort of accuracy. I was pulling my fourth hoodie over my shoulders and sipping a cup of coffee that had gone lukewarm less than five minutes after I'd poured it. Lydia stumbled in from somewhere and came to the living room to say hi.

"I hate this fucking cold weather," I groused.

"All we need is a dance party," said Lydia. "A no-heat dance party. I used to do this back when I lived somewhere that didn't have any heat at all." She went to the stereo and put on something good, and then started dancing with a fury and passion that was contagious. Ten minutes later, I was sweaty and happy. Ten minutes later, I'd forgotten all about the cold and lonely self that existed before. Even later, as my heart rate returned to normal, as the cold soaked its way through the layers of cloth around my body, I remembered that it didn't have to be like this; that I could change if I needed to. We had warmth that radiated, and a secret combination of moves that could turn the key to a place that I never knew existed before. When our cupboards were empty, and our stomachs were angry growling monsters, Xandria had this trick of getting a bunch of kale, a few potatoes, and a bulb of garlic. She'd toss it all in a soup cauldron and make soup for all of us. You wouldn't think that something like that could be so delicious, but it perked you up after eating only bread and bread products for days on end. It gave my body a little pat on the head, a little encouragement to keep running amok.

As if that wasn't enough, there were always other people over who were equally exciting. Snotty teenage runaways, intense old poets, over-enthused herbalists, stressed-out cigarette-smokers, rubber-stamp collage artists, people, people and people. Staying for a week, or for the evening;

coming from everywhere, knocking on the door and I peeped out the peephole and recognized them somehow, just like Jasmine had recognized me when I first stood there.

Sometimes these endless guests could get really annoying, like the crusty couple who let their dog shit on the carpet, or the pretentious performance artist who took hour-long baths in the house's only bathroom, but some of them were exceptionally great. One in particular.

CHAPTER 3

Lydia held a knitting circle in our living room every Tuesday night, and one night, I joined them. I don't like knitting but I wanted to hang out with Lydia. But she was busy on this particular night, making some elaborate hat for this intense 55-year-old lady she worked with. Jasmine was there too, but she looked tired. Still, I stayed, mainly because I had nothing better to do.

I was a little intimidated by the knitting circle, which may sound ridiculous, but they weren't some gossipy small-towners. They were a great and powerful force that just happened to be making scarves. Tough women (and one demure boy) with their needles clicking, talking about protests and girls and boys and dance parties. I sat there, in my holey hoodie and fireproof pants, chewing my nails and drinking a 40 and listening intently. I felt vaguely creepy, but I didn't know what to say. They were all older than me, all wearing wacky thrift-store clothes with a perfectly placed patch; all blessed with the magical ability to purl while delivering a complex analysis on the Spanish Civil war or police brutality. I knew Lydia and Jasmine would listen to my stories about the things I saw riding my bike and the crazy people I met every day at the coffee stand, but I didn't know if anyone else in attendance would really care.

Violet seemed a little off-kilter too, dropping stitches and making sideways eye contact with me. I didn't know she was Violet then. She was just some girl, and even though she was looking at me I figured that it must have been some mistake. Why would she be looking at me? My awkwardness was everywhere that night. It filled the room like balls in a ballpit.

After everyone went home, Lydia found me in the kitchen, languidly stirring some after-midnight why-not oatmeal. "Somebody likes you!" she sang tunelessly, and then placed both elbows on the kitchen counter and then looked up at me impudently.

Of course I blushed. And then I blushed because I was blushing, which never helps. "Uh, oh, uh." Lydia laughed. It was the kind of laugh that someone does because they know how you are, and for that reason it wasn't mean. "Um, who?" I stammered, my spoon-holding hand twitching slightly, sending a comma of oatmeal splattering to the floor. I left it there.

"My friend Violet!" I stared at her blankly. "You know, the one who was wearing the skirt with the heart patch sewn on, and the little red sweater?"

I looked at her even more blankly. "I, uh, don't usually notice what people are wearing..."

She looked at me: black t-shirt, black hoodie, dark blue work pants; the same outfit I wore all the time. I had four other outfits just like it upstairs, in my closet. "Well, she was the tall one with curly black hair? The one who kept looking at you?"

"Oh yeah, her. Why does she like *me*? I never even said anything to her. I, like, couldn't think of anything to say."

"I don't know. Maybe she thinks you're cute. Did you ever think of that?" Blush-o-thon. You'd think I were a damsel in distress or something. "Do you think she's cute?" I shrugged. "Oh, whatever. She's coming over tomorrow after work to return my shirt that she borrowed, if you wanna conveniently situate yourself in the living room." I said nothing, but that goddamn blushing gave me away. I concentrated on stirring my oatmeal furiously until Lydia changed the subject.

The next day, I *just happened* to be sitting in the living room, reading a book from the library, trying to pretend that I was interested in it. I jumped every time the door opened. When the door-opening finally bore Violet, Lydia hung out with us for a while, and then she mysteriously had to go. After that, it was all shaky hands and nervous laughter. All you need to know is that it culminated in a kiss, just like in any stupid romance novel that you could buy at the supermarket and toss away. That kiss was led up to by awkward conversation turned good, beer bottles opened against the lip of the counter, bruised hands as a result of the aforementioned, and a glance across the kitchen that lasted.

After the kiss, Violet pulled away from me. For a second, I thought she'd finally realized that a cute girl like her had no business making out with someone like me. But instead of running out the door, Violet closed her eyes and ran her hand over my face.

Her palm floated on top of the mountains of my cheekbones down into the valley of my eyes. She felt the curve of my jaw, the plain of my forehead. I felt like something really good, written in Braille. And we stood there like that for minutes, not speaking, her touching me.

The weird thing is that it wasn't weird at all. I could have stood there for hours and hours, listening to the refrigerator hum, her hand making laps around my face. After a few minutes, she opened her eyes and looked at me, smiling so big. No words. She pulled me to her by my hoodie collar, and we made out some more.

Eventually, Xandria walked in on us. She obliviously went to the refrigerator for a beer and left without looking our way, but we took this as a cue. My phone had been shut off, so she wrote her number for me on a corner ripped from the newspaper. I put it in my wallet, behind the clear vinyl where a picture should have gone. It was so tiny and the thought of losing it scared me deeply, even though I couldn't really articulate how or why, even though I knew I could just get her number from Lydia anytime I wanted it.

I stared at it a few times a day. The curves of her handwriting, the arrangement of the numbers. Randomly assigned by the phone company, but somehow they made so much sense. After a few days of staring at it and shaking, I mustered up every grain of courage in my body and called her from the house landline. She answered on the third ring, saying, "I was just thinking of you. Do you want to go for a bike ride through the graveyard?" Swoon!

Things went along like this for a while. We kind of pretended we weren't dating, going a few days without seeing each other and then having marathon hangouts that would start in the mid-to-late afternoon with a bad movie, accompanied by either coffee or whiskey, depending on what day it was and what time. They would usually end when I crawled out of her bed at 4:30 AM, put my clothes back on, and got on my bike to go to work.

Even when we hung out on my days off, she usually had school, work or a ridiculous drug study in the morning, and so I'd have to get up, too. I felt weird sleeping in her bed without her, so I'd climb on my bike and daze my way home. By the time I got home I was usually too giddy to sleep, thinking of the curve of her face or the texture of her breasts; or too sad, thinking of how I'd have to spend all day alone, and how we weren't really close enough yet for me to call her more than once every few days. And whenever I left her for work I was always so bleary and dead, working for eight hours in a daze and then heading home to my bed for a fitful, lonely nap. I'd wake up periodically, wishing her spine was pressed against my belly every day. But I didn't know how to ask.

Then, one morning, she surprised me at the coffee stand. I opened my sleep-heavy half-lidded eyes a full three-quarters, and smiled all big before I realized what I was doing. I gave her a big tall cup of piping hot coffee, with soy milk and lots of sugar, just like how she liked it. On the house, of course. I poured myself a smaller cup, black and steamy, and we leaned against the counter, elbow to elbow.

Suddenly Violet slapped her hand on the counter, eyes wide. "Oh my god. Did you see that guy? His shirt said 'I LOVE CRAZY BROADS.' I wonder if I should give him my number?" My heart sank. I guess she could tell, because she reached out and cupped my face in her hand. "Just kidding! I--" and then she was overcome by a giant sneeze, giving birth to a shuddering snot-ball that stuck partially on her cheek and partially on her other hand. Her face turned red, catching up with mine. I was still kinda reeling that she touched me in public. It makes me look as if I'm not invincible. Like I'm the kind of girl who gets her face touched, who almost collapses from the weight of it.

Violet had her own issue to deal with right now, and didn't notice mine. She was rooting around desperately for a tissue, making a little pyramid of pocket-debris on the gleaming coffeestand counter. Candy wrappers, a purple crayon, a few stray gloves (she picked lonely gloves up off the floor, because they made her sad), a few pennies. And then she pulled out the garlic bulb.

She had been sick for a while, with some cold or another, and I'd given her a bulb of garlic to eat, because eating raw garlic cures colds. This was weeks ago. In that time, she had gotten much better, or at least not sick enough to need garlic anymore. She had forgotten about it in her huge dark coat with the cavernous pockets. A few cloves were gone, but the rest had sprouted into a tiny plant, one that she just pulled out of her pocket. She wiped her nose hurriedly on her sleeve, held the garlic in her palm and said, "Hey, look!" and I was flabbergasted. "It's a...plant!" she gasped.

I'd never seen anyone take a living thing out from a pocket that was supposed to hold tissues and gum and cigarettes. And she didn't shriek or throw it away; she was just as excited by it as I was. Three inches of green sprouting from a flaky white bulb, the tiny leaf at the top bowed, as if in prayer. We sat there and looked at it, awed.

Even better, a bunch of gray-clad customers came by and wrinkled their noses at my girl. I guess it must have been weird to them, seeing a scraggly girl, her eyes hooded and her nose red and dripping, holding a plant all luminous in her hand. But I didn't think it was weird; I thought it was great. Violet was fucking magical. Big goddamn deal if these commuters didn't get it.

After I got off work, we planted it in a pot and put it on her windowsill. And something was different then; she really felt like my girlfriend, not just some girl who hit on me at the knitting circle, a girl who left hickeys all over my neck and thighs, who bit the skin over my heart and looked up at me expectantly. When she'd done that before, I'd looked away, not really sure of what I should do. Now I wanted to say, *Go ahead.* I wanted to say *take it*. And I didn't say it out loud, but somehow she knew anyway.

CHAPTER FOUR

My housemates and I got so much more than we could eat from those dumpsters, so much more than we could give away. We had a wealth of vegetables, some rotten, some not, most at some point in between. We got some of them from dumpsters, but most of it was from donations from grocery stores who were happy for us to cart their trash away. They were all for Food Not Bon-Bons.

The first time I did a Food Not Bon-Bons pickup, before I lived in this house, I helped these two kids cart it into their living room. When everything was in a gigantic teetering pile, I stepped back and looked at it. Seven garbage bags overflowing with bread, plus four boxes of produce. My jaw dropped. This was *one grocery store*. This was *one night*. We could never use all this food, even if we gorged for weeks. *One grocery store, one night*, I kept thinking, over and over again. The more seasoned Food Not Bon-Bonners in my midst were unimpressed. They'd seen it all.

Food Not Bon-Bons was run out of our house now. Those kids whose living room I'd marveled in had been evicted, Lydia had lost her battle, and her frequent sighs became a lot more pointed. Every Sunday, a whole bunch of people came over my house to separate the disgusting from the passable, to chop it up into tiny bits, to fry or bake or puree it, and to drive it downtown. All kinds of people came--thick-shouldered dudes who had a deep-rooted phobia of doing dishes, wild-eyed ladies who chopped vegetables at warp speed, silent angry boys who made the most delectable meals I had ever tasted.

Whoever had a functioning car that week would load the bucket-sized pots and pans and drive to a park downtown to hand out food to the homeless people, the down-on-their-luck people, the mildly curious people, and the crusties who talked of the inherent worth of eating dumpstered food and living outside of the system, but who were always mysteriously absent when it came time for chopping or cooking.

Ever since Food Not Bon-Bons moved into my house, I didn't go to the park for serving anymore. I had to stay behind and clean the kitchen, or face Lydia's unending wrath. Not that the kitchen was all that clean to begin with, or that it was especially clean after I was done, but if I didn't at least try it looked like a vegetable disaster zone. Since going to the park was the fun part, usually it was just me and the college radio station. I scraped, I scrubbed, and I emptied the bowl where the cooks had put their vegetable scraps. When I was done with that, there were usually buckets and bags full of rotting produce to deal with. I couldn't put them back in the garbage from whence it came. That was admitting defeat. So I did what came naturally--I composted.

Fortunately, we had a tiny non-concrete earthy corner of our yard just begging for some rotting vegetable love. I dumped all the rot into a pile-like formation, and I occasionally thought about turning it. I knew I should look for the rake and flip it, but usually I was too tired after cleaning the kitchen and cooking for hours. I knew compost piles needed air to turn garbage into soil, but standing on a shaky mound of decomposing vegetables and hacking the shit out of it with my shovel kinda lost its appeal when I could be doing something besides toiling. So I'd call Violet or pick up a book or take a nap while the vegetables festered away.

My housemates weren't exactly raring to turn the pile either. Lydia was busy working at the troubled-youth center downtown, sometimes sixty hours a week or more, and wasn't really interested in getting her excellent outfits dirty. Xandria spent most of her time asking for spare change down by City Hall, drinking away the pain of being a fucked-up teen runaway turned fucked-up adult, and carrying on a string of doomed romances with guys who had big dogs and outstanding warrants. Jasmine didn't work; she was too sick. She was home more often than any of us, but she was almost always pale and exhausted, and I felt like a jerk asking her to turn it when I knew that she could barely get out of bed.

So the compost pile grew. I mean, it *grew*. Scarily. It became a new dimension, the sludge leaking off the side, turning into a greenish-grayish mess. It stunk. It sweated. It wept tears of former food. The swarms of flies seemed to be buzzing some sort of insult I couldn't understand. Or maybe it was an odd form of thanks.

The pile actually fit in well with the rest of the neighborhood. Our backyard spilled into one giant lot with a back alley just wide enough to coax a car through. Contractors dumped huge mounds of construction debris that they couldn't get rid of legally without paying a huge fine. There were piles of branches and boards and sheetrock, and kids crawled to the top, hid underneath, played bizarre kid-games. Alley cats napped in tire-mounds. Potato chip bags blew in the street, like oversized confetti searching for a parade. Sometimes a car would be parked in the street, forcing me to climb around it, onto one of the mounds. So I would sidestep gingerly, only to see someone's head bobbing up and down in the front, somebody else's head lolling back over the headrest, his chin pointed to the ceiling. I played the urban game that I know so well—the one called *La la la, just taking a stroll, can't see you...* I rolled my eyes as far to the other side as they would go, trying to pretend I was just fascinated by something to my right.

In other words, the compost pile was a motley mound, but good-hearted when you got right down to it. Stinky, but non-threatening. Dirty, but sorta productive.

The trouble began when Violet came over one day. She was wearing a ruffly trash-picked skirt and playing her new accordion. I heard her music as kind of a doorbell, opened the door and we smooched on the porch. Then we went inside and Violet tripped over a rake I had left on the floor the last time I turned the pile, about three weeks ago. I guess it had fallen over or something. She was sprawled out in the filth, all legs and organza. Her accordion bleated sadly. The knees of her long stripey leggings had something that looked like mustard smeared on them from where she fell.

"Fuck!" she yelled. "This house is such a dump. Maybe you guys should become crackheads. I saw a crack house on the news yesterday and it looked *way* better than this place..." She went on, but all I heard was "blah, blah, blah." Violet hated the compost pile. She hated the way my eyes shone when I talked about it; hated the slurry that stuck to her shoes every time she ventured to the back of my house. Violet was cool; she just didn't get it. I mean, she was a *knitter*. She was a thrift shopper, a half-price margarita sipper, a photobooth kind of girl. None of these are bad things, just mystifying to me. I wore work pants that could get splattered with yuck and still survive. I drank beer so I wouldn't notice the smell of all that produce rotting. And fuck photobooths, I could barely look in the mirror sometimes.

"That isn't a compost pile, it's a landfill! How do you expect new dirt to form when you just throw all that shit out to rot?"

I sighed. I picked up the rake that Violet had just tripped over. "Do you want me to turn it? Because I will."

Violet looked mildly shocked. "Well, okay...I guess..." Clearly, she had thoroughly enjoyed complaining, but didn't actually want me to take time out of our day to do anything about it. She kissed me again, in the quiet dark hallway. Fingers locked around belt loops and all that. "It's good to see you," she whispered, although we'd just seen each other the day before.

It was a hot kiss, but I pulled away and smiled at her infuriatingly. "Geez, Violet, I don't know. I mean, I really *want* to stand here and fuckin' kiss you all day, but *someone* really thought I should turn the compost pile..." She gave me a light punch in the stomach, rolled her eyes and smiled at me all gap-toothed and cute. Sigh. She picked up her accordion and began to play a jaunty march, and we marched to the backyard.

I raised the hoe above my head and brought it down hard onto the mass. My boots squished and squelched. The hoe upset the top layer of vegetables and exposed a new layer to the sun, to the air. I used it to chop the bigger vegetables into smaller bits, so their tough skin wouldn't stop them from decomposing.

Violet played faster, cracking her jaw in time to the music, jumping from side to side in a self-conscious little dance. I was feeling pretty goddamn good, like I was actually doing something productive for once, my muscles waking up. And then my rake hit something that felt a little strange. It was solid instead of squishy. It didn't seem like a vegetable. I leaned in to inspect it.

Holy fucking shit. I peered down, thinking it was--thinking it wasn't--thinking it couldn't be--thinking it must be--

I turned to Violet. "Very funny."

"What?" she said.

"Now I know why you really wanted me to turn the compost pile."

"What are you talking about?"

I pointed to the offending spot. "This fake hand? Ha ha."

Violet took one look and started screaming her head off. She bent double at the waist, one hand over her mouth, eyes wide, terrified breaths escaping from the cracks between her fingers.

I ran to her and held her, patting her hair, smoothing it, feeling her body tremble against mine. I was a little shaky too, once I realized. The accordion lay crumpled in the dirt and we stood there, watching the hand, as if it was going to do something.

It was a right hand that used to be on a white body. The palm was exposed, the fingers curled. The fingernails were short; the fingers wide like a man's. It had a slight sprinkling of hair on the fingers I could see. It was not playing baseball. It was not typing. It was not pressed to the ground while the rest of the body was doing a handstand. It was not tying a shoe. It was not squeezing shampoo, or waiting for shampoo to be squeezed onto it. It was not giving the finger to an incompetent driver. It was not placing a pickle slice on top of a hamburger. It was not praying. It was not picking a nose. It was lying on its back, exposed to the thin winter sun. Why was it in my compost pile?

I wanted there to be a completely ridiculous explanation. I would have bought anything at this point. It could be attached to a creepy old man who has a fetish for rotting veggies. Or it could be attached to a kid who thought this spot would be a sure win at hide and seek. Anything. Anything. I wanted the pile to quake, have a real live human being stand up and bid us good-bye, slightly embarrassed. But the hand just remained there.

Violet and I looked at each other. "*Fuck.*" she whispered. "What are we going to do?"

"I don't know." I thought of my housemates. I thought of Lydia at work, flipping through files, making phone calls. I thought of Xandria, but she was too mysterious for me to imagine her days. I thought of Jasmine, knitting scarves to keep herself busy, brewing elaborate herbal teas that might make her feel better. All those hands, attached to people. Doing things. How could I say *There's a dead body in our compost pile.* How could I say *come home*?

"Do you think it's, like, a whole body? Or just a hand?" Violet asked me. I shuddered. I didn't want to look.

"Um, I don't know," I said weakly. "The pile doesn't look like it's gotten, you know, too much bigger. So, um, I guess it's not really possible. But why would there be just a hand?"

We stood there, silently, before this mound of vegetables that might be a gravesite. Finally Violet said, "I'll look." She gingerly picked up my shovel, and started poking through the pile, starting about a foot away from the offending hand. Her rake separated banana peels from eggshells, globs of rot from rotting globs. The hand sat in the corner of the pile, like a naughty child. The hand had to end somewhere, right? Would it be better if it ended abruptly? Would it be worse if it was a tributary to a larger body; if we had to see the face?

Violet got closer, closer. Finding nothing, she started picking around the hand. She found a crumpled bright-orange plastic bag, with the three intersecting circles that spelled to the illiterate what was written beneath it in bold letters: BIOHAZARD.

The bag was tattered and ripped. The stump, the end, whatever the hell you want to call it--was stuck in this bag, unmistakably from the hospital a few miles away. "Holy shit," Violet and I said in unison. We stared, utterly transfixed. It seems like such a little thing, right? That's all I could think, standing at the edge of my compost pile, staring at this tiny tiny thing. And it was a thing at this point, not useful anymore. Trash, like everything else in that pile. If it was so tiny, how could it possibly be so upsetting? But somehow it was. I looked around the lot. How had this hand gotten all the way from the hospital, I wondered. Unless…

Violet had already beaten me to it. She was standing next to a pile of huge garbage bags that were shredded slightly, as though an animal had clawed it. Through the slash marks, we could see the same shade of orange that was in our compost pile. "Those fucking assholes!" yelled Violet. She ran to me and buried her head in my shoulder. "I hate this world, I hate it so much."

I couldn't think of anything to say to that. I mean, how could I convince her that anything was okay when we had just found a hand in my backyard? Especially when we both knew that if we lived somewhere else we would never have to find severed hands when we were just trying to compost. We'd never know that things like this happen at all. We could read about it in a magazine, the Utne Reader or The Nation, perhaps. We could get kind of pissed off, or horrified. And then we could turn the page and forget all about it.

We wouldn't have to look at it: this hand, gnarled and dirty, hacked right off of some person who never knew that it would wind up here. We wouldn't have to look at the fingertips, wondering whose nose they used to pick. We wouldn't have to look at the biohazard bag it came in and get mad that it belonged in a landfill, get mad that someone thought my street was a suitable equivalent.

"So let's fix it," I whispered in her ear.

"How?"

"We can give it a proper burial, at least." So we got gas masks (I had them in my room, in case of emergency) and elbow-length rubber gloves. We dug a little hole in the leafy part of the lot, underneath one of the few trees. I stood on the shovel, pushing the tip down with my boot, while Violet hummed a funeral dirge. I mechanically dug, deeper and deeper, past the stones and the potato chip bags and vein-like roots of the stubby, sad shrubs.

Violet took the shovel from me when I was done, used it to pick up the hand and put it in the hole. It teetered at the edge, and then, with one tiny move, she tilted the shovel and the hand tumbled into the hole. We both looked away. We both heard it hit, and it made the strangest noise. So soft, so subtle, so unlike anything I'd ever heard. Violet and I just stood in the eerie silence afterward, not moving, until a faraway car alarm brought us back to life. Then she pulled a stray glove from her pocket and threw it in the hole, covering the hand. I couldn't help but smile.

I wished, for a moment, that I were still in touch with my family. We were in touch, theoretically, if "being in touch" meant that I had a tense phone conversation with my mom every few months. We didn't talk about anything real; it was more like a periodic confirmation that we were all still alive. They didn't know about my new house, or what went on inside, just that my phone number had changed. They didn't know what kept me lying awake at night or whose words kept me alive. And I didn't write to them, but if I did, the events happening right now would make an awesome postcard. "Hey Mom, I'm burying a severed hand in the ground with my lesbian lover. She's singing a funeral song and it's *so goddamn cute.* Tonight, vengeance will be ours! —But I don't want to write how, in case the FBI is reading. Love ya! --Tabitha"

Somewhere between finding my gas masks and digging the hole, we had thought of the perfect revenge. But we had to wait until the middle of the night to apply it. So we put our dirty rubber gloves into a trash bag and tied it up tightly, and then went to Violet's place. Normally I don't like hanging out there, but my whole house felt kind of contaminated right now.

Violet lived twelve blocks away in an apartment with two other girls. They were okay, fun to sit on the couch with sometimes. They didn't make my blood tingle like my housemates did, but they were good for a little quiet. Nobody was home when we came in, though, besides the cat. "So," Violet said. "What do you want to do now?"

"Ugh, I don't know," I said.

"I want to take a shower. Do you want to come with?" Of course. Not only did I like hanging out with my girlfriend naked, but her thermostat was always at least ten degrees higher than mine, elevating winter-time showering from a total ordeal to a pleasant reality.

We went into the bathroom together. She shut the door behind her and there was that momentary weirdness where I realized I was in the bathroom with someone else, and the world seemed slightly off-kilter, but then I was jolted back to the moment because I was in the bathroom with a cute girl and she was taking her shirt off. And I'm not a horny teenage boy;

really I'm not, but the sight of her breasts under the florescent bathroom light is enough to crash whatever train of thought I was riding.

It's weird, isn't it? I have a set of breasts, so you'd think the subject of breasts would be a tired one. And it is when they're mine, but it's not when they're hers. When they are underneath a brilliant smile, parenthesed by cute little tufts of pit hair. When they are pressed up against mine as the girl they're attached to pulls me in, with her skinny tattooed arms, for a hot kiss.

And so I slid my mouth down to the little hollow between her neck and her shoulder and started sucking on that tiny little delicate stretch of skin right above her clavicle, because I knew that will make her emit those sexy noises that make me shiver. Those moans, like she's in so much pain and I'm the only one who can make it better. I backed her into a corner, up against the wall, her body tilted towards mine. I kept my left hand spread flat against her luscious back, smushed against the cold tile of her bathroom wall, like a plateholder. I wanted to shield her from the reality of those cold tiles. And I brought my other hand up to one of her luscious breasts. I cupped it in my hand; felt the weight and the softness, squeezed her hardening nipple between my index and middle finger. I pulled away from her neck and we stared at each other for a second, with a distinct hunger.

We kissed again, lips pressed up against each other faster, more urgently. She scraped her nails down my back in such a way that I know it's a signal to fuck her. I reached for the thick curly hair between her legs and found it already damp. I looked up at her and smeared the dampness around a little, teasing her with a big, almost-bratty smile. Just when the look on her face was beginning to turn from lustful anticipation to impatient annoyance, I plunged my first two fingers into her. She let out a sharp sigh and grabbed a fistful of my back fat, dug her nails in hard as I fucked her. She put one foot up on the bathtub so I could go in deeper.

And I did, as far as her body would let me. My hand felt very meaningful all of a sudden.

Usually I'm all nervous energy. I'm all "ums" and "uhs". I fumble, I trip, I mess up. But when I'm fucking a girl I really like, I am an arrow pointed directly at a target. I'm flying through the air, headed straight towards a bulls-eye. I'm on a mission. The endless loop of every embarrassing thing I've ever done is momentarily put on pause. All I can think about is this breath, this heat, this girl in front of me, impaled on my hand, totally at my mercy.

She asked, "Could you go down on me?" and I happily obliged. The angle was kind of awkward, and it hurt my neck after a few minutes, but I could hear her cute little squeals echoing off the tile wall and I fucked her even harder, the palm of my hand bumping up against my slick chin. We could have been there for hours, or maybe a few minutes. I didn't know. I didn't care. I forgot there was a war on. I forgot that I was cold and hungry. I forgot about what had just happened in the compost pile. All I knew was this rhythm, this motion. Part of me wished that she'd never come, that I could keep on doing this forever.

But eventually she let out a really loud, hot noise that made my own cunt tremble. Her thigh muscles got so tense and then they went slack in a great rush. "Oh.......man....." she sighed. "That was...... fucking awesome." I pulled my hand out, but stayed crouched on the tile floor, smiling up at her. She pulled me up to her by my armpits and kissed my cheek in a tired way. I was hoping she'd reach over and see how wet she'd gotten me; how badly I always wanted her. Instead, she opened the shower curtain. "Well," she said, all business, "let's shower!" Without waiting for my response, she turned on the faucet.

So, we took a shower, standing in the steam watching each other in that tired-yet-happy after-sex way. There's always someone shivering in the steam and always someone underneath the warm water. Usually it was her under the water and me in the steam, but I tried not to dwell on it too much. Just the way she looked at me over her bottle of biodegradable soap was enough.

We got out of the shower and dried off and dressed again. We made a pot of coffee and drank it all. We played a half-hearted game of scrabble, in which I kicked Violet's sorry ass. We waited. We waited. Around one a.m., we got bored with sitting in the lap of luxury at Violet's house and headed back to my own.

Xandria was sitting in the cold, on the front steps, sipping some coffee from a travel mug. "Hey, dude," I said, and filled her in on what was going on.

"A hand? That's so fucked-up!" she yelled.

"Yeah, I know," said Violet.

"But we've got a plan," I said, and told her what it was. "You want to come?"

"Fuck yeah," she said, "but I have some kale soup on the stove."

"That's fine," I said. "It's too early anyway. There are still people out on the street. We want to be stealth, like ninjas." I saw a pouty look spread across Violet's face and I felt bad for a second. I hadn't even thought about how maybe she wanted this to be just our mission, but I'd been neglecting my housemates for way too long, and I missed them. And it's not like this was some romantic escapade. We were avenging a severed hand, for god's sake.

"Dude, why are you sitting out here in the cold?" I asked Xandria, who shrugged. I stepped over her and went into the kitchen, which smelled steamy and healthy, a scent I'd recently learned was chlorophyll. I peered into the bubbling cauldron of soup. Violet followed me and pouted again. "Want some soup, baby?" I asked her in a small, hopeful voice. She looked at me like she wanted to be mad, but couldn't help herself. She got two bowls from the cupboard and excavated two spoons from the dish-mound in the sink.

Xandria came stomping in. "Dammit," she said, "I was really looking forward to using that compost pile this summer." Xandria and Jasmine had found a giant plastic kiddie pool in the trash a few months ago, and had hauled it home. It sat patiently in the corner of the living room, waiting for holes to be drilled and dirt to be poured inside it. It was going to be our garden. "I'm so tired of eating that wilty-ass stuff from the stupid-market." That was what we called the supermarket at the edge of our neighborhood, filled with nutrition-free boxes and depressed produce.

The soup bubbled on, eventually the kale was tender enough to eat, and we three slurped our bowls in tired companionship. When the clock struck two a.m., we decided it was time. We added more black to our outfits, and lifted some cartons of grapefruit juice off the back stoop. These were the bastard stepchildren of the late-night dumpster runs: expired three weeks ago, sitting in the sun ever since. Winter sun, but still. Even when freshly dumpstered, they looked too beaten-up for anyone to drink. My housemates and I had avoided doing anything about it; it was just too gross for any of us to handle. Now, I was grateful for our laziness. Now, after burying a severed hand, nothing was too gross.

Violet and I loaded up our bike baskets with the slimy cartons of greenish-black juice, and Xandria, lacking a basket, packed some juice cartons into a plastic bag and dangled it from her handlebars. I piled and piled, until my basket was bulging with rottenness. Then, we shakily set off in the direction of the hospital, going fast, even with the extra weight of all the juice. I felt out of control with all that weight on the front. My bike turned sharply to the left when I didn't hold the handlebars tightly enough. I slogged on, gritting my teeth and bracing my elbows, trying to keep it steady.

Before I knew it, we had squeaked to a stop in front of a building marked "Tedibear Hospital--Administrative Offices." I looked at Violet; she looked at me. Neither of us wanted to go first.

Finally, in one fluid motion, Xandria grabbed a carton and untwisted the top. The condensation on the outside of the carton made it slide out of her hand, and it fell to the ground and splashed a little, released its noxious smell into the air. When she picked it up again, it was with extra rage. And when she threw it, it flew like the winning touchdown, if we cared about football. It flew like it was headed for something. It was a spaceship launching. It was a new planet we'd discovered: this flight, this landing.

Once she'd done it, it felt okay for me and Violet to do it too. I can't even explain how good it felt, picking up that sludgy juice container, twisting the top off, and hurling it at the wall of that fucking hospital. The splat it made, the firework of disgusting juice against the wall. It was beautiful. We were too wary to whoop and holler, but I was doing that inside. We both were. When we were done with all the rot, Violet wrote DUMP ON US? WE'LL DUMP ON YOU on the sidewalk with a thick black permanent marker, arrows pointing at our handiwork, her usually ornate handwriting made sloppy by all the excitement.

I'd have to go to work in less than three hours. My shoulder would hurt later from the force of picking up the juice containers and hurling them, but for now it felt tingly, now it felt alive. Once we were done we got back on our bikes, fast. We rode hard for about ten blocks, light-footed but gaspy-lunged. After we'd crossed some imaginary threshold, we slowed down, rode three abreast, taking up the whole road. There weren't any cars out at this hour, not really. We started talking, nothing really exciting: *wow I don't believe it/yeah that was really cool.*

We passed by some house party, the music spilling out into the street, making the closed windows shake with its intensity. "Oh, I *love* this song!" Violet said. I didn't recognize it. Some hip-pop thing that was probably on the radio. She pulled over, threw her bike on the sidewalk, and started dancing on the corner. I pulled over too, and stood there, bike slung between my cement-planted legs. The music was cheesy, but kind of infectious. I was nodding my head almost against my will, and banging out a rhythm with my thumbs on my handlebars. Xandria had stopped her bike, and she looked kind of annoyed for a minute, but then she wheeled over and joined Violet, and they danced together for a few seconds. Their moves complimented each other so well. I stood and watched.

The song ended for a split second and a very similar new one began. Violet came up to me, plucked my hands off the grips, and pushed my bike so that it fell, banging my inner thigh in the process. She didn't notice, more due to excitement than insensitivity, and pulled me over its fainted carcass. Xandria turned away from us, shaking her ass distractedly, as though she were a person who'd just been dropped on this street corner by accident and thought it would be a good idea to start dancing.

I didn't really notice her because I was too busy dancing with Violet. We danced: awkwardly, dorkily. If we were at a junior high dance, we would definitely have had something hurled at us for our multiple crimes against humanity. There was so much to choose from, a smorgasbord of offenses and punishments. An empty dixie cup with droplets of punch splashing out for the awkward way my hips moved in their sockets. A well-timed snort at our complete irredeemability as people. Violet would have gotten whacked upside the head with a ruler by a parent-teacher chaperon for the suggestive way she was dancing against me. And I would have gotten a grenade launched at me for the way I was looking at her.

But sometimes life isn't so bad. We were light-years away from junior high, from dances where you paid three bucks to be made fun of in the bathroom, from unspoken rules enforced by projectiles, by popular vigilantes. I was nineteen, she twenty-three. Thirteen was a decade away for her, and I felt like I'd aged a decade in this past year. So it was six years away if you went by the calendar, sixteen if you went by instinct. Either way: it was far.

Usually I hated dancing. This was the first time I'd done it outside of my house in years. Maybe the first time ever. But tonight it felt like the only way to express all that rage and all that joy. I usually didn't do it because I always felt so stupid, like my body was speaking a different language than everyone else, and there were no interpreters.

Plus, I didn't want to dance the way girls do, all hips and boobs and ass, because I didn't want anyone to look at me that way. I didn't really know how to dance like a boy, either, so I danced like a goddamn awkward confused butch dyke basket of rage: I stomped. I flailed. Occasionally I did a strange little shrug.

Tonight, the girl in Violet was taking over. She danced sort of like those boring safe girls did when they wanted some boy to look at them and fall in love. But when Violet did it, it was mesmerizing, not desperate or forced like it seemed when those girls did it, all body spray and tube tops. Maybe I just thought that because the dance was for me now. Her hands were dirty from all those juice containers, and it just reminded me that we had just seen something fucked up and actually done something about it. Not just complaining or maybe signing a petition or writing a letter, but actually taking something into our own hands. She looked strange under the streetlights, glowing, so beautiful. So brave, throwing her bike down in one of the roughest neighborhoods in our city, where the danger was more tangible and immediate than it was in our neighborhood. Trusting the universe.

My neighborhood had a time-bomb kind of danger, cheap rent because of the mounds of trash everywhere and the long shadows of the refinery down the street, the toxic clouds it gave birth to. The neighborhood we were passing through had danger in gunshots, in angry sidelong glances, in sidewalk syringes and every awful thing you can ever imagine happening. Another version of me would have rolled my eyes at her, would have hated her for that trust. I would have called her stupid, naïve, totally sheltered. I would have yelled, *how can you let your guard down* and *especially now* and *especially here*.

But I didn't think any of these things; didn't say them. I was just happy. Who wouldn't be, when there was a girl dancing in front of you, and you could see her love handles vaguely underneath her jacket, where her shirt hiked up when she did hands-above-the-head dance moves? And you knew what they looked like because you knew *her*, and you had to stop for a second and wonder why anyone would ever diet those away. And when your housemate was so strong and so brave, dancing in the street corner by herself, like you and your girlfriend weren't being totally barfy just inches away, and your girlfriend was so gorgeous and so tough, and both of them taught you so much every day; just by being in your life. And three months ago, you didn't know either of them, you came so close to missing them entirely. Who wouldn't be happy, when you went out on a cold night to commit illegal acts and dance with abandon on street corners? And you couldn't drop your guard enough to really relax, but you were almost there. You were closer than you'd ever been before.

Eventually the dance party burnt itself out. Our movements become a little more repetitive, a little too repetitive, and our pauses to catch our breath got longer and longer. "Uhh, I'm so tired," Violet mumbled. "And it's so cold out."

"I could stay out here all night," said Xandria. "It's not *that* cold. But this music sucks."

We looked at Violet's phone. 3:45 AM. I had to be at work in an hour and fifteen minutes. We picked up our bikes and rode home quietly. I was pretty tired, too, but the night air on my face helped perk me up. There was no point in going to bed now, none at all. Well, there was, in that

Violet would wrap her arms around me, and fall asleep with her head on my shoulder, but I was scared I'd get too comfortable.

I saw the street sign that signaled I was nearly home. I made the turn without thinking, pure instinct. Just a few more blocks. I figured I would take a power nap, which is never a good idea at 4 am. But what other options did I have?

We got home and locked our bikes to the fence poles in my backyard. We walked through the back door, past the sticky-floored kitchen, and up the stairs. Xandria pulled a book out of the communal bookshelf and poured herself another cup of coffee, sat down without saying goodnight. Violet and I went straight into my room. She took her bra off without removing her shirt; shimmied out of it in some way that always mystified me. I only wore sports bras, no hooks, which required the removal of my whole shirt if I wanted to take them off. She kicked her shoes off, put her glasses in one shoe and her watch in the other. Violet, as predicted, flapped and flopped all over my futon, which is thin and not really good for flopping. She winced slightly at the impact, at how little it cushioned her from the hard floor, then curled up on one side and wrapped a pile of blankets around her. She had no problem sleeping, as always. I lay down next to her, outside of the blanket, and I kissed her forehead.

Her hand reached around and rested on my hip, and it was nice, but not nice enough to sleep. I lay on my left side, my other hip pressed up against the cold hard futon, which was cozied up to the cold hard floor. It was that hip I paid attention to, not the one that was melting underneath my girl's warm hand.

All of this felt nice, everything—arms around my waist, dazed smiles in the morning, her quick, sure hand in my cunt and the words that she whispered. All of it felt good, but I worried about it. I wasn't used to being loved so hard, and underneath all the good ran a current of nervousness that I just couldn't shake. I knew that if I relaxed, even for a second, all of the good things would disappear, as quickly as they'd materialized.

And my house was so great, and it shook me up in all the right ways, but I knew it couldn't last. It was like when you're a kid, and you're blowing bubbles, and somehow you manage to utilize your tiny lungs to blow a bubble that's bigger and more shimmery than all the rest, and you can't take your eyes off it as it shudders through the air. I was just waiting for it to pop and splatter my face with a slight misting of rainbow slime. And what would happen to me then? I didn't have anything else to do. I didn't have anywhere else to go.

If I was weak, I told myself, I would crawl into her arms and fall asleep. I'd slap my alarm silly when it brayed at me. I'd call in sick. I'd lose my job. I'd have to go back to Ohio. I had to be strong.

I had to be strong, so I got up and I left her. When I pulled myself away, I saw her frown deeply and move her hand along my side of the futon, as if I were something very tiny she'd dropped, not a full-grown person who's hard to misplace. She started feeling around more and more frantically until I kissed her forehead. A huge, hopeful smile spread across her face. It broke my heart in the best way ever, but I couldn't give in. So instead I sat in my blue metal folding chair, shivering slightly, watching the slow sweet breath of my girl asleep, watching the digital numbers of the clock gain and gain and gain until they told me it was time to go to work once more.

CHAPTER 5

When I hauled myself off the folding chair, even Xandria was asleep on the couch, the book still in one hand, her coffee mug empty. I briefly hated her for being able to sleep, and then threw some cold water on my face, thought about combing my hair, changed into a collared shirt and shoplifted dress pants, and walked out the door to where my bike was locked in the backyard. The cold is always the most brutal at 4:45 a.m. How it got so much worse in the past hour and a half was a complete mystery to me.

The one good thing about working so early is that I can ride my bike nice and slow. There is something to be said about riding fast, but that's more like a late night kind of thing. Riding fast is good for adventures; it's good for things you're going to remember. It's good when you're late and it's good when you need some excitement. But on my way to work, I like to ride so slow I almost fall over.

I dazed around until I realized I was at the train station. Okay. Okay, I thought. I can do this. Just eight more hours to go, and then I can sleep. Yeah! Coffee stand coffee stand coffee stand! A few commuters were stumbling in, looking like they absolutely hated their lives. Some homeless people were sleeping while sitting up, relishing these few hours when most of the cops are at home in their beds, like everyone should be. Outside the revolving glass door, I could see a family screaming at each other and waving their cigarette-holding hands in the air. Some baby I couldn't see was yowling tunelessly.

I showed up to the main store and got the coffee, already inside the tall airpots. It's all part of the robot-routine, same thing every day. Load them into a cart, push it to the stand. Some suited humans followed me, just like dogs follow strings of sausages in old cartoons. Unlock the cash register and put my till inside; unlock the cabinet where we keep the cream and sugar and cups. I set everything up and there was already a little line. A woman with a mauve, shoulder-padded blazer gave me the most grimace-y smile ever. She's a regular, I guess, but we'd never talked before. "This is the high point of my day. It's all I have to look forward to." I struggled not to reel, in sadness and shock. She gets *decaf.* Everything takes on such resonance when you haven't slept.

"Um, that's, um, really sad." The resonance replaces the articulation. She frowns and leaves. I am so awkward. How did I ever get this job? Why did I even try to be humane to her? I am a coffee-bot, I should know better. I take crumpled dollar bills, I punch frequent-sipper cards. I redeem a few. Tenth cup of coffee, it's free. Usually the commuters treated me like I wasn't even there. When they did acknowledge my presence, it's usually just as the coffee-bot and not as a human being who doesn't like being yelled at and ordered around. Mostly it was just a blur of gray, and the faces are all interchangeable. Sometimes there's a word, a gesture, a reaching out that stays with me. But mostly it was a blur.

Once the commuter rush died down, the homeless-people rush picked up. I handed out cups of coffee. They handed me a dollar, I opened the register and handed back four quarters in change. I have security cameras trained on me, like executioners' rifles, so I have to do this play-acting. See, they're paying me. I ain't helping nobody who needs it, no way. That's how it looks on the tape, all grainy and gray.

The homeless people are awesome because they are bursts of color in the endless flock of gray suits, and because they actually talk to me, they see me as human. There is the woman who always wears garish red lipstick and hands nickels to everyone as though they were special prizes. There is the old guy who likes to rant about how much he hates the church. There's the woman who is either loudly singing about love or getting into fistfights with an invisible person. On good days, she looks deeply into my eyes and calls me "sweetie."

But my favorite homeless guy was Torquil, a chatty middle-aged alcoholic. He always has something to say, whether it's about the pigeons cuddling in the rafters or the McDonald's employees snorting coke off the top of the soda machine. He always wears a tattered Jaegermeister shirt underneath whatever weird coat he's scrounged up for the day. His coats rotate, but that t-shirt remains the same.

Torquil is so funny that sometimes I forget what his life must be like. One day he leaned over the counter and looked into my eyes and said, "Babygirl," (he never could remember my name, but when he said "babygirl" I knew he meant me) "I need a drink so goddamn bad. I wish I could just drink this damn shirt," he said, tugging at it with shaky hands, looking at the faded Jaegermeister logo sorrowfully. "I would just drink this damn shirt, if I could," he repeated. I pulled a five out of the register and gave it to him so he could quiet his shaking. He was making me a little shaky, too. I didn't ring up the next five dollars' worth of customers' coffee, so the register balanced out at the end of my shift.

Torquil usually stopped by at around 9:30 to get his first cup of coffee, but he was nowhere to be found today. Sometimes Torquil would disappear for a few days and come back with a new story about some hot lady he'd met or some weird odd job he'd gotten, so I wasn't too concerned. Life continued at the coffee/cigarette/newsstand as per usual. Lots of yawns, lots of refills. Occasionally, a counter was wiped in a bored manner. I tried reading the newspaper between customers, but all the letters blurred together.

I gave up on the paper and saw some girl was standing there, waiting for me. She wanted cigarettes, and I carded her and realized that she was my age. Nineteen, born in the same month, even. Her face inside the shiny little driver's license square looked fresh and hopeful. I didn't want to look at the bags under my eyes on my ID, didn't want to look at the angry DMV glare. I don't drive or smoke anymore, and I'm too young for it to be good for anything else, so it was able to remain buried in my sock drawer most of the time.

I hated this girl, briefly, because she was clean and wearing clothes that matched and didn't look tired, didn't look hungry at all. Because I had had too many nights lately when the dumpsters were empty, when I paid my bills and had only twenty dollars to get me through the week. When I chewed on crappy bagels all month until I felt bloated and exhausted and so used up, and felt like things would always be like this, that they would never get any better. Nights where I lay awake, shivering under my stained blankets from curbside freeboxes, nights where my breath clouded in front of my face in my bedroom, when I forgot what being warm was like. Where the cold turned me slow, when I felt like an iguana in search of a heated rock. Nights when the mice skittering around my room kept me awake and nervous. And then when the mice stopped the car alarms started, so I couldn't sleep unless I was on the brink of total exhaustion.

On good days, I looked at this as a price to pay for all the fun and danger, of not being tied into a cubicle or college or a boring, useless family. It was the price of being free, of being part of a whirling dervish of art and chaos and love. On bad days, I wanted a new life. I would take anything else. Anything.

The cigarette-buying girl probably had parents who gave her a car, who paid the insurance, who bought groceries and cooked dinner. She probably watched TV at night, sitting in a comfortable chair in a room where the thermostat was set at an unnoticeable temperature. She was probably not caught up in a whirling dervish of any sort, as anyone living in the midst of art and chaos and love would not wear that shade of gray, for any reason.

She paid with a careless $20 bill, coming out of a wallet that looked as though it had been bought new. She gave me a polite half-smile and I realized I was staring at her. For a second, I just wanted things to be easy. For me, for her, for all of us.

Still, I hated her. I hated her because I wanted to be nineteen sometimes, really be nineteen and not this raging old person in a nineteen-year-old's body. Because I wanted to have everything going for me, because I wanted a bright future, because I wanted old men to stop shaking their heads at me in disgust. I was so mad at this girl that I knew nothing about, at everything she had, at everything she took for granted. "Thanks, and have a nice day," I said, insincerely. She directed a smile-shaped scowl at me. She spun on her heel, blow-dried hair waving in her wake, and then she was gone.

I tried to subtly sniff my armpits by pretending that I was scratching my back, like my armpit happened to land right in front of my nose by accident. Not that my sniffing was doing any good: I'd forgotten what normal girls were expected to smell like. Was it sugary or spicy or just bland, just like nothing? When my boss handed me the coffee earlier that morning, she made a face as if she had smelled something really awful. Was I that awful thing? My boss had smelled like artificial strawberries. They were mechanical, planned, a lonely biochemist's idea of what a strawberry was.

My "subtle" armpit-sniffing session was interrupted when Torquil showed up. "Hey!" I said. "What have you been doing all morning?"

"Oh, babygirl, today I went for a long-ass walk. I went to the hospital, because a lot of times you can get cigarettes from those ashtrays out front, because a lot of times people will have a puff or two and get called away and leave a whole cigarette behind, you know?"

"Hell yeah," I said. I'd done it myself.

"So I see my cousin's friend Clay outside the building, scrubbing some shit off that smells fuckin' nasty. He sees me and says he'll give me five bucks to do it because he's got a hangover and doesn't want to deal with it. So I start scrubbing, but then some other hospital guy comes out to yell at me because I'm not wearing a uniform. So I said, 'Fuck you, I don't even work here!' He said he was going to call the cops on me, so I left."

"Here, dude, let me get you a cup of coffee. On the house." It was all I can do. I suck.

"Coffee? Fuck that! I took my five dollars and got some Old E. I'm starting my day off right."

"You want some chips? Candy? Anything?"

"Nah, I'm good. I gotta go. They're throwin' out roses at the flower stand. I gotta date tonight, Babygirl, I gotta impress her!" and then he ran off. Fuck. Last night it had felt like Violet and Xandria and I were really changing something. But today, in the harsh glare of the station lights, things look so different. Who were *we* to think that hospital administrators would see a crust of slimy juice and change their evil ways? Who were we to think we could do a goddamn thing? The hospital was so big. It was never coming down. And we weren't changing shit.

Torquil eventually left and I had a few minutes to myself to process what he'd said. Conclusion? I suck. That's usually the verdict in my head. No hung juries, no plea-bargains. Straight to the land of suckiness. As if to prove a point, The Nickel Lady came up to me and nodded her special nod. I poured her a cup of coffee with lots of cream and sugar, and as payment she handed me a bottle cap. The Nickel Lady's usual shtick involved handing us a nickel and blessing us five times. She was really into the number five, and nickels in general. So this bottle cap was something new, but I thanked her as if what she had handed me was in fact legal tender.

"Read the inside," she said, in a stern tone of voice. The Nickel Lady hardly ever spoke when she wasn't reciting a mysterious blessing, so I snapped to attention. I flipped it over, expecting to see *Sorry, try again* or

You've won! Instead, printed in no-nonsense computer font, it said, *Get a life.*

"Get a life?!" I said. "You think I don't have a life?"

"Mmm-hmm," she said meaningfully, and then she turned on her heel and walked away purposefully, like she had an appointment she'd suddenly remembered. I tucked it into my pocket, clinking with all the nickels she'd given to me. Maybe it was stupid, but I believed in her blessings, I believed in her nickels. Maybe she was just some crazy woman who lived at the train station, but I chose to view her as a portal to another world. She delivered messages with her nickels and her strange muttered prayers. She'd chosen *me*, somehow. That was enough. She didn't ever talk to my boss, or to the severe-ponytailed woman who replaced me at noon. I'd tried to make small talk about The Nickel Lady to Ponytail-That-Means-It, but she just stared at me in disbelief. That was her usual reaction to me, though, and to anything I said, so I didn't think much of it.

The rest of the day passed. I got through it, somehow. And eventually it was noon. Noon, for lots of people, means lunch. Noon means quittin' time for me. No-nonsense-ponytail showed up at 12:03 and I dashed for the main office to punch out. The benches and people and tiles were all starting to blur together. *Just get home!* I yelled at myself, silently. *Left foot. Right foot. Left foot. Right foot,* over and over again. And that's how I made it to the time clock.

On the walk back, I bumped into Torquil, a few beers into his day. "Daaaamn, babygirl! You look rough!" I just nodded and kept walking towards my bike. Unlocking my trusty steed, I limped home on sidewalks and back alleys, not trusting myself to react to a car on one of the main streets. And before I knew it, I saw the gigantic mound of festering vegetables that said I was home. My bike squeaked through the trashed backyard somehow. I unwrapped the thick chain from around my waist and wound it around my bike, snapped the rusty padlock around the ends, and then opened the back door and walked inside.

I found Jasmine and Violet going through a garbage bag of pastries in the living room, trying to find a single, perfect bagel. They took the moldy and stale ones and tossed them over their collective shoulders. One skidded off of my shin, but I barely noticed. Violet jumped up, apologized, and kissed me. I hugged her languidly, leaning on her with all my weight. She took me upstairs, led me by the hand to my futon from which she had risen only an hour before. I laid down hard, and she tried to pull her hand away, but I held it tighter. I only know this because she told me later. I was already asleep.

CHAPTER 6

A few hours later, I was jolted awake by someone talking loudly in the living room. I could pick Violet's distinctive laugh out of all the other noise, but other than that it was all a blur. I laid in the dark for a while and tried to gather the strength to lift the toppled bookshelf of exhaustion off my chest. But I wasn't strong enough, mostly because of a familiar gnawing below my stomach.

My brain sent an exploratory committee, in the form of my hand, down between my legs. It came back smeared with blood. I muttered, "Fuck," and rolled over and off my mattress, crawling to the collection of rust-stained rags in my underwear drawer. I folded one into thirds, like I was making a burrito, and safety-pinned it to the inside of my underwear. It seems so unfair that no matter how much I move like a boy, how much I get called "sir" in the ladies' room, my body never understood. It thought it was perfectly applicable to cause me all sorts of pain, thinking I'd get a baby out of it some day. My body didn't know that the filth in piles all around my house would kill a baby. It didn't know that Violet could fuck me all she wanted with her silicone cock and my womb would still be blissfully free of any child-parasites. I heard children screaming at the grocery store and I wanted to behead them, and there's a giant hole in the ozone layer that would fry up any offspring of mine before they got to junior high. Still, my fallopian tubes kept blithely sucking eggs into my uterus like everything was fine. As if there was any sort of a welcoming environment, inside or outside of my body, for me or the baby. Or for anyone.

Violet came upstairs to see if I was awake yet and found me curled into a ball. "What's wrong?"

"Uggh, cramps. Ugghh."

"Your uterus is probably feeling yucky because you drank so much coffee today."

"Yucky?! What are you, a kindergarten teacher?"

"Oh, fuck off."

"Argh. It needs to stop torturing me! I'll drink some goddamn coffee if I want to." I started pounding on the rounded mound between my hipbones, the one that always got in the way of the kind of pants I liked to wear, making the top button pop open at the most inopportune moments. I was knocking like I would knock on the door of someone who had seriously pissed me off. "Fuck you! Stop doing that! I'm not ever gonna have any babies, so quit it!" My pounding just made everything worse, and I knew it, but I was too mad to stop. The only thing that did stop me was the realization that I sounded exactly like my mother.

"Ssh," Violet said. She made me lie down, and put her hands on my lower stomach. She started massaging, gently. We lay like that for a few minutes, her working on me as if I were some sort of fragile dough. I began to feel the panic subsiding a little bit. Every month, no matter how much I think I'm ready for the pain, I'm never really ready. My brain blocks out how bad it is. But when Violet touches me, it's so sweet, so comforting, so genuinely concerned. It takes the edge off.

Eventually she lay down next to me, her hand never leaving, the front of her knees against the back of mine. "Your body isn't just this *thing*," she whispered into my ear.

"But—"

"No. There are no buts. Your body is pissed off, because you're treating it like shit. And the more you treat it like shit, the more it's going to hurt you."

"Hmph."

"You can hmph all you want, but you know I'm right." There was absolutely nothing that Violet adored more than being right, besides maybe having someone else tell her she was right. Her hand became lighter, jumpier against my skin, the joy spreading through her fingernails.

"How was your day?" I asked, wanting desperately to talk about something other than my body.

"Oh, y'know. I woke up, then I had coffee and bagels with Xandria and Jasmine, and we found this teen magazine in a pile of crap, so we gave each other the quizzes, but, like, we had to change the wording to fit our lives. Because I, like, can't relate to 'How Boy-Crazy Are You?' or 'Are You In the Right Gym Class?' So that was fun, and then I went to my drug study while you were asleep, and then I went home and did some dishes and changed my cat's litter box and made sure that my roommates aren't dead, and then I came back to say hi to you…"

Violet was always in these drug studies, as a way of getting some extra cash while she was in school. She was a women's/queer studies major at the big, impersonal university downtown, and she'd be graduating in the spring. She was currently in a study testing a new kind of yeast infection cream. "It was so crazy, because today, they had to, like, take a picture of my vag! With this super-expensive camera that must've cost more money than God's yacht. And it was hooked up to this computer screen, so I got to see my vag and then my cervix all large and in charge on the screen. And then they cut out a little chunk of it, like, one-sixteenth of an inch wide, just enough to look at on a microscope, and then they gave me two hundred bucks! Pretty sweet. Do you want to go out for Indian food? I'm buying."

I love Violet. "Yeah....but I'm *so* sleepy...." My voice took on a dreamlike quality, in bed with my girl. It's like her arms around me pressed some sort of button that made my tough-girl exterior roll down like a power window. Doesn't matter how much I cursed and yelled, or how much beer I drank, or how many targets I hit with my phlegm projectiles. I was just like a Boston crème donut that had been sitting in the dumpster far too long: my exterior was stale and cracked, but inside I was still full of this delicious goo. I didn't always mind when Violet took a bite, exposing my insides to the air; it felt kind of good. But if anyone else had seen me like that, there would be trouble. The goo would attract flies, it would turn hard and lumpy if exposed to the air for too long. It might get me smashed into hard little crumbs.

But Violet seemed to know how to extract the goo safely. It didn't hurt that she used to work in a pastry shop, that she had access to all sorts of tools for injecting fillings into fancy donuts and precious cupcakes and all sorts of things that I usually didn't taste before they hit the garbage bag. She knew how to do it without breaking my skin.

"How was your day?" she asked.

"Oh, it was stupid," I said. "I was sooo tired. And some bratty kid asked if I was a boy or a girl and didn't believe me when I said I'm a girl."

"You look like a girl to me."

"I know! I mean, *hello*," I said, pointing my chin at the outline of my breasts swaddled under my layers and layers of clothes. "I have these enormous embarrassing, you know, um, tits." Violet giggled at my ineptness at talking about my lady parts, and then I continued. "But I guess little kids aren't looking for those. But it's still annoying. Like, why do they care? I was just standing there."

"I love your enormous embarrassing tits," she breathed into my ear, cupping one in her hand and squeezing her face next to my neck. She gave me a bitey little kiss and pulled away, looked at me in a way that makes me shiver all over. "But I'm too hungry to fuck you now. Let's go get Indian food!"

"Yeah, baby," I said, in a sleepy voice. "Let's go get Indian food." She took my hand and hoisted me from the bed, or at least tried to. I was still so heavy with tiredness—that invisible bookshelf still balanced on my ribcage—that she fell on top of me, and we giggled cutely for a few minutes, kissed each others' faces softly. I plead the Fifth as to whether any noses were bitten. My tough lady credentials are going to be revoked for sure.

Eventually I pulled myself out of her arms and clobbered down the stairs to find Xandria in the kitchen, chopping up some battle-weary bell peppers and frying some kind of stuffing for them, filling the air with a thick, homey scent. Violet and I nodded our approval. "You want some?" Xandria asked.

"Nah," Violet said proudly. "I'm taking my girl out for some Indian food, courtesy of my cervix!"

"Ha," Xandria said, and kept chopping. "Man, I've been thinking about last night all day. That was so fucking awesome."

"Yeah, we showed them!" crowed Violet. I looked at her eyes, shining so bright with that memory. I smiled back at her, feeling tense and weak and liar-y. She gave me a psychic-girlfriend what's-wrong look, and I put my hand over my abdomen and headed to the bathroom for some ibuprofen. I was not going to bear the responsibility of being the fire extinguisher for those eyes, so I kept my mouth shut.

In the grimy bathroom, I twisted the cap on the store-brand pain reliever bottle that looked like it had been through a war. I tossed the caplets into my mouth, then turned my hand into an inadequate, leaky cup. I glared at myself in the mirror. I looked sleepy and pain-ridden, but otherwise okay. My hair stuck up in greasy angles that I thought looked kind of good, even if it made my co-workers sniff in disgust. A withering hickey was visible just above my collarbone. Something crashed in the living room, followed by a muffled round of giggling. I took the Nickel Lady's bottlecap out of my pocket. What does she know? I have a life, and I like it just fine. Usually I saved everything she gave me, kept her nickels in an old pill bottle instead of spending them, because I knew that they were her blessings. But this one, I didn't even hesitate. It clattered into my wastebasket, and then it was gone.

PART TWO: XANDRIA

CHAPTER ONE

After Violet and Tabitha got on their bikes and squeaked out the door, I kept cooking my stuffed peppers. The Food Not Bon-Bons pickup guy had dropped three boxes of them on our back porch yesterday, and we couldn't use them all at serving. So it's bell peppers today and tonight and probably forever, until their green skins shrivel and turn black; because I'm broke but at least not hungry, not while this box lasts.

I thought about Indian food, about curry and coriander and turmeric. I thought about ginger and chickpeas and potatoes. My mouth watered; I wanted it so bad. I never had curry until after I ran away. Curry is a dirty word in big houses in Minnesota. Curry is for other people in other countries, in other parts of town. I had never had any until I ran away from lockdown with Spleen.

Me and Spleen met at some private mental hospital. If things were a little different, we probably would have been in juvie, sex-segregated, and we wouldn't have ever met. But our families had some money, so we got sent there instead. Tough love. The kind advertised in the back of rich-people magazines. That's what they call it when your parents don't love you, but want to at least pretend. Spleen was in there because he was on heroin and sold his mom's golf clubs on Craigslist for drug money. I was in there because my dad was raping me and I told people. Since my dad is a pillar of the community, and not just some crazy slob, that made me a behavior problem. Incorrigible.

Maybe if I'd confessed tearfully in a school counselor's office, things might have been different. But I told by screaming and flipping out and cursing a lot, and it was when I was already in lots of trouble for a whole bunch of other things, so when my dad stood there calmly and said, "This girl is out of control," things didn't look so good for me. Nobody questioned why I was flipping out so hard; and nobody seemed to stop and think that maybe a rapist can be calm and charming for ten minutes. So I got sent away and he got to stay in that huge house with a swimming pool and a cleaning lady.

But it wasn't all bad, because it got me out of that house, and I met Spleen. When everyone else was screaming at each other in the bullshitty group therapy, Spleen and I would look at each other and smirk. We started sneaking cigarettes in the courtyard and soon there were rumors that we were fucking, but that wouldn't happen until after we ran away. Inside, we were just friends. Really good friends. We didn't need to talk to understand each other. I could finally relax around him. And when he told me that he had a plan and wanted me to come along, of course I went.

When we got to Minneapolis, a very long, cold and dirty train ride later, we walked around, looking for Spleen's friend who owed him a favor. We went to this park where he usually hung out, and he wasn't there, but we found a Food Not Bon-Bons serving. The people there handed me a plate of something that was so delicious. I hadn't eaten in so long, I would have eaten anything, but it actually was really good. Potatoes and chickpeas and onions and garlic. *What's this?* I asked Spleen. *Curry,* he said, *and maybe some ginger and coconut milk.*

It was almost as good as the train ride, the first second the train pulled away and started chugging along, when we realized we weren't going to get thrown off, when we felt so fucking free. The woods going past the open boxcar door, and I looked at the scenery like I might look at a lover if I believed in that shit. This spice tasted like the first minute of that train ride, before the cold and the sleeplessness and the hunger. *Yeah, this is some good shit*, I said, like I knew what I was talking about. He nodded distractedly and said *we have to get out of here.*

We walked forever. He took me to a squat in St. Paul that he used to stay at when he was using. He got a friend who owed him a favor to front him a bag, and he cut some lines for us with the edge of a butter knife, right on the kitchen table.

"Aren't you supposed to use needles?" I asked. Such a stupid girl. I didn't know anything back then.

"Nah, that's what people did in the 70's, back when it was weak. You don't have to go to all that trouble now. Plus, if you sniff it, you don't need it so bad. At least not at first. Here, watch how I do it," and he trimmed the straw with his knife, inserted it in his nostril, closed the other side with his finger, and the line disappeared. He tilted his head back and sniffed. A lazy smile crept across his face and his whole body relaxed visibly. "Fuck yeah," he said.

He handed the straw to me. I vacuumed up the line with my nose, and I felt this sense of relief that I'd never felt before. I felt so completely calm. My ankle that I'd twisted running for the train didn't hurt at all anymore, and the general feeling of total horribleness that I'd just mistaken for my life went away for a little bit. My stomach was so full. Life was kinda okay, even if we were sitting on a cement floor littered with broken glass and fast food wrappers. Even though everything in our lives was totally fucked, and always had been. I'd gotten all kinds of high before, but it was never like this.

I was in love. Maybe with Spleen, maybe with heroin, or maybe just with curry. I don't know. Out of those three, all I have now is a shaker can of curry that Jasmine got at the dollar store a year ago. Not the good shit that the Twin Cities Food Not Bon-Bons people had. I've never had a meal as good as the one me and Spleen had on a paper plate, shivering in the cold on a park bench. I've also never gotten as high as I did that first time, either. I peaked when I was sixteen, apparently.

Now I'm twenty-two and everything is still fucked. Now I scoop filling into trash-picked bell peppers, in a house with electricity, with a working stove. I guess it's better. I don't really know. The filling was made out of whatever crap we had laying around. It smelled okay, but it looked so watery. I popped the peppers into the oven and set the timer, and then crumpled against the counter, suddenly too tired to stand. I've been drinking for days now; days and days. Years and years, actually, but who's counting? Cheap 40's with some old traveler friends, rotgut whiskey by myself, down by the river. Boxed wine at the art gallery opening I walked into with Lydia and Tabitha. Something pretentious was on the walls that didn't speak to me, so I just started gulping cup after cup of wine. The other gallery patrons avoided me, but I've learned to think that that kind of thing is funny.

I went to my room and pulled a bumjug of cheap wine out of the case I'd bought earlier in the week when I had some money. I liked to spend all my money on booze in bulk. Get rid of all my cash at the liquor store. That way, I knew I'd never have enough to buy a bag again. I lugged it downstairs, my wrist twisting with the weight, and hauled it onto the kitchen counter. There weren't any clean cups and I didn't feel like doing the dishes in the huge dish-mound, but I found a mason jar that was pretty clean. I poured the wine out and took a long sip, winced at its warmness, sipped again, put the bumjug in the refrigerator.

Lydia, Jasmine and some nerdy-looking boy all tramped into the kitchen, where the stuffed peppers were stewing in their juices. "Oh, yum!" Jasmine yelled. "That smells so good! You're gonna let us have some, right?"

I looked at the huge tray of peppers stewing. "No," I said sarcastically, "I'm going to eat these things all by my fucking self." Secretly I was glad they were home. Whenever I was alone too much, I started feeling really crazy. Started remembering things I didn't want to.

"Well, damn, tiger," Jasmine said, running some tap water into a washed-out margarine tub and taking a giant gulp. "Thanks for cooking."

"Xandria, this is Steve. He used to be friends with me and Jasmine back when we were girlfriends," Lydia said. The guy looked at me and didn't say anything, which is fine. It's not like I'm Miss Manners. Plus he looked kind of boring. He was wearing overly ironic nerd glasses, with a shockingly blue cardigan hiding his twig-sized wrists.

"Back when I was nuts!" Jasmine yelled, and they both exchanged a look. Lydia and Jasmine were always talking about when they were girlfriends, like it was *so wild!* Their current relationship wasn't that different from being girlfriends. Even though they were both always fucking other people, they still had something that they excluded other people from, and they liked it that way.

They all started talking about all this shit I didn't know about and didn't care about. Old housemates, old inside jokes, things like that. Lydia kept calling the guy "Juicebox" and Jasmine would laugh so hard that someone had to pound her on the back so she wouldn't choke on her water.

"Hey, Juicebox," Jasmine gasped, "remember that time we found a bagel on the parking meter?"

"Uh huh," the boy said.

"Oh yeah! I forgot about that. That was sooo funny." Lydia crowed.

Jasmine looked at me and said, "One time, back in the day, we went for a walk with Juicebox over here..."

"My name's Steve!" cried the weird dude, and Lydia and Jasmine erupted into a fit of helpless giggles. I pulled the bumjug of Carlo Rossi from the refrigerator and topped off the mason jar I'd been swilling from.

The wine was cooling down a little, so the evening wasn't a total wash just yet.

"Anyway," said Jasmine, after she'd pulled herself together, "Juicebox wanted to go to the beer distributor on Chester Street, and so we went for a walk—it was really late, like, after midnight anyway, and it was hot out so everyone was on their stoop. And Lydia had convinced me to wear a skirt for some goddamn reason—"

"Because you look *good* in them!" interrupted Lydia. "Butch, my ass." I opened up the oven and poked a pepper with a fork. It seemed done enough to me, so I pulled a plate off the dish-mound, gave it a little rinse, shook it off, and plopped two peppers onto my plate.

"Hmph," Jasmine said, "anyway, so me and Lydia were holding hands, because we were girlfriends—*ew*—and we walked by this stoop that was all, like, junior high girls, and one of them was like, 'Oh, you're gay?' and we were all like, yeah! And then one of them yelled, 'IS THAT A *MAN* IN A *SKIRT*?' and the other ones were all like, 'Nooooooo,' like she was so dumb for not being hip to genderqueer style, and we were all laughing about that, like so hard, and then we found this giant bagel! On a parking meter! It was, like, the size of a record!"

I laughed, despite myself. "Whoa," I pronounced. "Did you eat it?"

"Nah, it was stale," said Jasmine. "But we did take it home. One of Lydia's housemates spray-painted it silver and she hung it in their kitchen for so long. Until they moved out."

"That was such a fun night!" Lydia crowed. "We laughed so hard, I think Juicebox peed his pants.".

"Shut up!" yelled Juicebox/Steve, who had been quietly eating his stuffed bell pepper throughout the story, directly from his outstretched hand, chewing with his mouth open. "I did not!"

"So, Xandria," said Lydia, sensing my growing boredom with the conversation, "I thought you had some guy coming over tonight. What happened to him?"

"I don't know," I said. "I guess he's not coming. And his phone was shut off, so I don't know where he is. I guess he'll show up if he wants to show up." I wasn't really all that disappointed, or even surprised.

"Those guys are always doing stupid shit to you. You should totally play for the other team," said Jasmine.

"Ooh, are you hitting on me?" I said half-heartedly. "Sorry, I don't date people who like to process. I like guys because they don't say anything." I saw Lydia and Jasmine exchange a look. "See? You guys just said about twenty sentences about me without even opening your mouths. That would make me crazy."

"So you don't want to date anyone with anything to say? Isn't that, like, kind of unfulfilling?" Lydia interjected.

"I don't *date* anyone. I hang out with people. Sometimes we fuck. It's really not a big deal, and it's really not your business, either." I took a big, forceful bite of my stuffed pepper and I heard a weird crack. It resonated deep within my head. I felt something hard in my mouth, mixed in with the soft squishy pepper, and spit out half of a bloody tooth.

"Shit!" I yelled. Everyone stopped talking about my sex life for a minute. Lydia and Jasmine crowded around me while Steve/Juicebox sat in his stool, looking awkwardly to the side.

This wasn't the first tooth I'd lost. A shitty boyfriend back in Minneapolis had punched me in the face once because he thought I'd done the last of his drugs; there went my left eyetooth. I was fucked-up at the time so I hardly felt it. He was right, I had done the last of his drugs.

And a few of my teeth had rotted and I'd gotten them pulled at the free clinic a few years back. I didn't brush them a lot. I spent years without running water. I didn't have a toothbrush, usually. Who the fuck cared? Worrying about my teeth seemed as ridiculous as worrying about my Bermuda vacation fund or stock portfolio. Dentists were for other people, leading other kinds of lives. People who thought they'd be around for awhile.

So, yeah, I'm missing a few teeth. But I thought I was beyond all that. I thought I didn't have the kind of life that teeth ran screaming from anymore. Looking at this bloody little tooth in my palm, all I could think was *my past will never be behind me*. I shuddered, and it almost fell from my palm.

"Ew," said Lydia, "Let me see." I opened my mouth wide and she pressed a few buttons on her cell phone, turning on the screen so the light shone in my mouth. "Oh, gross!" she yelled admiringly. "It's, like, this piece of tooth just sticking out!"

"Like a gravestone on a hill," said Jasmine, peering in.

"You can go to the dental school. They'll probably dig it out for free." Lydia suggested.

"Fuck! Not another one," I sighed sarcastically. "How am I ever going to be a lawyer now?"

"You're going to need a lot of Derma-Blend too. That tattoo's gonna clash with your power suit," said Lydia.

"Yeah, I guess I'll just be a toothless fuckup, forever and ever amen." I took another sip of my wine to punctuate my statement.

"You could be a fortune-teller!" Jasmine cried. "You could have a card table and sit under the bridge and be spooky and tell people devastatingly accurate things about themselves. You don't need a full set of teeth for that."

"Yeah, that's a good idea. That's a great idea," I said, staring off into space.

"Or, like, back when I lived in Brooklyn, I used to date this girl who used to date this girl who was in the Coney Island freak show. She was a sword-swallower, and she had a big old tattoo on her face. And she was everyone's favorite freak. She would just stand in front of all those tourists and swallow a huge sword with a big old smile on her face."

"Yeah, I guess I should practice that," I said. "I know how to eat fire—"

"Oh!" Lydia interrupted, "do you remember Wileen? From Trouble Squat? That girl with all the lug nuts in her hair, who's in India now?"

"Oh, yeah, I forgot about her," said Jasmine. Juicebox nodded.

"She lost a tooth, just from, like, not brushing them enough or something. This was before you moved here, Xandria. And so she had to get it yanked, and she was really sad about it, so she got Crazy Benny to give her a commemorative tattoo. She couldn't think of a design, so she said he could just do what he wanted, because she already had almost full sleeves and just had a little blank spot near her armpit. So he made this beautiful tattoo of a tooth with wings and a halo, flying straight up to heaven. And there was a banner underneath it and in scripty font it said, 'Farewell Faithful Friend.' And every time I saw it I would just laugh and laugh. I think you should get that tattoo. I need a good laugh."

"But this is my fourth tooth that I've lost. I'd have to get four tattoos. And you laugh all the fucking time."

"You could get a tattoo of them so they look like the Beatles," the weird boy said. "Like the cover of Abbey Road, but with teeth!"

Lydia and Jasmine shrieked with laughter. I rolled my eyes. "Uh... no." I kept running my tongue over the sharp, pointy edge that used to be my entire molar. "It's so weird. It doesn't hurt at all. You'd think that your tooth breaking in half would really hurt. But it doesn't. The last time I got a tooth yanked, it hurt so bad."

"You probably missed the nerve," Lydia said. "But you need to get it pulled so that it doesn't get infected. This boy I used to date had that happen to him, and he couldn't sleep or anything after a while. His life was hell. So, seriously, make an appointment now. Don't wait for it to get bad."

I wonder when I'll stop losing teeth. When I'll stop being a fuck-up so bad that everyone notices. When my nights won't end with blood or screams or pieces of my body staring up at me from my hand, asking, *Hey, what are you gonna do? What the fuck are you going to do now?*

CHAPTER TWO

The next day, I woke up with a big hole in my mouth, just like I had when I'd gone to sleep. But there's always that moment, when I first wake up, where I feel okay. I wondered, for a second, why my mouth felt so raw. Then everything that happened the day before, and all the years before, crashed back down and I remembered.

I don't really care about my tooth. It's just another thing. My head ached from all the wine I'd drunk last night, and I wished I were dead. Then I wished I had a bag, then I wished I had a cigarette, and then I wished I had a beer. The usual morning lineup. I rolled off my futon and onto the cold hard floor with a long, sharp sigh. I had to get out of bed this way, every day. Throw myself from the warm blankets onto the floor, or else I'd just stay in bed forever.

I blearily walked downstairs in a daze, holding onto the splintery banister so I wouldn't fall on my stupid face. The stairs ended in the weird pinkish-red kitchen, which was good, because I always went straight to the coffee maker and made a pot. Thick and sludgy, just how I like it.

There's a gigantic metal shelf-thing in the corner and it doesn't really fit, it's a little too big and it gets a little too close to the counter, so you have to squeeze past it. No matter how steady you think you are, some part of you always brushes against it, and it rattles and it feels like everything is just going to fall on you; all the dollar-store spices and washed-out spaghetti sauce jars full of dried beans, all the fluttery coffee filters and random napkins and boxes of rice and pasta piled high. That's where we kept the coffee, in a wrinkly paper bag, "donated" to the house by Tabitha's coffee stand job. I grabbed the bag, then turned around and opened the lid of the coffee maker and dumped the used grounds into the compost bucket, which was full of festering potato skins and carrot tops. I shook the bag over the basket of the coffeemaker. Then I rinsed the coffee pot in the sink, which was hard because it was so overflowing with dishes that I could only tilt it in sideways. I poured the light-brown water into the machine and leaned against the counter, watching it drip, waiting, waiting, waiting to feel human again.

After a cup I felt good, or at least good enough to go on with life. Here for another day. I went back upstairs to my room to grab my giant, festering can of tobacco and some rolling papers. I sat on the stiff, cold porch-couch and rolled a cigarette. The cold air stung my face a little and I sucked the bitter tobacco taste deep into my mouth and lungs. There was a monster living in my ribcage; it needed cigarettes tossed to it every few hours or else it would sink its claws deep into me. With every puff, the claws retracted, but they were still waiting above my skin, waiting for the next time it got too hungry.

Then it was time to call the dental school and yell at them a lot. Those fuckers wanted me to wait almost two weeks with this huge hole in my gums. I yelled about how I was an emergency, how a tooth had fallen out of my head, how it could get infected and kill me. I got bumped up from next Thursday to this Monday. That's one thing my dad taught me—ask and ye shall receive. He was such an asshole, but that skill has gotten me places in life.

When that was over, I pulled a dumpster-bagel from the freezer and stuck it in the crumb-blackened toaster oven. I pulled it out and slathered some pale buttery spread from a giant container. I chewed on the bagel, poured another cup of coffee, put some good music on the sticker-covered boombox that belonged to Jasmine when she was in junior high school. And then, slightly hyper with all the coffee in my veins and all the yelling on the boombox, I started cleaning up the kitchen. I wiped the counter down with a graying sponge, I swept the floor. I started picking through the Food Not Bon-Bons donations and throwing out the rot, but

I got overwhelmed and had to stop. Something about all that green, and then all that black.

One thing that sucked about living in this house was that all the bad shit that I thought I'd buried came rising to the surface, like pond scum. When I was squatting, I didn't have time to think about how my dad raped me, how my mom let it happen, and everything else. I thought about that sometimes back then, but just when things were getting too crazy inside my head, a window would shatter and we'd all have to scramble trying to patch it with plywood and garbage bags. Or else the cops would come and we'd have to find somewhere new to live. Or someone would have a seizure or they'd take too much or something and we'd have to figure out how to save their life, remember which emergency room didn't call the cops on junkies. And whenever things were quiet, I could always score a bag and not have to think about anything.

Here on Asterisk Street, little things would happen, and everyone would make a huge deal about them. We'd get a high gas bill and everyone would freak out about paying it. Or a dish would sit unwashed on the counter for two weeks until the grease got permanently stuck onto it. Angry or passive-aggressive notes would be written on the dry-erase board on the kitchen. Stuff like that. Everyone else acted like it was the Apocalypse, but it was never enough to jolt me out of myself, so I didn't care.

In this house, I either laid around pointlessly or else I paced the house a whole lot, full of nervous energy and something else I couldn't name. It made me ball up my fists so hard that my nails dug into my palm. It made me bite the inside of my lips and cheeks until they bled. I couldn't cry. I wouldn't cry. I would have conversations with the past. I would yell, "Fuck you!" to the empty house until it echoed. That's all I could say. I said it a hundred times a day, until someone came home. Then I would just say it under my breath, when I thought they weren't listening.

Sometimes I talked to Spleen's ghost. He'd been dead for almost three years now. I couldn't remember exactly when he died, I just know it was when I was in jail. I didn't find out he was dead until the day I got out. I was down by the underpass, by the Mississippi river. It was cold out, but one of those sunny cold days that gives people false hope. I saw Dionne, sitting there with her dog. Dionne was always out there, no matter how shitty the weather was.

"Hey," I said.

"Hey. Where have you been? Haven't seen you in a while."

"Jail."

"That sucks."

"Yeah, I got the sweats pretty bad," I said, and we both laughed a battery-acid laugh. Those same sweats had leaked from her pores. It wasn't funny. "Yeah, I called our dealer twice, but he hasn't been calling back."

"That sucks."

"So what's been going on?"

Her face dropped. "Oh, shit," she said, "You didn't hear about Spleen?" and I knew what she was going to say. I knew that tone of voice. I heard it a lot back then. One girl froze to death, one guy was killed by a trick. One guy jumped in front of a train on purpose and one girl was hit by a car on accident. But mostly drugs. And mostly I didn't care; they were shitty people. Even when they weren't so shitty, I didn't really care about anything besides getting high back then. Spleen said it was because your brain gets confused, because the chemicals in heroin are exactly like the chemicals your brain releases when you feel love or feel excited or whatever, and so it stops making those chemicals. Sometimes little things broke through: dancing at a show, sleeping with somebody new, the moment when the train pulled away and started going kind of fast. But usually I barely thought about the dead junkie of the month, because there was no room in my head.

But I could feel this. I'd been clean for a few weeks and my brain was torturing me yet again, loud and clear. Spleen was always good to me. Always finding food and sharing it with me, always good for a walk by the river when there was nothing else to do. Always good for a bag.

One of his favorite things to do was to steal books from Barbs & Novels, the huge chain bookstore in the middle of town. I don't really know how he got away with it; he was obviously a mess, always so dirty. But he still had a sweet, charming smile; maybe that's his secret. And he would come home and read to me. It wasn't reclaiming our precious tattered childhoods or any bullshit like that. Sometimes grown-ups need bedtime stories too.

I'd never really liked reading. The words would always get tangled up until I could never pick them out. But listening to Spleen's voice, reading Bukowski and Burroughs and Philip K. Dick, made me understand why people liked reading. For hours, he would read, the candles flickering, his voice the only thing. I never got bored. I could have laid there like that forever. When he got tired he'd put the book back into a big sandwich bag, so it would keep looking like new. That way, he could return it for store credit, and we could use it to get coffee and bagels at the little cafe inside the bookstore. We'd always sit there together, warm for once with all the yuppies keeping a safe distance from our stinky pits and dirty clothes. And even though Spleen had lots of friends, he never included any of them in this little reading ritual. It was always just us.

Spleen wasn't my boyfriend. I had a crazy-house crush on him, which morphed into running away together, which eventually fizzled out. Sometimes we fucked when he gave me drugs, more of a trade than anything romantic. None of that really mattered; Spleen was my boy. I knew what he'd looked like under the florescent lights of institutions. I knew that his real name was Robert Miller and that he came from a rich suburb right by my rich suburb. He'd brought me to Minneapolis. He'd handed me that straw. I was his, and he was mine. Just like that. And I still feel like talking to him. So what if he's dead? I do it. I tell him stories about my life, about everything that happened since he's been gone. Sometimes the details are fuzzy and I have to make stuff up. He doesn't mind.

When I felt hyper but didn't feel like talking to Spleen, I cleaned the kitchen a lot. Usually I hate places that are too clean, like that awful house I grew up in. The cleaning lady had everything spotless, and my dad flipped out if anything was out of place. So my bedroom is a fucking mess, full of mold and crap and clutter. But cleaning the kitchen always gives me something to do. The water running in the sink drowns out the noise in my head. The best part is that I know this house will never be clean, no matter how hard I work. Being anywhere like that would be way too hard.

This manic morning I set out to attack the dish-mound, the tray that held the stuffed peppers that I'd made the night before, and every dish since the last time I'd had energy. I unearthed a plate with gooey frosting from a cake Lydia had made a week ago. "Fucking bitches!" I growled, but I wasn't really that mad. I scrubbed and I raged for a while until the drying rack was overflowing. Then I needed to do something else. I was like a shark—if I stopped moving, I'd die. I poured the rest of the coffeepot sludge into a cracking, peeling travel mug and stuck it in the cup holder of my beat-up mountain bike. You know, like where I'd put a bottle of Gatorade if I were healthy.

I rode all day long. For once it wasn't cold as hell. Maybe spring would be happening sometime soon. I rode to the park all the way on the other side of town where the punks always sat, but there wasn't anyone I knew over there. I rode over to the coffee shop where my friend worked, thinking about cinnamon buns and scones. But she wasn't there, and some boring-looking girl scowled at me when I asked. She looked like a manager, so I headed for the door quick.

Somehow I wound up at the bike path by the river where a madman had built crazy sculptures out of garbage every mile or so. At every sculpture, I stopped my bike, pulled my giant can of tobacco out of my black backpack, pulled my rolling papers and lighter from my pocket, and had a cigarette, watching the sun sink onto the river, lower and lower with each stop. My ribcage-monster stayed quiet.

It wasn't long after dark before I got so hungry I couldn't ride anymore. Time to go home and eat some more bell peppers. Bell pepper stir fry, bell peppers and rice, bell peppers 'til I puked because I didn't have money for kale or chicken or a hamburger. But there was money for two pints, and I stopped and picked them up before I went home. I slung the cheap black plastic bag over my handlebars, remembering that horrible time when I tipped over and they smashed and I didn't have money to get any more. That memory made me extra-careful now.

I squeaked in behind the house and locked my bike to the chain-link fence, winding my heavy chain around the top bar. I tiptoed through a whole lot of rotting crap, defeated cardboard boxes, trash that had blown in through the street, the scary compost pile, made even scarier recently. It didn't look much different from how it always did, but I thought about what Tabitha had told me and shuddered a little.

Tabitha was in the kitchen when I got in. I went straight to the random-crap drawer, pulled the bottle opener out, and opened one of my pints. My hands were already starting to shake. I took a long drink, wiped my mouth on my hoodie sleeve, and made eye contact with her, smiling real wide. "I'm thirsty, you know? I've been riding my bike around all day."

"Yeah, I know how that is," she said.

I pulled out a few bell peppers and washed them off. "Do we have anything else to stir-fry this with?"

She looked in the refrigerator. "Nah."

"Not even an onion?"

"We're fresh out, dude. We need to go dumpstering again soon."

"Yeah," I said, and took a bite out of the uncooked bell pepper. It wasn't really what I wanted after riding around in the cold all day, but it was better than nothing. I chewed it like it was an apple, and then put some water on for rice. "I guess I'm into raw foods now," I pulled soy sauce and powdered ginger from the spice rack. "You know I went to jail for dumpstering, right?"

"Yeah, you told me once, but I never heard the whole story. How could they get you on that? Like, I don't understand,"

"The judge called it trespassing. I would have just gotten probation, but the cop who arrested me filed a report saying that I called him a name, which I don't even think is true." I thought about it for a second. "Maybe I might have let one slip while the fucker was kicking me in the back…" I trailed off.

"Well, who could blame you?"

"Oh, they don't care. They aren't human. So I got taken back to jail. I had just turned 18, so no juvie for me."

"But that's so stupid! You weren't doing anything wrong." Tabitha cried. She sounded more upset than I did when it happened.

"Yeah, I don't get it, either. It's kind of funny, with all the shit I did back then..." I paused, but I could tell she was listening, so I kept going. Why the fuck not. "I used illegal drugs every single day, I stole everything I possibly could, and I was a hooker."

"Whoa, really?" She leaned forward intently.

"Only sometimes. When I needed money bad enough."

"Whoa, dude," Tabitha said, "I didn't know you used to be a...a prostitute. That's intense."

"Whatever," I said dismissively, thinking *I wasn't any more of a whore standing on the corner in a skirt than I was in that big mansion with a cleaning lady. The difference was that when I was working I at least got something that made me feel better when it was all over.* I took a long drink again. Shit, the bottle was nearly halfway empty. I was 25% done with all the beer I had for the night, and it was only 6 p.m. I was usually making calculations like that in my head; I had always been good at math. I still had some wine in the bumjug, but I didn't want wine. The booze was beginning to loosen my jaw, making me feel a little warm and relaxed. Not warm and relaxed enough, so I kept going. Maybe if I made her feel bad for me, I could get another beer out of her. I took another swill and continued my story.

"I had a few priors for shoplifting, but I'd never done any time. I thought for sure I'd get probation on this case too, cause, like, I wasn't doing anything wrong. But I got put away this time, for eating food that nobody else wanted. The judge I got was one of those judges who thinks he's changing your life by giving you a tough sentence. One of those judges who wants a fuckin' thank-you card." Tabitha nodded along, but I could tell she had no idea what I was talking about. "This thing"—I pointed at the tattoo on my face—"didn't help convince him that I was a productive member of society. He yelled at me about it from his podium, and all these other fuckers sitting in the courthouse giggled at me. I got 21 days in addition to time already served."

"Three weeks," she said, "that's not too bad, right?"

That question stopped me dead in my tracks, at the complete ignorance of it. The complete innocence. I suddenly hated Tabitha for her idiocy. I hated her for her curiosity about me, about her questions, her easy presence, her wide-open face that made me just want to talk and talk and talk when I knew that wouldn't do me any good. "Obviously, *you've* never been to jail," I sniffed. I let the sentence hang in the air for a minute while we both thought our stupid thoughts.

"Those 21 days took years and years," I began again. "Terrible. But it was good, because I couldn't get heroin in there. I mean, it was there, but nobody trusted me enough to let me know how to get it."

"Why not? Like, wouldn't they want your money?"

I laughed a vinegar laugh. "They could tell I didn't have any money, or anybody looking out for me on the outside. Plus, I was the smelly, dirty girl. And the girl with the giant tattoo on her face." Everyone thought I was nuts, which spared me a few fights, but left me shaky and sweaty in the corner, feeling my veins twitching and moaning and needing just one more hit before I fell over and died, trying to hold my soaked t-shirt away from my body so it wouldn't make my cold sweats colder, but there was always one part that touched me no matter how much I tried to get away. I'd been through little withdrawals before, when I was out of money or when the dealer was slow returning my pages. But this time, I knew there was no hope left. Nobody was going to bail me out. I couldn't go down to Spleen's squat and beg for some drugs. I couldn't put on my fishnets and heels and wipe my pussy with a baby wipe and stand on the corner. I was stuck in this cage, and nobody was coming for me. Probably nobody even knew that I was in here, and definitely nobody cared except for Spleen.

"But anyway, here I was, stuck in jail. I tried to sleep through the worst part. But you know what's fucked up?"

"What?"

"Withdrawal won't let you sleep. It keeps you awake so you can feel every inch of your body deteriorating. It keeps you up so you can think all day about what a little bitch you are for this drug, when you swore you'd never be anybody's bitch. It makes you realize you'd just traded one hell for another. And you thought you were so smart. Yeah, real fucking smart." My eyes stung. I took another slug off the bottle to keep my voice from breaking. Stupid, I shouldn't have started telling her this. Now she's going to want me to finish. So stupid.

"Even if you could rest, jail doesn't ever let you rest. You have to line up and say your number. You don't have a name. You have to line up for all kinds of bureaucratic bullshit. It doesn't matter if you just got to sleep for the first time in three days, or whatever. You can scream about it all you want, but they'll just throw you in solitary. You can bash your head against the wall, but you'll just wipe your face on somebody else's dried blood or crusty shit, plus you've already got a headache anyway. Or you can just stand there quietly and take it, because there's nothing else you can do."

"I don't even know what to say. That sucks. I'm so sorry you had to go through that shit."

"Yeah, it was pretty bad. The first few days were so horrible. Realizing that I was where I was, and my body begging for something that I couldn't give it. And do you know what the worst part was?"

"Um, no."

"When you're kicking, you get the shits really bad. And unless you've had the shits really bad on a cell block toilet, you don't know embarrassment. You don't know..."

I trailed off, thinking about sitting on that filthy, cold stainless-steel toilet, my guts turning themselves inside-out, whoever was around yelling, "That smells fuckin' nasty!" The guards were glad to have something to amuse them, laughing at every squirt and fart. And it fucking hurt and I would have blown just about anyone for a bag; anything, anything to make this all stop. Stupid fucking body, all it did was make me miserable. It was a whiny child screaming in the corner, and I was the bad mom who couldn't get it to shut the fuck up. I clutched my fists to my bare thighs, digging my fingernails in deep. The slight pain from the red half-moons on my white thighs was not even a birthday candle flame compared to the nuclear explosion in my stomach. I bent double and another painful, loud tide came out before I could stop it. Another comment from one of the bitches in the room with me, another wave of laughter from the guards. I wanted to scream, but I knew they'd just make fun of me some more. The toilet paper was scratchy and raw and just made everything worse. Not that I was expecting a quilted puff of luxury or anything. It was so thin that the shit went right through to my hand. Someone would inevitably yell "Don't you get shit in my sink when you wash your nasty hands, bitch!" at the top of her lungs. Repeat this scene several times a day.

"But anyway," I continued, "after a few days I felt a little better. Not that I felt great, or anything. I was in fucking prison eating dog food. I was getting called a bitch by the guards for not standing up straight. I was still a number. But my brain felt a little clearer than it had before. It wasn't a good thing, but it was something new. Instead of thinking about how much withdrawal sucked, I got to think about how much jail sucks."

"How much does jail suck? I mean, I know it sucks. But how much?"

"It was like all the worst parts of junior high, times a million. And you're locked in a *cage*. The only people who can let you out are the dumbest, meanest people in the whole world, who stare at your tits and curse you out all the time. Who look at you like you aren't even a piece of shit on the floor."

"Goddamn, dude," she said, "I'm so sorry. I can't even imagine. You're so tough, for going through that and still being able to function in the world."

"Yeah," I said, tipping the dregs of my pint down my throat, "I'm really functional. I'm a fucking picture of mental health."

"But you still, like, get out of bed in the morning. You still laugh when something's funny. And you still go dumpstering! That's bad-ass."

"Well, shit," I said, "they didn't send me to the chair. I'm still here. Plus, that was a long time ago. That's all behind me now. Hang on a second," I said. I pulled the change from my pockets. Thirty-one cents. The absolute cheapest, shittiest, most-guaranteed-hangover brew I could get was a buck fifty. "Dude, I need another drink, after all that." I said. "Lend me two bucks?"

Tabitha looked at me for a second too long. I wanted to head over to the refrigerator, but something held me in my seat. "Tell you what," she said, "I'll buy you a beer. I just got paid today. I'll buy a six-pack, and you can have two, because I'm a four-beer queer."

Two beers plus my other pint sweating in the refrigerator would be a good start to the evening, and I had some more wine in the bumjug for when that ran out. It was a good tradeoff, after playing teacher all fucking night. "Yeah, that sounds good. Let's go to the deli after this rice cooks," I said, pointing my chin at the bubbling, peeling pot on the stove. I stirred it with a chopstick.

I cracked open the second pint, and we talked about other things. I was feeling wary, kind of pissed that she needed to ask me all those questions, that she didn't already know the answers. I wanted to scream *when I was your age I didn't have a nice girlfriend. I didn't live in a house with nice people. I was a whore and I went to fucking jail.* The thought echoed loudly in my head, but I smiled and nodded, because she was buying me beer. I usually didn't talk about it with anyone. There'd been a lot of people who'd gone through so much worse. It was only three weeks. But, it really did change me, and I didn't like admitting it.

The rice was finally done. I left it on an unused burner. The house was cold enough that it wouldn't still be hot by the time we came back for it, but I wanted beer more. But Tabitha spooned out a bowl for herself, and I clenched my fists. "Sorry, dude, I'm just hungry as hell," she said.

"Yeah," I said, scooping a steaming pile into a bowl of my own. Might as well eat something, it would keep my legs from twitching. I dumped some soy sauce on top and ate the rice as fast as I could, felt my gut gurgling and filling.

When Tabitha was finally done eating, she left her dirty bowl on the counter. I gritted my teeth as best I could, my jaw all full of holes. We wrapped scarves around our necks and I put on my extra down vest.

Tabitha got a canvas bag to put the beer in so she wouldn't be responsible for consuming an evil plastic bag. We walked out the door and down the street.

"Hey girl," a passing dude sneered, "what's that shit on your face?"

"None of your fuckin' business!" I snarled. He walked away with that *crazy bitch* look on his face. Tabitha snickered. I hated people asking me about my tattoo.

Except this one time, back when I was in jail. One day one of the scariest girls came up to me in the cafeteria and my body tensed up so hard. But instead of starting with me, she just looked at my face. A cold, hard stare. We stood there, watching each other, for a few seconds. It felt like a long time. I tried to hold my body like I wasn't afraid of her. I wasn't sure if I should make eye contact or not. I looked into her eyes because I didn't want to seem scared.

"Why'd you do it?" she asked, not completely unkindly. I didn't ask her what she meant. I didn't have to.

I thought about the day I'd done it. Dionne had gotten a tattoo gun somehow and was looking for people to practice on. And I thought, *oh why not, why the fuck not*. I was probably pretty fucked up at the time, because I always was. I couldn't really remember.

So Dionne etched a huge spiral on my face. My tattoo started as a thick black line, almost two inches wide, at my pulse-point on the left side of my face, right beneath my ear. It curved over my eyebrow, right next to my nose, narrowing all the way, spiraling tinier and tinier until it ended with a point in the center of my cheek. She did it only a few days before I got sent to jail; still a little red around the edges. It hadn't really healed well. It's not like I got county-issued lotion or anything.

"I got it," I said to my fellow inmate, looking her straight in the eye, "so I wouldn't look like my father anymore." I hadn't thought of that before, but once I said it out loud I realized it was true. Every time I looked in the mirror I was haunted. Nobody could deny that I was my father's daughter; it was all there. His crooked nose, his thin lips, his icy blue eyes. Now, with a huge black swirl across my face, I looked unrecognizable. I loved it.

The inmate (I wasn't sure what her name was) didn't say anything else, but she knew what I was saying, and I knew that she knew. It was the closest I'd ever felt with anybody. We didn't need to process, we didn't need to waste time going on and on about our feelings and fall into each others' arms sobbing like all of the dramatic dykes I live with now. The rest of the time I was in jail she told people to shut up every time they called me ugly or weird or whatever. And we nodded whenever we passed. That was enough. That was all I needed from anyone.

"God," Tabitha said, "what the fuck do they think it is? It's not, like, a mole. It's, like, so obviously a tattoo."

"Aah, fuck 'em," I said, and then we were at the corner store. The same old lady worked the late shift, until 2 a.m. every night. She knew all the drunks, like me. I nodded hello, and then stood to the side of the opening in the bullet-proof glass, so Tabitha could shout her order inside.

"I'd like a six of Fat Tire."

The woman looked at her skeptically. "I.D.?" She shouts. Tabitha patted her pants and jacket pockets in fake desperation. "Oh shit," she said. "I forgot my wallet back home."

"Then how are you going to pay?" asked the lady in a seen-it-all, heard-it-all voice.

"I always keep my cash up front!" Tabitha crowed. I winced. Did she want to get mugged? "I'm twenty-two, honestly," she said.

"Yeah," I piped up. "I live with her, I know how old she is." It's true: nineteen. The woman sighed deeply, rolled her eyes, and put the Fat Tire in a cheap plastic bag.

"Oh, I don't need a bag," said Tabitha, pushing a wad of crumpled bills into the little tray that ran beneath the thick, grimy layer of glass. The woman pulled the bag off and threw it away. She slid Tabitha's beer through the special armed-robber-proof door, and we grabbed it and went away into the night.

"I don't feel like going home," she said.

"Me either," I said. "I know this abandoned quartz refinery that's pretty fun to hang out in," I said. "We can climb to the top of it. There's a ladder and stuff."

"Cool," she said, and we walked there in silence. It was only fifteen blocks or so from the house, across the train tracks, and down a little hill. I walked fast. Tabitha was behind me, struggling to keep up. I ignored her. I'd be ok; I just needed another beer. I hopped over the little wall and made a beeline for the ladder that would get us to the top of the quartz refinery. I didn't look back to see if she was still behind me; I could hear her beer bottles clinking together. She was fine.

Once we got to the top, I could see the bright lights of downtown on one end and I could kind of see the faded lights of the stars on the other. Tabitha's head popped up over the side of the building. She was panting a little bit. "Whoa," she breathed, looking at the view. She hoisted herself over the lip of the roof and sat next to me.

"I told you it was cool," I said, reaching for a beer.

"How'd you find out about this place?"

"Snacky D took me a couple of years ago."

"How'd he find out about it?"

"I don't know. It's something that you just know about." Tabitha cracked open a beer too, and we sat and drank. "Fat Tire, huh? I didn't know you were such a big spender!"

"Dude, it's got *bikes* on it. Beer and bikes are two of my favorite things. And now they're together! How could I say no?" She smiled all big and proud and took another sip.

"Can't argue with you there," I said.

And we sat there, drinking our beers and watching the skyline. We don't really believe in big buildings and all they represent. I'd protested in front of some of the buildings that we were staring at, and I know Tabitha had too. I like dirty things. I liked fucked-up and broken things. Sitting in the weeds of this crumbling factory I felt more at home than I would have next to those fancy shiny buildings. But it was still nice to see them, glowing in the distance. It made me feel small in a good way. Like I was a part of something.

I looked over at Tabitha and stopped being pissed off at her, mainly because she's the kind of person who knows how to appreciate a good silence. We could sit next to each other and think our own thoughts. I could hear her breathing, and the deep quiet, all around. If we were attracted to each other, it might have been romantic. But since we were friends, it was about something so much bigger than just us.

Sitting up there, it seemed almost impossible that there are jails in the world, and that I used to be in one. Someone told me once that when you've been caged, no matter how short your sentence was or how long you've been out, you can't go back to how you were before. That there's always a little piece of you stuck in that cage.

And she's right; but up on top of the quartz factory I felt like the window had been opened up and that little piece of me still stuck in jail in Minnesota was peeking out as far as it could, straining to see the stars, breathing air that hadn't cycled through thousands of fucked-up lungs. And they were the same stars that the rest of me sat under, and the rest of me was so free. No jobs, no bosses, no fathers. Definitely no cages anymore. My dreads, usually so heavy, blew around in the wind and my head felt as light and airy as if I had shaved it. I shook my head around and laughed like a crazy person. We couldn't feel the wind in jail.

I stood up, my vest open, my hoodie open, my t-shirt the only thing protecting me from the cold, and held my arms out like a scarecrow. Tabitha looked at me quizzically, but I just leaned back and let out a big whoop, as loud as my lungs could go. I stretched my hands far above my head; my t-shirt rode up and my belly was exposed to the harsh winter air. The cold felt good; it was evidence. It was proof that I was outside now. Proof that they hadn't killed me; that I was still alive.

CHAPTER 3

The endless supply of bell peppers somehow came to an end. The shelves were all bare, and I was tired and grumpy. Kale-potato soup would fix it, at least for a little bit. Kale-potato soup is probably what keeps me alive. So cheap and warm, so filling. "I'm going to the stupid-market," I said, poking my head into the living room. "Anyone wanna come?"

"You'd better go while you can," Lydia said, looking up from the newspaper. "They're closing."

"What!" Tabitha said, throwing down her boot-black rag and wiping her hands on her pants. "That sucks!"

"Yeah, but what are you gonna do. It happens," Lydia sniffed. "Especially around here. Their last day is the 30th."

"Now we're going to have to bike all the way to Fancy Town to get our groceries?" Tabitha wailed.

"Fancy Town's better anyway," Lydia said. "The stupid-market produce is all wilted. And the cans are all dented. And the assistant manager talked about my ass once, remember?"

"Oh yeah! That jerk!" Tabitha balled up her dirty fists. "But it sucks that we're going to have to go to Fancy Town. That's, like, three miles away. And up a hill!"

"I think today's the 30th," said Lydia.

"No, it's not. It's the 28th," I said.

"No, it's the 30th," she said. She pulled out her organizer from her purse, flipped it to a page scribbled with notes. "See?"

Lydia was right. "So?" I said.

"So today's the last day. We should all go there. We should do something."

"Like what?"

"I don't know, like take pictures. Like document it. Like be there."

"If you guys want to come, you should come," I said. Tabitha wiped her newly shiny boots off and stomped her feet into them. Lydia ran upstairs, muttering something about a camera. "I don't know what the big deal is," I continued. "It's not like there's going to be a parade or anything. It's just a shitty grocery store getting shut down."

"I don't know, it might be interesting," Tabitha said. "Plus, we could probably steal a lot of stuff." Lydia came rushing down the stairs, a complicated camera in hand. She placed the camera in a purse and slung it over her shoulder. She went to the front door and stalked outside confidently, while Tabitha and I followed like confused puppies.

The four or so blocks to the store passed without incident. The sidewalk wasn't wide enough for the three of us to walk next to each other, so Tabitha race-walked to catch up with Lydia and I trailed behind them. They chattered about something that I couldn't quite hear.

Before I knew it we were at the store whose weary neon sign scripted out "Harold's", although I personally had never once called it that. We squeezed our way through the small concrete pillars designed to keep the shopping carts away from anyone who might actually need them for anything real. Taped on the gigantic windows, where it normally said things like "PORK CHOPS—99 CENTS PER POUND!" were hand-painted signs that said "CLOSING! LAST DAY MARCH 30TH." I guess I hadn't been to the stupid-market in a while.

"Whoa," Tabitha pronounced. "Everyone in here looks so...grim."

"And that's different from any other day…how?" said Lydia, adjusting her viewfinder on a single, abandoned piece of white bread lying on the dirty linoleum. "This is a dank-ass, depressing store. What do you expect?" She snapped the picture and a haggard woman pushing a cart loaded with soda and potato chips turned around to see what was going on. She stared at us for a full minute and then turned back to her load. By that time, Tabitha was laying on an empty shelf like she was dead and Lydia's camera was snapping away. "You get in there too, Xandria!"

"No. No pictures," I said.

"Oh, Miss *Celebrity*, if you don't want pictures of your face, you can just put this over it." She tossed me a dusty bag of marshmallows. "Come on. Quit yer whining and get in the picture!"

I thought, *oh, what the hell.* Tabitha rolled off the shelf and onto the floor. "No, Tabitha, you stay on the shelf closer to the ground. Xandria, do you think you can make it onto the shelf right above her?" I crept up, slithered between the shelves, my back to Lydia, my dreads spilling over my shoulders and off the shelf, like a shitty curtain that Tabitha hid behind. "Good! Good!" I heard the shutter clicking. "Now Xandria, extend your arm!"

"I can extend my arm. I don't know if it'll be dramatic enough for you," I said.

Lydia sighed theatrically. "*Try.*" And so I slid one arm away from me, over my head, let it dangle lazily. More clicks. It was an uncomfortable position, so I shifted my weight slightly. And then I heard the shelf crack. I tumbled onto the floor, hit the linoleum with a thud, and opened my eyes to see the potato chip woman shaking her head, slowly and with great disgust, as if we were too pitiful to even comment on. I got to my feet quickly, Tabitha rolled off her shelf, and we all walked to the next aisle.

Tabitha was the first to crack up, then Lydia, then me. We laughed in the spice aisle, with the few remaining bottles of pepper and thyme. Tabitha snickered, raising her hand for a high-five. "You okay?"

I slapped her hand half-heartedly. "Yeah, I'm fine. I need to get some potatoes." I tramped over to the produce department, which was usually bad enough to make me want to kick things. Today it was only a little worse than usual. Someone had scattered lettuce leaves all over the floor. Carrots died a mass death in a pile.

I picked out a few potatoes that weren't sprouting too badly and a wilted kale bouquet. I tucked the kale into my bag quickly. Not sure why I even bothered being stealthy, nobody here gave a shit, especially not today. I saw some boxes of veggie bouillon. Those went right into my pocket. But I was gonna have to pay for the potatoes since they were way too big to steal. Lydia was looking around intently, like she was trying to memorize everything. Tabitha had the camera now and was snapping pictures left and right.

I got in the long, grumpy line. My housemates eventually wandered over to me. The cashier robotically scanned the items of a woman whose hot pink eyeliner matched her Spandex leggings. Out of nowhere, Spandex woman turned to us and said, "Motherfuckers."

"What?"

"They're *going* out of *business*! But none of this shit is discounted. What the hell are they going to do with all this food? Today's the last day! After all these years of shopping at this store, you think they'd give something back. Shit."

The cashier looked up. "They ain't treating us workers much better. They're just throwing us out into the cold. None of the other Harolds' are hiring."

"That's big business for ya!" Lydia chimed in.

"Yeah!" Spandex woman crowed. "They're all a bunch of jerk-offs! Just a bunch of jerk-offs!" The cashier stopped scanning the items and clapped her hands. Lydia and Tabitha joined in. Even the potato chip lady, still shopping, put her hands together for that sentiment. Before I knew what I was doing, I found myself clapping, too. We clapped until it felt weird, and then we all looked at each other, smiling like we were old friends, until the moment passed and we were all awkward shoppers again.

I tried to imagine this hot pink woman at Fancy Town, buying organic quinoa and watercress. I tried to imagine her voice yelling,

"Motherfuckers!" next to a box of organic maple-walnut cookies that cost seven dollars. I could not. I squinted at the woman, trying to store her in my head, the way she was, in her natural habitat. She was an endangered species, now. We all were.

CHAPTER 4

Another morning-afternoon arrived, eventually. Still hungover, still crazy, still trying not to think. Another dive from the futon to the floor, another huge steaming pot of coffee. And then what? One weird thing I liked to do when I felt bad was listen to this one CD that was always hanging out in the kitchen. It said "Whiny Teenage Songs" in Jasmine's handwriting. I put it on track 6 and listened to the guy sing about panic on the streets of London, wondering if life would ever be sane again, and demanding that the DJ be hung. I loved that song. For some reason, singing the word "panic" with him, drawing the word out a little bit, made me feel less panicked.

Today I needed to hear the song so goddamn badly, but the CD had gotten scratched somehow, and the guy's voice sang out, "P-p-p-p-p-p-p-p-..."

I growled and whacked the CD player, hard. "Come *on*," I yelled.

Jasmine was in the next room. "Sucks," she said, "it sounds like we've gotten a visit from the Goddess of Skips, who thrives on ruining everyone's favorite songs..."

I breathed in and out, hard. I didn't look at Jasmine, just stood over the sink like I would do the dishes once my breath came back to me, clutching the slippery stainless steel like it was the guardrail of a steep cliff. Just play the song. Then I'd be okay. I'd do the dishes and drink the rest of my coffee. I'd be okay. Just *play the motherfucking song!!!*

I picked up a glass and started scrubbing it frantically, like that was going to change a goddamn thing. Like the sponge was a lethal weapon, like the glass was what was wrong with me. Just going over it again and again, even though it wasn't really all that dirty in the first place. Just a water glass, barely smudged.

"Uhh, are you okay?" Jasmine asked. Something about her voice made me jump, and the glass slid out of my soapy hand and smashed on the edge of the sink. I didn't realize that I was cut until I looked at the sponge, covered in red blotches. Then I was forced to look at my hand, a thin stream of red winding down my wrist, and I started laughing hysterically. Just cackling as hard as I could. The blood dripped all over the counter, making little dots.

"Dude, are you, like, okay?" Jasmine asked again.

"NO!" I shouted. I gasped for breath. I squeezed the edge of the sink with my other hand until my knuckles turned white.

"Do you need to scream? I'm pissed off too. I need to scream. Let's scream together, okay? One...two...three..." and together we let out the most spectacular noise. It felt kind of good. A little too group-therapy for me, but good, anyway.

Jasmine took me by the arm and sat me down on the tall stools around the kitchen counter. She looked into my eyes for what must have been a full minute. I wanted to look away, but I couldn't.

Finally she said, "What did they do to you?"

I looked at her and stammered, "I don't—I—I don't—"

"I know that scream," she said. And then she told me her story, about her stepbrother, when she was 11 and 12, when he was 17 and 18. About mouths and dicks and hands, about being held down, about being silenced. About the daily sneers, the words about her whispered so low that their parents couldn't overhear. About the milk snatched out of her hands at the breakfast table, and the mean-spirited laugh as he held it just out of her grasp, and how it hurt so much worse than normal big-brother brattiness, because of everything else that had been stolen.

She told me about not fighting back at all. And hating herself for it, hating herself for everything. How she knew it wasn't her fault, because she read lots of books that said so, but she realized that she was up against something huge and insurmountable. That he was the straight-A jock and she was the troublemaker. That nobody would believe her. And how after a while, she just gave into all that hatred. She let herself believe it. And how that was the worst part, worse than any physical violation.

While she was talking I pressed my hand into the cuff of my sweatshirt, letting the blood dribble onto the fabric, drying hard and crackly. I barely noticed; I clung to every word she said, because it had happened to me too. Not that exact way, but I knew what she was talking about, so much that I was shaking. And then, somehow, I told her about what he did to me.

I didn't go too far into detail. I didn't really want to talk about it. Everyone who knows what happened wants to hear about my father. What he was like, what he did to me, like it's some witty little anecdote. Fuck my father. I don't want to talk about him. I want to talk about me, and how my whole life has been ruined because he couldn't keep his dick in his pants.

I don't really want to talk about me, either, but I am tired of pretending nothing had happened. I am tired of pretending to be a survivor. I haven't survived shit, because it hasn't ended. It's still happening in my head, all the time. I told her in short, guttural phrases, with lots of stammering and cursing. It was so weird that we were even talking about it in the first place; so weird that it had come up at all.

"I didn't talk about this shit for years," she said, when I was done. "Mostly because nobody wanted to hear it. But also because I was so angry that I didn't want to start. I didn't want to let it go, because there was so much of it, and because nobody wanted to deal with it."

"Yeah," I said. "Yeah, I know."

"One thing that sucks about having people think you're fun is that they don't want to deal with you when you're not being fun. They don't want to see that you have all sorts of shit in your life, and just because you can tell a good story doesn't mean anything. It doesn't mean that you're not going through hell, you know?"

"Thank God I'm no fun anyway," I said, half-joking. And since it seemed like the only chance I'd ever have, I told her. About the dreams, the ones that I hated, the ones that came when I wasn't drunk enough to forget, the dreams that were just re-plays of what had happened in real life. The hand over my mouth, the underwear tossed aside, the shoulders on my shoulders.

And I also told her about the dreams that I loved. The ones where I drove back to that house, broke the window, turned off the security alarm, went to his bedroom, and killed him. Where I held his throat in my hands and pressed my thumb on his windpipe, where I stabbed the knife through his heart, where I held the shotgun to that face that looked so much like mine. Where he begged for mercy and I ignored him. Where he begged for compassion and I laughed, just like he'd done to me. Dreams where I finally felt safe; his blood on my hands, his voice silenced forever.

When I wasn't too drunk or fucked-up, the nightmares would come. When the dream came instead, I woke up feeling so good. I woke up truly refreshed. And the next night, I wouldn't get so drunk, hoping that dream would come again, hoping I could kill him again. Usually I was rewarded with another nightmare.

I never told anyone about those dreams because who cares about dreams? Lydia and Jasmine liked to talk about their dreams and it bored me to death. And I might get locked away forever next time if I talked about how the thought of killing my father was the only thing that made me happy.

But Jasmine said, "I know exactly what you mean," and I knew she did. She said, "When Chad first went to college, I was flipping through the channels one afternoon and I saw this special about how college freshmen die from drinking too much. And I got down on my knees and prayed that he would die like that. That he would get in a drunk-driving accident or choke to death on his fucking beer bong. Anything. Anything so he wouldn't come home for winter break. And then I felt horrible. I couldn't believe what a psychopath I'd become."

"Is he still alive?"

"Yeah, but I lucked out. His junior year he went to Budapest on a study-abroad thing, and he liked it so much he decided to move there. He married this Hungarian girl and he's a dual-citizen there now and he almost never comes home. And I always make sure it's when I'm not visiting. So I haven't seen the bastard in years."

When I was in the hospital, we had group therapy and we were supposed to talk about this shit. But nobody did. About half the kids I was locked up with were cool, like Spleen, but the other half were dramatic backstabbing bitches from hell. Usually those "group therapy" sessions degenerated into petty whining about who said what to who and what drama was going on in the hall at that point in time. So even if I'd wanted to tell them about the daily scorn I'd grown up under, the sneers, the spitting in my face, and how that was almost worse than being raped; I couldn't have squeezed it in between Carla screaming at Jenny that she was an ugly bitch who should quit stealing her shampoo and Jenny screaming at Michael for liking Shawnda and Michael saying that Jared kept hitting on him and he hates faggots and Jared saying...on and on and on. It was enough to drive you crazy, just in case your life hadn't already. I wasn't going to cry in front of them, either. And I didn't cry in front of Jasmine, but I felt something. I'm not sure what. Like the feeling of release, minus the tears, minus the embarrassment.

Jasmine and I kept talking until the conversation burnt itself out. It didn't take long. When we were done, Jasmine hugged me, maybe for the first time. It felt like a life raft. "I'm sorry to dump all this shit on you, man," I said.

"It's okay. If you don't dump it, you become, like, a landfill. You fester and rats run all around your insides. You need to flip the compost pile in your heart sometimes. Air that shit out and try and make something good, you know?"

I shrugged uncomfortably.

"All I'm saying is, I'm here for you. You don't have to explode. When you sit around and think how nobody gives a shit and you're a terrible person and nobody wants to hear it, please know that it isn't true. It just isn't true."

"Uh, thanks," I said. My forehead was all sweaty and my hands were all shaky for some reason.

"No, really," she said, taking my hand like she was asking to marry me. "That's what saved me," she said, making intense eye contact, more serious than I'd ever seen her. I looked away. "I used to do drugs too. And drink too much. And cut myself. And fuck people who were just awful. And one day I was taking this really long walk—I'd taken the bus all the way to Mosside for a job interview and I didn't get it and I decided to just walk home, seven or eight miles, and I was thinking about everything for so long, and then I just realized. That I'm not a terrible person. That I'm not a piece of shit. That my life is worth it. That I'm worth it. It sounds so little, and so cheesy, but that's what saved me. Well, I mean, not just that. It was a lot of hard work. But that's where it all started."

"What are you, a missionary?" I said, meaner than I'd meant it, and then laughed uncomfortably.

"Maybe. Maybe I'm a missionary from the Church of Don't Fuck Yerself Up. Maybe I am a nun from the Heavenly Order of Ladies Who Don't Take Shit. But I did take shit, and I did fuck myself up, until I realized. And I ain't no saint; I still did lots of bad stuff after. But I didn't feel like I had to, you know? That was the difference."

"I hate missionaries. I hate nuns," I sneered.

"Well," she said, looking very old and very tired all of a sudden, "I hate having conversations like this. But sometimes I have to." I didn't say anything. I've never had a conversation like this before, but I already hated it. Our eyes met. She looked away first. "You wore me out, dude," she grimaced, "I'm going back to bed." And then she shuffled away and I was left with dozens of dirty dishes, and so many drops of my own blood.

PART THREE: JASMINE

CHAPTER ONE

Spring was on its way. The house was finally more stuffy than cold, which meant that it was time to rip the billowing plastic from the windows. Xandria stood on a chair, knife in hand, and stabbed the layer of filmy plastic that had sort of kept the drafts at bay all winter. She made a little hole with her knife, and ripped it with her other hand until the plastic hung in tatters, duct-taped to the frame. Gloomy, rainy light burst through, slightly illuminating the room.

"Fuck yeah!" said Tabitha, sitting on the couch next to me. It was a tacky overstuffed shade of green that must have made sense to someone, once, but its offensiveness was made up for in its unparalleled comfort. The couch was from the 80's, just like me.

"Yeah, for real," said Lydia, perched on the blue velvet armchair. "I'm so tired of these gas bills. And staying in this dirty-ass house all weekend because it's too cold to go out." She wrinkled her nose in the general direction of the piles of Food Not Bon-Bons dishes that Xandria had just brought back from a serving in the park, and left in a big pile on the floor, next to the couch. I was picking at the scraps. Some kind of eggplant-noodle dish. It was cold and kind of gummy, but still so spicy it made my nasal cavity burn.

"Oh, come on," I said, half in jest, half because I was tired of Lydia's endless bitching. "This house is, like, so not a big deal. Back when I worked at Wal-Mart there was this old guy who was, like, a visionary seer stuck in the body of a floor-sweeper—"

"'Visionary seer' is redundant." Lydia interjected in a snotty grammar nerd kind of way.

"I am NOT being redundant! He is not just a *visionary*, he is not just a *seer*, he is a *visionary seer*, and he was sweeping the fucking floors at fucking Wal-Mart, and, like, everyone thought he was crazy, but he was actually so cool. And one day we were taking an unauthorized smoke break behind the dumpster and he told me this brilliant theory he had, like this precise math equation about how interesting you are is inversely congruent with how clean your house is."

"Ooh, *wow*. If only your redundantly-visionary-seer-mystic-psychic-mad-scientist friend were here to compute an equation about all of us and tell us how *interesting* we all are, then we could feel better about living in this dump. That would be just *awesome*." Lydia's voice shot arrows.

Xandria and Tabitha looked uncomfortably to the side, like they always did when Lydia and I fought with each other. Lydia and I were ex-girlfriends who had somehow melted into good friends. She was the youngest-sibling-Leo-Latina-firebomb and I was the chatty-Aries-abuse-survivor gasoline puddle. What do you get when you mix us? Good sex, good laughs, loud arguments. Explosions, in every tongue. Ripping open every crevice imaginable. Our smoking wreckage made people uncomfortable, even though it glowed the most gorgeous shades of red and orange.

But right now, I didn't give a shit about making anyone uncomfortable, because I had the most uncomfortable thing of all lodged in my gut, spreading itself through the pathways of my body. "Dude! What the fuck do you want me to do about it? You bitch about being stuck in this house, but you get to leave every fucking day, so don't *tell* me about being trapped in the house!" I said. "I am sick! I am so fucking sick! I can't get out of bed half the time!"

My voice was beginning to get raw and scratchy, and I could feel the announcement I had been carrying around for several days begin to roll down the hill of my throat. It had been perched on the top, waiting for the right moment. I saw Lydia begin to roll her eyes. *She doesn't know any better*, I thought, to dam the flood of hatred that hit me. *She doesn't know yet.*

Xandria and Tabitha were exchanging a *they're crazy* look. I almost never raised my voice this much, even to Lydia. "Don't you roll your eyes at me!" I snapped. I saw Xandria fold her knife in two, hang it from its hook on her belt, and head towards the door, as if this was some normal drama that she didn't want to deal with. "No, Xandria, wait." I said. She spun on her heel and looked at me with a half-questioning, half-annoyed look. I tried to pretend I was onstage, so my voice wouldn't quaver. "There's something that I have to tell you. All of you."

I must have had a pretty intense look on my face, because even Lydia stopped her bitching for a second. "Um." I said. There was a long silence, in which I could hear the kitchen tap dripping, the mold growing, the bus roaring by, the air bouncing off the thin plaster walls. I listened to the sound of us breathing, the four separate pairs of lungs expanding and folding again and again. I am a storyteller, but there was no story for this. There was no good metaphor, no hilarious conclusion. I am a storyteller, so I usually hate silence. I am an abuse survivor, so I usually fight against silence. But for now I was embracing it. Now it was the buffer between me and three tiny words. I was going to stretch this silence as far as it could go. Because I didn't want to hit the end, the raw dead stop. But I knew if I didn't say anything, they would get bored and wander away. Pump my veins full of poison, let my body attack itself. Just don't call me boring.
I looked at the window, with its swags of plastic hanging down, thinking about the night we taped them up, a group effort from a November that

seemed so impossibly far away. Lydia played a bunch of 7" records while I held the plastic sheeting against the top ledge of the windowsill because I'm the tallest one in the house. Tabitha held the plastic to the window frame at the bottom, and Xandria duct-taped frantically. After that, we all sat on the couch, enjoying the slightly warmer and less drafty house. For some reason, this memory was making my eyes well up. We had no idea what was coming for us. I had no idea about the time bomb I was blithely carrying in my womb.

Crying before The Announcement would be really bad. Extra-bad; so I plunged ahead. "I hate to get all Lifetime Movie on you guys, but..." I looked into their three faces, noticing the details, the tiny flaws—the slight smudge of grease on Lydia's glasses, the zit erupting beneath the darkened flesh of Xandria's facial tattoo, Tabitha's rather unfortunate dandruff problem. I took a deep, shaky breath, or as deep as I could. There had been a band of thin invisible steel wrapped around my lungs ever since the doctors told me. I had to keep reminding myself to take deep breaths. I had to keep reminding myself that I wasn't dead yet, that I had to keep inhaling, exhaling and inhaling again.

I am sick. Really sick. Everyone that knows me knows this, but they didn't know how bad it was. I didn't know how bad it was until a few days ago. I've been feeling this searing pain in my gut for a while, almost half a year. But it's not just the pain that's so bad. It's the sweats that wake me up in the middle of the night, this endless heaviness, all around; the feeling that something in my body is out to get me. My body and I, we used to be pals. We used to hold hands and run up stairs with a secret glowing glee, us, us against the world.

When I saw this queer performance artist speak during a rough time in my life, she looked at me from onstage, in the middle of her performance, me out of all of those people, and said, "Don't worry; no matter what, you'll always have yourself," I hugged my knees, sitting on the floor, and thought *yes yes yes*. And a shiver went through me, like a renegade orgasm trampling across the mighty plain. If that statement had come to me on a Hallmark card I would have rolled my eyes at it, but the eye contact and performance art made it real to me, made it spark, made it the IV that I could plug into my veins. Ha ha ha, aren't these medical metaphors all so funny now that I might actually die? Now that I might actually have an IV attached to my arm? Now that...

"I have cancer." Their faces, as though attached by a string not visible to the naked eye, fell in unison. It was almost hilarious. In fact, I had to stifle a laugh. In fact, were it not probably the most serious moment in my entire life, I would have been hysterical.

"What?" said Tabitha.

Lydia put her head on her knees and started sobbing loudly.

"How?" asked Xandria.

"I was stupid, I guess. I thought I could smash a million TVs at the dump. I thought I could swim in polluted rivers. I thought I could eat food from the garbage. I thought I could live in this world." I said, and we all thought about it for a minute.

But really, who can say what caused this? Who can say when the refinery is injecting its unfunny clouds into the conversation, when there's medical waste in the compost pile, when I used to smoke on my breaks at Wal-Mart with photo chemicals all over my hands? Maybe it was the endless double prints that I developed that did me in; the tan and green developer chemicals sloshing all over me when I re-filled them. I didn't bother washing my hands when I touched those chemicals, because I wanted to die back then in a teenagerish way, because I didn't think I would really die. And I only wanted to die because I thought this was all there was: fifteen-minute smoke breaks with a chance to see the sky; and then back to the photo lab where the fake smiles glowed so white they burned my eyes. Visionary seers stuck behind brooms. High school, high school and more high school. Chemicals absorbed through thin skin, hiding and waiting. And didn't they pick a great time to make themselves known, now that I have a life worth living?

Tabitha asked, quietly, "How did you find out?"

"I just found out two days ago. Violet gave me the number to her drug study for yeast infection creams. I figured I could make some money off this body that's been sputtering and stalling and making me hurt so bad. I figured it would be just a tiny, little thing, not a big deal at all. Just a few pap smears, a few photo sessions with the VaginaCam" (as Violet liked to call it) "I figured out how much energy it would take for me to get on the bus, sit in the waiting room, lie on the table, sit on the bus again and go home. It would get me a few hundred bucks, and I needed that few hundred. And—" I didn't want to go into the whole story again, so I just said, "They saw a visible growth on my cervix. They did a hollow-needle biopsy of it to see if it was malignant, and they did some blood tests and X-rays to see if it has spread. And they called me a few days ago. And..." I looked around. "Well, you know." Meaning: I don't want to talk about it anymore.

Before I went to the drug study of doom, I rested for a long time, like putting energy into a savings account, and got on the bus, and endured the bus ride somehow, and slogged my way into the elevator at the hospital, and through the white hallways that never seemed to end. I was already panicking when I got to the waiting room, my face covered in the cold unfashionable sweat of exhaustion, wondering how I would ever make it through this and oh god why did I come why was I so stupid as to think I could make a buck off this body that had apparently dumped me and left me standing at a phonebooth, with a dead cell phone and a tiny scrap of paper, dialing and dialing and just getting the fucking machine?

I smiled and nodded through the question/intake phase. I got a snarky little thrill out of boldly squealing "lesbianism!" when they asked what kind of birth control I use. Some things just never get old. I didn't mention the fact that, oh, my whole life had been derailed, because whatever had felled me didn't have a name. When they asked me if I had ever had cancer, I could answer "no" honestly without even thinking about the festering uneasiness below my gut.

The nurse, who was around my age, and dressed in scrubs printed with Disney characters, said, "OK, Jasmine, we're going to have to do a routine Pap smear and STI testing on you, just to make sure you don't have any abnormalities that would affect the outcome of the study, okay?" I nodded and signed the consent form.

Picture this: hairy legs raised in stirrups, thin blue papery cloth that reminds you of a picnic table cloth covering your legs, so you can pretend that a total stranger doesn't have their hands in your crotch; and also allowing the total stranger whose hands are in your crotch to see you only as a vagina and not as a person. Psychological barriers. And imagine the insertion of the speculum, the snap, and then an involuntary gasp of horror from the person inspecting your vagina.

Even though, from birth on up, you got the impression from the world that your cunt smells bad, looks bad, and is generally the most disgusting organ a person could have, you only believe for a second that yours is particularly distasteful. You remember that this person has seen thousands of cunts, probably, and yours cannot possibly be the weirdest.

No, you know this is something serious. Serious as the bills clicking shut, serious as the gynecologist's gasp: "I'm going to need to get another doctor in here. Hang on." You know it's serious as the clock loudly ticks and you're still on your back, all alone. And when two doctors come in, they re-insert the speculum gently (while telling you what they're doing; they're good doctors), and there is a tense silence, and you put your hand on the crinkly blue paper hanging between your knees and push it down to see two faces looking at each other with dread, not speaking, you know that there is no possible way this can be good. Your knees look like mountains, you think, as you feel the sweat begin on the small of your back pressed up against the white paper beneath you.

"Yes?" I said, expectantly, like they had said my name, like I was merely responding. These doctors couldn't even know my name, I was patient #JZM411. Drug study confidentiality, so when I run for president nobody can ever say that I sold the terrain of my vagina for money once.

"There is...a...serious abnormality...on your cervix," a doctor said, in a stern voice. "I think you need to get dressed and meet me in the office next door."

When he said that, I knew what it was. When he said that, all of the saliva drained out of my mouth and stuck right in my throat, forming a knot, forming a four-leaf-clover traffic pattern, the cars all speeding towards nowhere. I couldn't swallow. I couldn't cry.

The doctors pulled the utilitarian curtain around the bed and exited the room. I spent approximately two hundred years getting dressed. My socks were still on, fresh from the stirrups. I found my rumpled boxer-briefs tucked into even more rumpled long underwear. I stretched them over my legs, feeling for a moment like a svelte femme lady putting on stockings. Was I dying? Next, the burgundy corduroy pants, with a finger-print of white paint stretched across the thigh. They were a lot more loose-fitting as the days wore on. I hadn't felt like eating in a while. I snapped my belt shut, the one with the cowboy-hat belt buckle that I'd stolen from a bizarre highway rest-stop on a drive across Texas a long long time ago.

I summoned every ounce of strength I had left in me and went into the room next door. I told the doctor all about my break-up with my body; the night sweats, the fevers, the lack of strength, the vague memory of what it was like to ride a bike up a hill or dance or do anything, really.

The days in bed, the nights spent floating in an unknowable terror. The long empty afternoons, time stretched so thin that holes were fraying in the center.

He said that there was a visible growth on my cervix and there was a strong possibility that it could be a tumor. The symptoms I was describing didn't sound good. He said that they could do a hollow-needle biopsy today and send it to a lab and I'd have the results in a few days.

So, I undressed again. They took a giant swab and applied a local anesthetic and put this huge needle into my cervix, and sucked out a little tiny bit. I hardly paid attention. I wondered how I would tell everyone I had cancer. I didn't need a test to tell me what I already knew. Cancer. The word my body had left me for, the secret lover who had been stealing my girl all along. The worthless jerk: it didn't matter. It had her.

The doctors told me that I could sit up now. They said they needed to draw some blood to see if I'd had a recent upsurge in my white blood cell count. I hardly noticed. I hardly cared. I wanted to say, *don't even bother*. Why hadn't I thought of it before? It made such perfect sense.

"So, what are you gonna do now?" Lydia asked, yanking me from my flashback.

"I don't know," I said, honestly. "I haven't called my dad yet. I guess I'll go on Medicaid and disability and chemo. I guess I will wait and see. It's, um, spread pretty far. So, like, I don't know..." I knew if I said anything else I was going to cry in front of them. I hate crying in front of people, even people who are crying about me. I pretended I was sniffing my armpit so they wouldn't see the daredevil tears getting ready to cliff dive from my eyelids.

The doctor's voice on the phone had been polite, yet somber. Cervical cancer that had spread into my lymph nodes. I was going to need surgery and then chemo. I was going to have a hysterectomy and grow a bad-ass mustache from the wild imbalance of my hormones. I was going to need lots of financial resources that I didn't have. And even if I got the money somehow, I still might die. I still might die.

"I know some people at the Disability Office," Lydia said. "I can hook you up with expedited processing so there'll be less waiting. And I can tell you who's the least condescending, so you don't have to roll over and beg for dignity."

"Thank you, Madame Bureaucrat," I said, and tried to smile. Since I hate faking it, I only got about halfway there. A subject change seemed wise. "Um, I think if I tell my dad, he might try and make me go back home. And, like, I don't want to do that. Because, like, even though he has cable and the internet and all that, I don't want to leave. But I might have to..."

"Dude, if you need anything..." said Tabitha. Oh, so many ellipses today. So many words we choked on. I wanted to say *Thanks! I need some new blood circulating through my veins, I need a new cervix, I need some energy, I need someone to crawl in my bed with three-month-unchanged sheets and wrap their arms over my shoulders as if they were a loving, comforting human backpack and hold me through the long cold-sweat sleepless nights and I need fresh-fruit smoothies and I need someone to go down on my disaster-area vag before I go on chemo and all my pubes fall out and I get embarrassed to have anyone see me like that and I need my fucking mother to not be fucking dead and I need someone to call my dad and tell him I'm dying and I need someone to tell me that I'm not dying in a way that I believe, which is going to be difficult because I'm pretty convinced that I am, you know?*

Instead I just smiled and said thanks. I think I am going to have to re-assess my position on fake smiles. Nobody likes a downer, even a downer with cancer. People with cancer are supposed to be hopeful and brave. We are supposed to emit a beacon of pure white light straight from our shiny bald heads. "Oh, come on, you guys," I said, poking a jovial elbow into Lydia's quivering backside. "I'm sure I'll be fine."

I guess I didn't sound too convincing, because Lydia just sobbed louder, and Xandria punched the wall really hard. The plaster cracked in little threads all around where her fist had met it. "Fuck," she said again, and quickly stomped out of the room. I thought, briefly, of the intense conversation we'd had a few weeks ago, of hugging her for the first time, of how she was just starting to let me in past that hard crusty exterior. Tabitha just sat there, looking shell-shocked. After a while of sitting uncomfortably, listening to Lydia cry, avoiding Tabitha's eyes because I had nothing more to say, I said, "Well, I'm going to bed," and then slowly, with great effort, hauled myself up the creaky staircase and back onto my mattress. The sun was just beginning to set. On my long and terrible journey upstairs, I grabbed the cordless phone. My cell phone was shut off two months ago because I just couldn't pay the bill, so now I was tethered to the landline.

I pulled out my supermarket phone card and punched in an endless string of numbers. I had already made my real family cry; now it was time to make my other family cry too. I dialed my dad's number, the familiar area code, activating a phone in the suburbs of Boston that rang three times. "Hello?" The voice answering belonged to Judie, my stepmother. I was hoping it wouldn't be her, because I hate talking to her so much.

"Hey, Judie, it's Jasmine." She still has no idea of what her son did to me. Absolutely none.

"Oh, hi, Jasmine." I could hear a TV in the background, and her voice had a tinge of annoyance. Probably not for the same reason mine did. Do people really not notice these things?

"Um, is my dad there?" Judie and I rarely had anything to say to each other beyond this exchange. I couldn't say anything more, because then I might say everything, and there would be trouble. I heard her call, "Henry!" to the house, and then the pause before my dad got on the line.

"Hello there, Jasmine," he said. "How are you doing?"

"Uh, not too good," I said. Then I told him. Our conversation went along predictable paths. I could have been in a freakin' made-for-TV movie, is all I'm saying. If you ever want to make everyone in your life start spouting clichés, all you have to do is contract a possibly-terminal disease.

My dad is not essentially a bad guy. He's had his emotions stolen from him in the way that many men have. They have everything, control of the whole fucking world, but they can't feel anything. I have absolutely nothing and I'm probably going to die penniless really soon, but at least I can feel it all. The shitty parts are horrible, yeah, but the good parts were so fucking good.

Sometimes I feel bad for my dad because he sits at a desk and then goes home and sits in a chair. He doesn't jump up and down until he is tired. His eyes don't get bright, ever. So who is worse off? Me, obviously. But still...

"Dad," I say, "I don't know what to do. It doesn't look good. I might—uh—I might—"

"Jasmine, please don't talk like that. Of course—of course you'll be fine," says my dad. His voice was ragged and his breathing got funny.

"I'm not really all that sick yet. I mean, I'm sick, but—I don't know, maybe."

"Jasmine." I don't know why he keeps saying my name. "Jasmine." My momma died young too. Older than I am now, though; and it wasn't a disease or a drunk driver or anything like that. She did it to herself; she chose to leave us.

She was the one who named me. Jasmine Zora McGillicuddy, after her favorite tea and her favorite author. We are both remembering this, long-distance, across the phone lines. That terrible hum starts. It's barely perceptible during a normal phone conversation, although it's theoretically there all along. You can only hear it when nobody has anything to say. "If you need anything, you know I'm here. And if you want to come home..."

I shuddered, visibly, at the thought of going back. Frozen dinners and having to look at that terrible family portrait. My dad's wearing the kind of glasses that have the thin wire right beneath his eyebrows. He's forgotten to shave and his smile is bordering on desperate. Judie's hair is a shade of blonde that is not quite right for her features; and she's wearing a floral-print dress that is not quite right for any non-lobotomized human. My stepbrother Chad is standing behind me, wearing his cap and gown with the local high school's colors. He has a smirk on his face and his hand is resting on my bare tank-topped barely-pubescent shoulder, a little too close to my freshly-minted breast for brotherly affection. The look on my face says it all. I look like I absolutely want to die. His hand had burned itself onto my shoulder like hydrochloric acid, and looking at that picture made me feel the exact shape of the scar again.

The worst part was when Judie, in her dusting of the various uninteresting pictures on the wall, would stop in front of that one and sigh deeply. "This picture would be so nice if you didn't have that sourpuss look on your face," she'd sniff in my general direction. I had absolutely nothing to say to her usually, and even less to say on that subject. So I just got a new sourpuss look to match the old one. Nothing changed. I knew that if I had to look at that picture every day, my heart would simply stop beating. Even though my uterus was full of tumors, that picture would be the thing to knock me dead.

"I am home," I said to my dad.

"But how are you going to pay your rent? Are you still working?"

"I've got that taken care of, at least for now. And I'm trying to get on Medicaid and emergency food stamps."

"So you're going on welfare? You think that's going to solve all of your problems?"

"No. But I, like, want to eat and have chemo. And maybe, I don't know, have a chance of beating this thing. And if I have to go on welfare, I'll go on welfare."

"But what if—"

"You can come out here if you want. But I can't leave. I can't and I won't. This is my home now." And there just wasn't anything to be said beyond that, so after listening to that hum echoing and echoing again, we said good-bye to each other and hung up the phone.

When you tell a secret, there is supposed to be a weight lifted. But I just felt heavy with the sadness of all these people who thought I was going to die. My house was a hub for gossip, and pretty much everyone who mattered to me would hear within the week. And they would come to me, and they would cry, probably, and I would be expected to comfort them, since I couldn't cry yet. And I would crush underneath the weight, all the tears.

I'm not going to lie: the attention-whore part of myself was kind of intrigued, thinking about all those people thinking about me. But it was mostly muted by the crappiness of everything, the worst-case scenario come true. I sat on my mattress numbly, the cordless phone in my hand. I knew I should get up and put it back in its base, that it would lose its battery charge and then nobody could use it, but I was just so goddamn tired. Fuck it. I hurled it in the general direction of a pile of dirty clothes on the floor. See, I'm still kind of considerate. I don't want to break the phone, because then I might not be able to call up people I love and ruin their day.

The impact of the phone hitting the pile scared a member of The Cockroach Family, and it scampered across my floor. Maybe it was on its way to a club located underneath my dresser, where all the most attractive and charming cockroaches hung out. Maybe it was going home to its family, full of news from the other side of the room. Maybe it would still be frolicking away while I lay rotting in the ground.

Normally, I didn't kill the cockroaches in my room—not because I particularly enjoyed having them around, but because my imagination is a great and luminous force. I imagined cockroach mothers bringing trap-poison back to their children, and looking around in bewilderment as they all died. I imagined the baby cockroach funerals. I imagined cockroach news anchors talking about the sudden wave of mysterious killings that had befallen their community. I imagined the terrible earthquake-like trembling my boot would bring to their happy land, the anti-foot rallies that would be held by a scared-yet-brave populace. I couldn't live with myself if I were the instigator of all that.

But you know what? Fuck it. I'm going to take them out with me. I want the floors to run with their greenish-blackish blood. Let them remember me as the biggest calamity to ever befall them. At least somebody will remember me for something.

I raised my combat-booted foot and slammed it with all my might on the cockroach's little head and body. The ground shuddered slightly, and a few more cockroaches ran out of the little hangout in my dirty laundry pile to search for their dead. I stomped on them too. Let them all come. Let them try to have a mass funeral for their beloved; let their cries ring out throughout my room. I didn't care anymore. I stamped and stomped until I couldn't see any more cockroaches, until the sweat and tears were thick in my eyes, until I literally did not have the strength to stand anymore and fell onto my mattress.

I gasped hysterically, in a way that might resemble crying if I had any mechanisms left inside me that would allow me to cry. I was a murderer. A *murderer*, and of course I deserved this tumor beneath my bellybutton. I deserved it because I wanted too much, because I told too many secrets, because I laughed too loud and because I lived too hard. Because I'd only had a few marbles worth of life in me and I played them all at once. I thought there would be more. I thought I had time for movies and TV and being lazy. I thought I had years to write my books and try to save old-growth forests and sing in a band and have a baby. Decades to fall in love, dance in the street, raise my fist at a monolithic building and scream until I was hoarse.

I saw a cockroach lying on its back, one frail leg waving languidly in the air. I saw another cockroach scurry up to it frantically and stop. It placed its feelers on the other cockroach and stood still, touching it. That was all it took for whatever rusty mechanisms in me to slowly creak into life and make me cry like a fucking baby. I lay there, shivering underneath my blanket, for the longest time. I felt the word *cancer* descend upon me, like a gigantic blow to the head, delivered by a girl who just doesn't know what else to do.

CHAPTER 2

Before I got sick, I worked at the hipster cupcake shop a few neighborhoods away. I couldn't get a job that would make my dead mama proud, sitting at an office re-arranging the pictures in my cubicle all day, because I'd gone and gotten those "FIGHT BACK" tattoos on my knuckles (the "F" and the "I" are on one finger, as I am not an exceptional 11-fingered girl). I got them so I'd never sell out, because I'd never be able to. I'd never get in that door with the razorblade handles, oiled with the blood of the working class. Or something. That's what I told people who questioned their job-stopping ability.

Really, I got them because I was super-full of fighting energy. Because I had a knife and knew how to use it, and because that made me feel better than thousands of dollars worth of therapy had. I got them because I thought I'd finally found the secret to being okay and I wanted every girl to know it too. Right up front, black capital letters with pink accents, serif font, no mistaking it. No layers of metaphor to peel away, no guesswork. FIGHT BACK I said, riding my bike in traffic. The people on the sidewalk saw "FIGHT" on my right hand, while my fellow motorists just saw the "BACK" on my left. That's right, BACK, behind me as I sneeze through the traffic. And FIGHT goes out to all those girls on the street, the ones with short skirts getting called bitch and ho and slut; the ones with short hair getting called dyke and fag and sir. "Fight," I stated simply, without opening my mouth. And usually that word passed unnoticed, but sometimes it attracted a nod or a smile or the look in someone's eyes like they really needed to hear it. And for that reason, for that reason alone, I could never regret them.

Everyone else I knew with knuckle tattoos was straight outta prison or straight off the freight train. I felt kind of stupid next to those hard-asses, my tiny fluttery hands resting on my corduroy pants. And maybe I am wussXcore, maybe I get a little misty-eyed at sunsets and write poetry for christ's sweet sake, but my old housemate Teta said *fuck those people, you've earned them* while staring at the blackened letter-shaped scars on my hands.

With those six words, she said what needed to be said. She said, in those seven syllables spoken quietly but with the utmost assurance, "Although thick-necked boys and crusty punks like to act like they have personally invented knuckle tattoos, as though they and they alone have the right to make bold, uncompromising, un-take-back-able statements, and although they might try and make you feel like you've done something wrong, *fuck those people*, because you have suffered under a great many un-fightable things: the weight of your step-brother's body on yours, and that family portrait, and how nobody noticed; the guys who think you can't fix your own bike and the girls who look at you like you just haven't figured out how to do your makeup yet; and the weight of everything else, every other thing—you can still fight back with whatever's left, and put that message on the body part that will be delivering the blows, and you should not—for even a millisecond!—feel like you are not good enough or tough enough or punk enough for those tattoos, because for the above-stated reasons and about a million more, *you've earned them*."

I needed that validation so badly I hadn't even realized it until Teta spoke that night. The worst kind of need is the one that is so huge it is unnoticeable, like the air around us. And that sentence lightened the weight on my hands, yet made them twice as powerful. I walked a little harder, I rode my bike a little faster, I held my head a little higher.

So the tattoos giveth, but they also taketh away. They gave me the strength I needed to keep on living and encouragement during rough times, stored literally at hand. But they also doomed me to a life of working lousy jobs. I guess it wasn't just those tattoos. Like I said, I'm a poet, and everyone knows poets are good for nothing. Luckily, I was also a dishwasher. Poetry can be as shimmery as a soap bubble and as stubborn as a tub full of buttercream frosting that's been sitting out all morning, so I understood these dishes well. And whenever I was getting too whiny, one thing always inspired me.

I was eighteen, on my first Greyhound ride that spanned more than 24 hours, my first night and day and night again on a bus. It was also my first time traveling through the desert and I couldn't sleep; the hours and hours of dark highway punctuated by the odd fast-food sign; the screaming babies and poky seat-mates and the distant memory of being comfortable, once, made larger and more luminous by the complete lack of comfort. By the time we pulled into a McDonald's at 4:45 in the morning, I was ready to end my troubles by diving headfirst into the milkshake machine and filling my lungs with that chalky slop.

The workers there looked like they were pondering suicide too, and really, who wouldn't be? It was so late, yet so early. Grease was everywhere. And then, this short-haired woman came in, her McDonald's uniform looking stylish the way she wore it, her hands full of flowers. She stepped behind the counter and started talking in rapid-fire Spanish, and all the dead-faced women just perked right up.

The short-haired woman buzzed around the room, so fast, so efficient, yet more graceful and dance-y than the McDonald's employee handbook probably recommended. She tucked a flower behind each woman's ear, sneaking in next to them without interrupting the rhythm of drink refills and French fry dispensing. The gloom lifted in a way that was visible. I tried to make eye contact with her when I placed my order, but she was too busy with the women. She belonged to them. I was just an intruder in the palace she'd built out of wilted lettuce and soda-ringed tray-paper.

The driver herded us back on the bus soon enough, and munching on my salty tallow-soaked potatoes, I saw my first sunrise over the desert. If you've ever seen one, you know that they're too big to squeeze into these tiny black and white letters. If you've never seen one, please know that they are big enough to erase any doubts that you're on the right path.

So, I had that shining example to draw from when I grew exhausted and cupcake-spattered. I knew I could never be as bad-ass as that woman, but because of her I knew that bad jobs can become good jobs if you bring flowers and are magical enough, and if your co-workers have the slightest bit of hope left. Sometimes you don't even need flowers. Sometimes you just need stories and impeccable timing. Sometimes even a good facial expression will do it.

When my co-workers were too busy baking cupcakes to stand around and listen to my stories, I told them to myself. I let the blobs of food in the rinse sink turn into shapes in the way that I'd let clouds turn into shapes were I on my back in a field in the sunshine. Soaking the porous plastic lids in a special bowl of soapy water, I christened it St. Rita's Home for Wayward Lids. I had to move it into the sacred rinse sink, which is supposed to be free of any dirty dishes, but if I let these lids sit in the harsh neighborhood of the pre-rinse sink, where buttercream toughs roamed the streets, who knew what would happen to them? They'd get greasy in a semi-permanent way that would just make everyone's lives harder.

I didn't tell any of my co-workers about this new branch of social services in the kitchen, but it made me happy thinking of the lids discussing among themselves how great it was to be out of the pre-rinse sink and on their way to being clean. How happy they were to be free of the tyranny of the gobs of food, the unwanted fruit bits and un-tossed Splenda packets and cupcake linings. I imagined a corny movie being made where a bitter old bowl has had it with life, and then takes in some troubled young lids and learns, through a winning combination of hard work, frustration and cute moments, how to love again.

I liked being the crazy wild-eyed dishwasher chuckling in the corner. I liked riding my bike there early in the morning. I liked it, even when I had dishpan hands and a sore back and the knees of my pants were perpetually dirty, covered in blackish kitchen-floor slime. Even when the dishes kept coming and coming and coming. Even when it was bright and balmy when I walked into the kitchen in the morning and rainy when I emerged eight hours later, like I'd stepped into an alternate universe.

When I got off work, usually around four or five in the afternoon, the city was mine for the taking. At the beginning, I was too tired to do anything after work; but after a few weeks I got really strong. I didn't need sleep; I needed to live my life. So I was on my bike and the possibilities were endless and I wrestled with the tired that threatened to knock me over, because I was young and alive and goddamn it, *I was not going to let these dishes win.*

Sometimes I'd meet up with friends for appropriate dinners: pierogies and beer with the bike messengers; Indian buffet with the intellectual grad-school dykes; 40s by the river with the crazy old men who played chess in the park all day; coffee and cigarettes with the other poets. My faggot friends and mystical healer friends would just come into the cupcake shop, so I didn't have to track them down.

My friend Tatyana and I MC'ed a monthly poetry open mic at the cafe on the north side of town. It kept me dancing on the edge of my typewriter. If I didn't have anything new to read, that meant I wouldn't be able to look out on that sea of faces, every eye trained straight on me. Sometimes my voice clunked against the wooden floor, but sometimes it pointed so resplendent towards the wall, it bounced right off, it broke and filled the room with a bright and shiny energy and I knew I had them.

Of course, I could still go on stage and be the witty MC and people would laugh and clap, but that wasn't the same thing at all. Nobody came out to see me and Tatyana bantering; they came because they wanted to witness that moment of truth, when the words were perfect, when they were strong enough to take us all somewhere else. When my hand was curled around the metal microphone, damp with nerves, I was fully present, an arrow shooting through my whole being, every neuron firing pleasantly, my skin aglow with a fire I never felt anywhere else. The furnace exploding, in the best way imaginable.

So yeah, that was my life before I got sick, and it was pretty damn good. Poems + friends + food + work, and sprinkled in were some other things= bills, blood, the occasional romantic encounter, a bite taken lustily off a tomato and chewed with finesse, fights with housemates about petty shit, blasting music behind closed doors, life-changing conversations with those same housemates who'd been pissing me off the day before, stir-fry, whiskey, train tracks, skies hidden behind buildings, late-night dumpster runs, funny conversations overheard by strangers, daydream-y visits to the Greyhound website, but never any actual leaving.

I'd get letters in our creaky rusty mailbox, full of reasons to leave. There was Jerome, who I lived with when I first dropped out of college, writing me postcards from Chicago. His slanty handwriting spoke of disenfranchised teens and odd encounters with humanity and the spare room in his apartment that was mine if I wanted it.

Kristi, my high-school girlfriend, would send me elaborately rubber-stamped envelopes from. She was going on tour with a bunch of radical crafters, teaching people how to make beautiful paper out of old crap they had laying around the house. Her spiky handwriting swirled around onion skin and little paper-bumps. Did I want to be their roadie? There was room in the van for one more....

Teta sent me long loopy-script letters from the farm. It was going great, she felt so much peace and quiet, but she was bored without us, without her city. There was plenty of space for me if I wanted to come and stay for a while...

And I put these letters in stacks, and I answered them, and I meant to do all those things and more. I just needed a little extra money; I needed to find someone to cover my shifts at the cupcake shop, or else I needed to save up enough money to quit entirely. Soon, soon, I was always telling myself. After the Food Not Bon-Bons conference, after this month's open mic, after I make enough money to pay that gas bill, after I seduce this new cute girl and she breaks my heart, I can leave town. I can do something else. Then I got sick.

CHAPTER 3

One day I was biking to work, late as usual. Work was a 20-minute bike ride when I was headed that way with no particular agenda, and 15 minutes when I was late and I cut corners, ran red lights, and generally risked my life for a few trays of cupcakes. I usually rode to work the 15-minute way. My thighs and calves straining, cutting off a honking SUV and laughing, full speed ahead all the way. But this one morning, I just could not speed up. I felt like I was expending the same amount of effort as usual but riding so goddamn slowly.

"Huh," I thought, "that's weird." And I locked up my bike and was berated gently by my boss for being late. "I'm sorry," I said. "I just couldn't go any faster."

The next day, the same thing happened again. I checked the bottom bracket on my bike; it was fine. I started waking up earlier so I'd get there on time, and as a result I started going to bed earlier. I stopped hanging out after work. I started spending a lot more time lying in bed, staring at the ceiling. I started doing the dishes slower and slower. I took vitamins, I drank more coffee, I started sleeping a whole lot more. But I was still so tired. And then there was that odd low-level pain in my gut, making me even more exhausted, like relatively mild menstrual cramps that never fully went away.

After a while, even sleeping made me tired, because I'd be woken by terrible sweats, complete drenching, so strange. Before, I could pretend that maybe I was just tired because it was winter, because I did too much, or some other convenient lie. But the sweats scared me. I would wake up and go to the bathroom, hoping maybe I just had to pee and this was my body's weird way of telling me. Making eye contact with myself in the mirror, at five a.m., my eyes looked so bright blue, so terrified, so wide.

They looked like the eyes of someone who was in trouble. Serious fucking trouble.

A day off from my job turned into a week, which turned into a month, which turned into the realization that I was kidding myself thinking this was just a little time off, that it was just a normal sickness. The management at the cupcake shop was sympathetic, but I knew they'd never hold my job for me. Those dishes needed to be washed whether or not I was sick.

I went to the health clinic at the edge of my neighborhood, only to find that they didn't have sliding-scale health care for people with no insurance. Clearly this was a common plea, as they hustled me into a social worker's office where a woman wearing a purple sweat suit and sipping coffee from a teddy-bear-themed mug was just waiting for a sicko like me to give her life some purpose.

She walked me through the welfare application, saying she would help me with all the big words, like "destitute." I wanted to show her the well-worn dictionary in my room, the one I occasionally took into my arms and squeezed as though it were a living, breathing thing; the only way I knew of to show my deep esteem. I wanted to tell her that a peek into my bank account would reveal the definition of the word "destitute," that I knew it well enough.

Instead, I smiled and nodded and took the application home. I didn't fill it out. I didn't know where my pay stubs were, and I didn't really want to go into the cupcake shop to get copies and let everyone see how sick I had become. I wasn't on the lease, so I couldn't prove I paid rent. And honestly, I didn't pay rent anymore. Lydia had been paying it for me ever since I had to leave my job, three months ago. She had a good job as a social worker, where she worked a shit-ton of hours and, not coincidentally, made a shit-ton of money. Maybe we wouldn't have thought so if we were living in condos and buying cars, but for low-budget ladies like us, Lydia had hit the big time. She could afford things like fancy groceries and movies out. She could pay my rent without it hurting her at all. The first time, we had to have a teary, intense talk about it. The second time, it was less intense. The third time, I didn't even have to ask her. She collected Tabitha's rent, withdrew fifty bucks from the stash that Xandria had given her at the beginning of the year, and wrote our landlord a check without saying anything to me. I felt relieved and terrible all at once.

Sometimes I looked at the house—don't get me wrong, I love the house, but I looked at it with its piles of dirty dishes, the cockroaches leading their complicated lives, the bubbling walls, the drafty windows, the rust-rimmed toilet—and I feared little Lydia would be swept away into Responsibility Land, into a clean, well-heated, well-scrubbed apartment. Not that there's anything wrong with that, but I wanted Lydia to stay here with us in our sweet and friendly flophouse forever. I knew the dirt and grime drove her crazy in a way it didn't me or Tabitha or Xandria. I knew that, unlike any of us, she wasn't tethered by the weight of an empty bank account. Yet, she stayed. She grew up in a loud, crowded house where there was always something interesting going on, and I think she worried that she'd be lost without that noise and wildness.

Plus, we had followed the grand dyke tradition of former lovers being great friends. Family, actually: knowing each other on the cellular level. Being the space between heartbeats, the voices in each others' heads. We were so young when we were girlfriends, and now we were grown-ups together. It made me feel so good, seeing the seeds I'd sown within her turn into nutritious bunches of kale, delicious globes of tomatoes. And the seeds she'd sown in me were now marigolds, dahlias, and the beginning of a mighty oak tree. She planted well. She fertilized.

We had met at a party in the collective house I'd moved into once I'd dropped out of school. This house was called The Slophouse and it had spraypainted turnips stenciled on the kitchen wall, it had a freebox which magically met nearly all of my clothing and/or amusement needs, it had eight occupants and needed a ninth for the smallest, least desirable room. Only a hundred and fifty bucks a month; bottomless coffee; roommates who weren't afraid to dance and scream. I gladly traded in my top-40-blasting, endless-rivers-of-party-vomit dorm room.

I'd seen Lydia around before; she went to the school I'd thrown away. But we'd never gotten to talking before that night, sitting on the ripped-up couch sharing a cigarette bummed from a loud dude who kept trying to hit on Lydia, until she threatened to castrate him and I laughed until I couldn't breathe.

Months later she confessed, "I was so fucking mad at you that first night we met, when you bragged about dropping out of school like you were some hero. I had to work so hard to get to school. I had to fight to get into honors classes at my shitty-ass high school, and I had to be the perfect brown scholarship baby to all these people who wanted to give money to poor disadvantaged students like me. You had all that handed to you and you just threw it away."

When she said that, I was stunned into silence and I realized I'd never thought about it before, I felt like such a stupid privileged asshole. It had truly not crossed my mind. I couldn't even think of a dignified, intelligent response that wouldn't be condescending, wouldn't be humiliating, or would be worthwhile at all. Instead I said, "So why didn't you scream at me like you screamed at that guy who gave us a cigarette?"

"Because I thought you were hot, and I didn't want to scare you away." I leaned in to kiss her and she turned her head away sharply. "But now that I've got you by the *cojones*"—she grabbed at my boxers in a way that was partially seductive and partially terrifying—"I can tell you that you're an annoying white person!"

"Yeah, I know. But I got scholarships too. I dreamed about college too. But once I got there, it was just such bullshit. It wasn't what I wanted to be doing. I learned so much more just riding the bus there and talking to people. I learned more fixing bikes, I learned more at two in the morning. And school was just getting in the way of all that, you know?" She nodded.

"Like," I continued, "right now I could be writing a paper about white privilege for some women's studies class. Or I could be having this conversation with you that I'm never going to forget. My sources cited are my beautiful girlfriend and the injustice of the fucken world, not some dusty textbook."

"Yeah, school is bullshit, but you need it. And you're still so lucky that you could just toss it aside when it got boring. And there's nothing you can say that will make it not true." I've always appreciated a beautiful woman who'll kick my ass when it needs a kicking. Not out of meanness, but out of a love for the truth, a passion for setting the record straight, a joy in righting the myriad wrongs of the world. So what was left for me to say, besides "I love you"? I said it and there was this small, sexy, confusing moment, where we could have fought or we could have fucked. Where a chasm grew between us, and yet, a wall burst into flames.

I loved Lydia so much, even if she did wind up leaving me for that stupid tranny boy who had better sideburns than I could ever have in my wildest most utopian dreams. I still love her, even though things were never easy. We had to question and yell and challenge and break each other, again and again. We're grown-ups now, sort of. Some things have changed, and some never will. I'm still a dork and a stupid white person; she's still a loud smart-ass. She's chubbier and more beautiful than when I met her. And even though we've processed and apologized and cried about it on more than one occasion, I'm still kind of mad at her for dumping me, even though it's been years now. I've tried to get over it, but my bitterness nourishes me like a well. It's cold and clear and never seems to run dry.

Maybe I'd be less bitter if I had a real girlfriend, but this house makes me feel like I don't even need one. I loved so hard I felt like my chest would explode, and to my great surprise, it didn't have to have anything to do with sex. It was the kind of romance that was never going to be in a movie showing at the cineplex, never be in a novel with Fabio on the cover. The romance of a friend saying exactly what you needed to hear; of tires meeting pavement; the romance of the road out; of the stars spinning a little in the sky because you were drunk but safe enough to be outside, because you were all together and you had each others' backs no matter what. Nights like that, I felt unstoppable. When it was so late, and we all had jobs to go to, or something to do in the morning, but we couldn't leave the front porch. Starry nights, cigarettes passed around, and our stories holding us together like twine. We were one gigantic hammock. Frayed but comfortable, and hopelessly enmeshed. Somebody would say something that turned the key into a secret lock in my heart, opened all sorts of trapdoors inside me. The laughter was a blanket. Nobody wanted to be the first one to go to bed. Nobody. This was all I needed: pairs and pairs of bright eyes and the glow of streetlights. I didn't need to lose my breath looking at someone; I didn't need to come with someone else's hand inside of me.

When I have a girlfriend, I don't have nights like that. I lose myself. I forget to write. I am raw, unvarnished need. I forget about anything besides burying my face in her armpit and inhaling. I forget about anything besides inside jokes delivered under blankets, besides small soft moments, besides the way her bones move in her skin. So I've done what all addicts do when they realize they can pursue their high or they can live, but not both: I've cut myself off. I can live without girlfriends. No, really, I can. Most of the time, anyway. Some nights I tossed my vibrator aside in bored disgust. I dreamt of lying in bright green fields with girls, kissing them, and it felt so real that I would wake up and reach for my girl, and then realized that I was alone in my rumpled bed, and an ache rippled through me like an echo.

But if I had a girlfriend, I'd be lying in bed by myself thinking, "Where is she? Why isn't she calling?" I would waste whole days being sad because she had done some little thing wrong, and then giddy with joy because she'd done something cute to make up for it. My vegetables would wither, my typester would get silky with cobwebs as my poems languished unwritten, my friends would roll their eyes at my absence while I tumbled in bed with a cute girl like sheets in a dryer. At the end we were fluffy, and unwrinkled by loneliness, but don't clothes always smell better drying on a rope in the sunshine? Out underneath the blue sky, flapping in the breeze? Next to each other, but still blessedly separate?

There were days when the clink of my keychain drove me completely insane. Because it's weighted down with keys, like a high school janitor, even though the only things left in my life that require keys are my house (one key for the knob, one key for the deadbolt) and my bike lock. But I still had five or six keys on there that belonged to the houses of ex-girlfriends. Girls who'd thought of me enough to go to the hardware store and get a copy of their key made, so they could hand it to me and say, *sure, come over anytime* with that special smile on their face guaranteeing that the next occasion that I turned that particular key in that particular lock I was going to come multiple times shortly afterward.

And I'm not the stalker-type so the girlfriends didn't demand the keys back when they decided they'd had enough of my bullshit. The keys were left to clink uselessly on my keychain forever and ever amen. To throw them out would be admitting a strange sort of defeat. To throw them out would mean admitting that I'd be standing out in the cold forever.

Hell, I still had the key to Lydia's old house, eighteen blocks from here, even though I know exactly where Lydia is. I know exactly where she isn't, too. She hasn't been in my bed in a while, hasn't brightened up when

I walk into a room and rushed over to kiss me, her arms around my waist squeezing me so tight I worried I'd throw up. She hasn't made me come in a long time, hasn't called me before she goes to sleep when she's away from home. That old house she used to live in has been full of weird boys for years now; and I doubt they still have the same locks. But I'll never throw that key away.

Sometimes I shivered naked in the steam of a shower that was taking too long to warm up, and I'd glance at my jutting-out hipbones, and remember the first night Lydia and I slept together, when she ran her hand down the side of my body and stopped. She touched my hipbone gently, like it was the rarest most endangered fuzzy baby animal that she'd found on the sidewalk, and then looked up and said, in an enchanted whisper, "This is my favorite part," and just like that, I was hers. And then she proceeded to fuck me like I'd never been fucked before, her small curved fingers thrusting deeply in my cunt. And I couldn't remember anything feeling so good, ever. I'd fucked a girl or two who screamed, and I thought they were just being dramatic. But Lydia pressed some kind of secret button inside of me and I howled. She just looked at me, a tough-top smirk on her face, but I could tell that she was delighted.

I remembered dancing with her in the grocery store, her arms wrapped around my hips, The Bangles playing on the background Muzak and then she suddenly leaned me against the edge of the dairy section, her teeth tugging on my lower lip, not caring who saw. Remembering that made me miss her like hell, even though she was still my best friend, still living a few feet from my bedroom door. Why didn't she remember, too? How could she stand knowing that my magical hipbone was only a few yards away, on every single one of these long cold nights, and not touch it?

Maybe those moments with Lydia were something beautiful for me to store in a jewelry box, but they weren't enough to live on. Maybe I felt better lying in bed by myself, thinking of the vegetables I'm gonna grow and the books I'm gonna write and the good conversation I just had and the friend who's going to come over and fix my brakes on my bike tomorrow just because I said *I need help* and she heard me.

Being alone made me happy. I figured shit out all by myself. I recited poetry to the bedroom walls. My voice bounced off the corners and sounded rich and so full, and I was bathed in the glow of all those words. I sang while separating grossness from less-grossness in the Food Not Bon-Bons vegetable boxes. I moved like a dervish, I loved like a phenomenon, I drank like a mercenary, I fucked like a hurricane, I wrote like a machine gun. I was alive and I loved being alive. I felt it sparkle, felt it twist and shimmer with possibility. Then I woke up one morning and got on my bike to go to work. It was so hard, all of a sudden. I just couldn't speed up, no matter how much I tried.

CHAPTER 4

After about a month of laying around the house, sipping herbal tinctures that Xandria had concocted to kick my immune system into high gear, of realizing that I wasn't going to magically get better on my own, of realizing that I'd never get the paperwork together for the clinic in my neighborhood, I'd bundled myself up and went to the free clinic downtown. I'd waited for hours and hours, trying to read the Gabriel Garcia Marquez book I'd picked up at the library on one of my few excavatory trips out, but I was feeling too shitty for surrealist fiction. So I was reduced to reading the crumpled waiting-room veteran Family Circle, which was more around my level of intellect at that point in time.

The doctor who saw me was of the nose-wrinkling variety. "Jasmine Z. McGillicuddy? That's quite a name."

"I'm quite a gal!" I said, flashing him a toothy smile. He didn't laugh.

"What's that on your hands?" I obligingly made my fists cuddle for him, keeping the same toothy smile that I hoped would project the sentiment *Don't I look like someone who's deserving of health care?* He squinted and read them back to me. "Fight back? Against what?"

"Against, you know, oppressive forces." Long silence.

"Um-hum. Well. What brings you here today?"

I tried to tell him about feeling as though my body was a girlfriend who was dumping me. I didn't know what I'd done wrong. I knew in a general way, but I didn't know exactly what had done it, and I didn't know how to make everything better again. All of my normal tricks for wooing back girlfriends were rendered useless. I could write the most heartwrenching letter known to humanity but my body couldn't read. I could make the best mix tape in the world, one that perfected the blend of poignancy and danceability, and still I'd lay exhausted from all the work of pressing the record button. I wanted to put the spark back into our relationship, but the wood was hopelessly soaked, and the flame wouldn't catch. I tried telling him this in layman's terms, but I'm sure I sounded crazy as usual.

I guess I must have sounded even crazier than I thought, because the doctor, after a few cursory looks at me, said that he thought I had a drinking problem, even though I told him I'd been too sick to drink for months. He diagnosed me with alcoholism and depression.

"Wait, wait," I said. "I've been depressed before. This isn't like being depressed."

"You're exhausted, but you can't sleep. Or else you sleep all the time. You can't eat. You're this. You're that. And you're talking so fast it seems like you're in a manic phase." He looked very tired. "Perhaps you thought you were depressed before when it was really life's troubles that were getting you down. Perhaps you never knew what depression really was until now."

"I thought you said I was in a manic phase. I thought you said I talk too fast. And what about those night sweats I've been having?"

He gave me a withering look, massaging his temples like my very presence was giving him a migraine. I walked out with a prescription for Prozac.

And I believe in myself. I do. Even though I'm a poet, and that means I'm always apologizing for the fact that I exist, even though I'm a woman in a world that hates women, and a queer in a world that hates queers; even though I leave the soy milk out on the counter, and talk too much, and genuinely hate old ladies, even the sweet doddering ones who earnestly mean no harm to anyone at all—I still believe that I am worth saving.

I knew this doctor couldn't save me. I knew he didn't give a shit whether or not I was dead in a year. Still, I thought maybe—*maybe*—he was right. Maybe I actually paid attention that day in preschool where we learned what a doctor was, how they wear white coats and we should respect them because they are Always Always Always right! Even when they don't listen to a word you say! Even when they know nothing about you and can't be bothered to read the intake questionnaire that you painstakingly filled out!

I did used to drink a whole lot. I did feel a little off-kilter. I did feel like I was too full of love and rage and sadness. And so I went to the pharmacy, I filled the prescription, and I took the pill. I held out my tongue and placed it in the center. My tongue, no matter how I try, just will not stay still, so the pill looked like a little sheep on a field at the beginning of an earthquake. The pill slid around until I took a swig of metallic tap water from a cracked mug that read "#1 Grandpa" Then it went down my throat, heading straight for my gut.

I made eye contact with myself in the bathroom mirror, my face obscured by the bottom of the mug. I drank until I couldn't anymore, and then let the mug clank onto the sink. My face looked dirty, tired and scared, in that order. The dirtiness probably had more to do with the mirror than me, and I didn't know enough to really be scared yet, so tiredness won out, and I slunk back to my room to rest for a while. The waiting room, the bus ride, the condescension had all exhausted me.

My mattress was overly familiar. I had spent so much of my time these past few months lying on it, day after pointless day. I used to think my dishwashing job was such a curse; the sweaty hands in clumsy rubber gloves, the way it made my wrists hurt so bad at the end of the day. The tiny specks of batter and frosting and coffee grounds that just would not come clean, that appeared at the corner of a dish I'd just scrubbed, like an overzealous neighbor on a TV sitcom. Now I would give anything to have it back, to have the energy to lift up a huge, greasy tray again and dunk it in the sink. To ride home covered in dirty water that turned cold in the evening air.

Maybe I am depressed, I thought. I knew in my heart of hearts that this pill wouldn't change anything. That there was no way it could. But I was so tired of fighting that I let myself believe. I should have chosen that moment to rotate my wrists, cross my arms, and look at my knuckles. I should have fought back. But instead I took my pill every day, like showing up to a job. I still felt just as sick as I had before. The idea that I had cancer, and that I felt worse because I was letting it rage through my body, did not even occur to me. Sometimes, I think that's the worst part.

But I didn't know, so I just lay there, pondering the impossible task of getting up. I'd think, *in five minutes, I will get up.* But in five minutes, I was still too tired. Usually I would lie there until I had to pee so badly I couldn't stand it anymore. I would stand, dizzy with the effort, and stumble towards the bathroom. From there, I would make the epic journey to the foreign land of the kitchen.

The kitchen was a good spot because it had the coffee maker, food, sunlight streaming in sometimes, a few chairs with backs and usually a housemate or two utilizing any of the above-named attractions. So I would drag myself to the kitchen and do some things. Made coffee or herbal tinctures. Nibbled on some food, although I didn't feel much like eating, usually. Caught up on the gossip, dissected various aspects of life. Even though I felt like shit, my voice hadn't left me, and for that I was glad. I told everyone the stories of the complicated dramas the Cockroach Family played out on my wall, the intricate patterns the dust mites made in the air, and the stories that rose to the surface of my brain after hours of mattress immersion.

When I ran out of stories to tell about myself, I would tell them stories of things I'd heard on the radio; and honestly, if it weren't for that goddamn radio I think I would have lost it completely. It was next to my bed, positioned for prime snooze-alarm-slapping back when I worked. Now, it was at the perfect length for me to extend a weary arm from the mattress and turn the dial. Usually I listened to college radio, where earnest nerds played noise and punk and soul and salsa; sometimes I flipped it over to NPR and listened to that. That radio, it was amazing. It gave me something to think about and talk about besides my own despair.

I only told them the funny stories, not the bad ones that were starting to come up, things that I'd tried so hard to forget, things that I was supposed to have drank and smoked and pilled into oblivion, that crowded their way back into my brain simply because I had run out of other things to think about.

One day I was sitting on the toilet, noticing the way the toilet paper hung, and remembered when I was ten, when Dear Abby ran a whole week's worth of letters debating which was the correct way to hang a roll of toilet paper—over or under? At the end of the week, she commented that she'd received more letters on this subject than she had about Operation: Desert Storm.

My parents were already divorced at this point in time, and my dad had custody of me, since my mom didn't have a job and collected SSI and sat around the apartment chain-smoking silently all day. But my mom had me for weekends, and I read that Dear Abby column in her nicotine-stained apartment. I had salvaged it from a pile of crap, because my dad had dropped me off five hours before and my mom had hardly said a word to me, just sat in a rickety chair and stared at a dead spider plant hanging from the ceiling, entangled in a macrame plant holder. Occasionally, she'd walk over to it and twist it around until the plant holder could twist no further, then she'd let it go and watch it spin. This small action seemed to delight her far more than my presence did.

So I started reading the pile of old newspapers, as a distraction. I commented aloud on a few of the more absurd stories. She would make a faint, odd noise in response. Then I read the Dear Abby column and thought it was just so weird. I needed some adult guidance, even if the only adult within shouting distance was a million miles away, on Planet Spider Plant or something. I explained to her what I read and asked why people care more about toilet paper than they did about a war. She turned away from the plant, slowing in its rotation, when I said that. She turned towards me, for the first time since I'd been there. She took a minute to respond, a full minute of silence where I wondered if I should ask her again, wait longer, or just leave her alone.

She looked right at me and her eyes were so big, so blue, and so empty they sent shivers up my spine. "Because people are idiots," she said, her voice flat. "They only care about things that aren't important." She lit another cigarette and stared at the spider plant, which had stopped spinning and was just hanging in the air. I stayed with her in the eerie silence until the clock struck 8, and then I scurried to the TV to watch "Beverly Hills, 90210." My dad wouldn't let me, but my mom didn't care.

She killed herself a few days after that, mid-week sometime. My dad was the one who found her when he was dropping me off for the next weekend. I was getting a soda from the vending machine in her apartment complex. Otherwise I would have been with him when he found her body. As it was, I walked down the hallway with a can of orange soda in my left hand, for me, and a can of Tab in my right hand, for my mama. And I twisted the doorknob, and began to open the door, and the door slammed shut, hard. I thought it was just my mama having one of her moods. I put her soda down to pound more effectively. "Let me in!" I crowed. And my dad opened the door a crack, and eased his body out into the hallway, with the door open as little as necessary. An awful stench followed him and I knew better than to make any fart jokes. The look in his eyes told me that fart jokes were absolutely not appropriate at this moment. And he told me to wait in the car, and I said *why,* and he said *do it,* and I said *it's cold,* and he squeezed my forearm really hard and said *do it.* And I left the can of Tab in the hall, just in case my gut instincts were wrong. I saw him at the pay phone in the lobby, making some kind of desperate call, and an ambulance coming and him letting them in and I knew, I knew before he came out to the car and told me, *Jasmine, your mother is dead;* his face wrenching away from me after spitting out the words.

She hadn't said anything to me after her Dear Abby comment. Silent that whole weekend. She handed me a bowl of oatmeal for breakfast and I was so shocked that she had even remembered that I was staying with her.

Even now, fifteen years later, I wonder if she thought of that Dear Abby column when she was laying out the pills. If she thought about a world where people were being murdered, systematically murdered, and how other people thought that wasn't as important as having the toilet paper hang a certain way. I wondered if she had hesitated before that first pill, and then thought about how people are idiots, all of them, and decided to go through with it. If only I hadn't told her.

I'd never told anyone, and I hadn't let myself think about it for years. It was too weird. It sounded so crazy. But lying on my mattress, I had time to wonder. So I wondered, even though it hurt.

I thought about other things too, funny things, hilarious makeouts and misguided adventures. Those are the stories I would tell the housemates in my daily dispatches. I never really talked about my own despair, but it hovered over everything I did. It was my accent and my punctuation. Lydia knew what was really going on, sort of, but that was out of sheer necessity, so she would continue lending me the money to pay my bills. It was like if you sponsor a child in Morocco or Latvia through a Save the Children magazine ad, you occasionally get a letter from the child you're sponsoring, so you don't feel like you're just throwing your money away.

But I didn't dare even hint at it to anyone else. Not Tabitha with her puppy-dog excitement for the way we lived our lives; I couldn't let her see the end result. What if she started shopping at the mall? Not Xandria, who had that sad history. She would just think I was whining. Not the people who came to visit me, because I knew they didn't bike all the way over here to hear about my late night barf-o-thons or abdominal pain that made me lose my breath sometimes. I know they didn't want to hear about how the days just limped on and I was beginning to wonder what was the fucking point.

I missed the outside world. But every time I went there I was so overwhelmed by weariness that I could hardly see anything about it. I had been tired before, of course—I was your typical burning-the-candle-at-both-ends, can't-let-a-job-get-in-my-damn-way kind of lady. But this was different, an exhaustion that sunk its hooks into the marrow in my bones, with weights hanging off every incision. A fishing trip gone horribly, horribly wrong. As a kid, I had hidden my dad's bait before he went on fishing trips so that the fish would be spared. I didn't think I deserved to have my story end like this, but here I am, lying on a mattress, waiting. For what, I'm no longer sure.

CHAPTER 5

The day after my C-bomb had been dropped, Lydia took a personal day from work and made some phone calls. She jerked me from my bed with a, "Come on, we're going downtown." She plucked her eyebrows in the bathroom mirror while I sat on my bed stupidly and took my wrinkled "Pride '02" shirt off at iceberg speed and put on something a little more dashing for the welfare office.

As I stirred sugar into my coffee, Lydia got her I-mean-business coat off its hanger, put on her go-to-hell shoes, and got ready to hustle me out the door. I hustled as best I could, coffee sloshing from the sides of my porcelain mug. She started the car with a cigarette in her mouth.

"Uh, Lydia? Maybe you shouldn't be...." She gave me a Look—nobody tells Lydia what to do—but she put the car into park, motor still running, got outside and smoked her cigarette in the early-spring chill. I sipped my rapidly cooling coffee and tried to pretend that we were on our way to some adventure, just like back in the old days. We were just going downtown to...ice skate! And then go to the coffee shop with all the really hot baristas, and embarrass ourselves by loudly talking about which one we wanted to make out with. Yup.

Lydia got back into the car and we drove the rest of the way in companionable silence. She hit a pothole on the way and coffee splashed all over me. She laughed at me and I resigned myself to the fact that food and drink gets all over me, no matter what the fuck I do. I took another sip and laughed right along with her. Lydia and I can never shut up, unless we're around each other. We like to joke that we are an old married couple: years of companionship, deep love but no sex. Hours of silence while she knits and I whittle or some such hobby from our Victorian childhoods. She calls me Herbert and I call her Mabel. Cardigans and old lace. It's cute, and mildly funny, and now I can't do it, because it connotes getting older. Mabel will go to the Old Spinster's Home all by herself, tying a yellow ribbon 'round the old oak tree for good ol' Herbert. I can't laugh anymore.

In the waiting room, life amused us by sending a whacked-out Vietnam-vet-turned-hippie. He wore a painter's mask over his nose and mouth with a peace sign painted on it. "My name is Sandstoan," he said, talking loudly so I could hear him over his muffled mask, "and I am here to tell you that America is Gemini rising! Gemini is the sign of the two-faced tiger, the twins of anger and more anger, and it's coming to bite us if we don't look out!"

"Amen, pal," I said.

"See, I knew I could talk to you. I saw you two girls and thought, those girls, they're fighters. They can slay whatever dragon jumps out of Uncle Sam's birthday cake."

"We're fighters? Wow, however did you come to that brilliant conclusion?" Lydia asked irritably, pointing at my knuckles. She was a social worker, and couldn't be amused by wingnuts anymore, as wingnuts don't fill out their food stamp applications properly, don't submit their required verifications in a timely manner, and often needed things to be explained to them in triplicate. She was supposed to be patient when she was on the clock, but off the clock she could be as snarly as she wished. She sighed pointedly and flipped open a magazine.

But I don't get paid to deal with wingnuts, so I can still love them. I thought this guy was fun, because he took my mind off my impending doom for a few seconds. "Are you, like, saying that Uncle Sam thinks dragons are as arousing as strippers?" I asked.

"I'm saying that America is changeable. I'm saying that it's like a snake, all curled up, and it wants to bite. I'm saying that you've gotta fight sometimes, and you've gotta stab. You've gotta fight whatever the hell is killing you. Or else," he said, his eyes wide and spooky, "it's going to get you!"

"I'm trying, dude. I am trying," I said, my voice quavering a little. Why was nothing actually funny anymore? Why did everything have to have the undertone of death?

"That's all you can do," he sighed. "I ain't got long for this world. I've got the TB."

"People still get that?" I asked incredulously. Lydia nodded yes. Social workers are so unshockable. "I have cancer," I offered, and saw Lydia wince.

"Damn, girl, you're almost as unlucky as me."

"Almost?" I asked. I wanted to say, *fuck you. You're twice my age. You've had twice as many years. Nobody is as unlucky as me.*

"Yeah. I got terrible luck. Terrible. And you know what did me in? All those years as a garbageman." I said nothing, so he continued. "Ya ever hear that saying? Break a mirror, it's seven years' bad luck?"

"Yeah," I said. Lydia shifted her magazine slightly, and I knew she was listening too.

"Well, I usedta be a garbageman." He said this like it was a punchline to a joke, and then looked at me expectantly.

"I don't get it," I said.

"Think about it," he leaned in. "Think about all those mirrors, sitting on the curb. Nobody wants 'em. So us guys come and we throw them in the truck. We push the button that compacts them. Do you see what I'm saying?" I nodded. "I got at least 1,490 years of bad luck to serve out. My grandkids'll have bad luck. They'll have three heads because they got a no-good rotten bum for a grand-dad. I shoulda saved them. I shouldn't have pressed that button. I shoulda just kept the damn mirrors. I coulda hung them all on the side. I'd have the shiniest garbage truck in the city.

But instead, I was just stupid. I wasn't thinkin'. Just following orders. And look where that got me."

All of a sudden, I loved Sandstoan. I broke into my first genuine smile since I'd heard about the tumors throwing a rager in my body. I thought about him on the back of a garbage truck, so shiny it was completely blinding, reflecting the city to itself. I imagined him healthy, his mullet flapping in the breeze, his face as luminous as his shiny garbage truck. Free of all the bad luck.

He let out a jarring, phleghmy cough that shocked me from my reverie. He wasn't on that parallel-universe garbage truck. He was here with me, in the world of the waiting room, with its nailed-down chairs and sad smiles. We were both stuck in this universe, in this world. His name was called and he shuffled off slowly towards the main office. He didn't say goodbye. Lydia and I made eye contact with each other and smiled, and she went back to her magazine and I went back to my own personal hell.

The rest of the day wasn't too interesting, just a haze of bureaucracy. We started my application for Medical Assistance, temporary disability cash, and food stamps. I learned where the food bank was. I was so proud of myself for having my Social Security card and my birth certificate, finding them even in the midst of all this bullshit. But nobody else was proud of me. According to the bureaucrats I still needed copies of my lease, every pay stub from the past four months, my bank account number, and a whole pile of other impossible things. I wasn't on the lease, I wasn't going to have a bank account soon because I don't have anything to put in it, and I have never saved a pay stub in my life. It made me dizzy to think about. Lydia tried arguing with them for me, at first in her perfectly professional, we're-all-in-this-together mode, and then getting louder and more insistent. Still the bureaucrats wouldn't budge. We left the office hours later, with a stack of photocopied paperwork in our hands, feeling slightly defeated.

On the drive home, I said, "Do you want to go to Feeding Trough and get a milkshake?"

"Ew, that food is sick." She winced slightly as she said it, and I knew she was regretting her choice of words. I didn't mind. It's not like I had stopped thinking about it or anything.

"I know, but I need something totally junky and horrible right now."

"Yeah, I know what you mean. That place is kinda funny sometimes. It might be fun."

"Okay, but I feel really shitty. Do you think we could just go to the drive-thru?" Lydia nodded her assent and we squeaked into the line of cars. She ordered two milkshakes, one chocolate, one vanilla, and a medium fry. Her treat, of course, she's healthy enough to work.

We got home and collapsed on the couch with our booty. Tabitha wandered in to see who was home and caught us savoring our junk food. "I can't believe that you guys went to Feeding Trough. Their beef is raised on rainforest land!"

"Dude, I have *cancer.* I need a fucking milkshake to make me feel better. Feeding Trough is close. Feeding Trough is cheap. And I don't wanna hear it, okay?!" The intensity of my voice would have scared me, if I had given a shit about anything anymore. Tabitha looked kind of nervous. She turned her bright little face from me to Lydia, and then left the room without saying another word.

I looked at Lydia. "Fuckin' kids," I said, and we both started laughing so hard. We used to be like that, too, full of reasons why nobody should do anything. That made it even funnier. What had made us stop? Age, exhaustion, defeat? I wasn't sure. I spit my milkshake-sip into a rough gray napkin bearing the Feeding Trough logo so I could continue laughing unencumbered. Its sticky coldness dripped all over my hands, spilling onto my thigh in uncomfortable little dots.

When we had composed ourselves, Lydia said, "At least you can win more arguments now. You kind of sucked at debating before. But now you've got this trump card."

I said, "Yeah, good thing."

"We were all wondering why you were being such a weirdo before. And now we know why. And now, nobody's going to think you're a pain in the ass. Because you have cancer."

I stopped laughing. "You guys thought I was a pain in the ass?"

"I mean, not always," said Lydia. She had that look on her face; she knew she'd gone a little too far and was trying to cover it up. "But sometimes, you'd just be going on and on and on, telling us all those weird stories that had nothing to do with anything, and we'd all be like, what the fuck is she *talking* about?"

I looked at her, horrified. I was so proud of myself, thinking I'd pulled one over on whatever the hell had derailed me. Still telling stories, still talking shit. But I had only been fooling myself. And there is nothing I hate more than deception, especially self-deception. What can I say: I'm an Aries. What can I say: I grew up under the weight of lies, and once I got free I swore I would never do that shit again. And what was worse than finding the lies inside of me? Floating around in my bloodstream; eating away at everything I had built. I know, I know—the metaphors are too obvious here.

I looked at her and I forgot what had been so funny, forgot why I had ever laughed about anything in my whole life. All I could see was my face reflected in her glasses. Two little me's, in miniature, looking as thin and transparent as ghosts.

CHAPTER 6

After all that, I went to sleep, exhausted. I was awoken a few hours later by the surprise of Lydia in my bed. "What are you doing here?" I asked, sleepily. A small, excited part of me thought maybe she had fallen in love with me again, that she was coming back into my bed for good.

She was sobbing into my shoulder. She pulled a fistful of my hair, hard, just like she used to when we were having sex. So hard, but it had never really hurt before. So hard, but now it felt misplaced without her teeth on my neck, without her other hand squeezing my nipple urgently. She used my hair as leverage to pull my head off the pillow, so that it faced hers.

"You can't die!" she wailed, right into my half-awake face. "You can't fucking die!" Then she let go of my hair and collapsed into me.

I knew one of the reasons she loved me was because I didn't bullshit her, and so I couldn't say, *no, of course I won't.* So I was silent. I wrapped my arms around her and I was silent and she knew why. She knew why. Her body convulsed with grief and I could do nothing but hold it. The longer I held her body in silence, the worse her sobbing got.

While I held her, I thought about all the nights I'd lain awake next to girls, or else just lain awake thinking about them, imagining the myriad ways that they could be taken from me. The sniper, the anvil descending from the sky, the side-swipe, the car explosion, the homophobe with a baseball bat, the derailed train, the random gunfire, the flesh-eating virus, the runaway elephant on a trampling spree, the drunk driver, the psychopath, the hunger of the world for beautiful girls.

And that was, I thought, the worst part about being in love with somebody—the fact that, at any second, they could be taken away. They could be sucked up into that vacuum that existed right outside of my arms, and I couldn't let them go into it. I wouldn't let them go into it. But there was nothing to be done. They had to leave my arms eventually. Every time I left, for work or for school or the grocery store, I left like I'd never see them again. Every time they were late to meet me, I mourned violently. I planned what I would wear to their funeral. Maybe if I went through all the craziness of losing them, I wouldn't really lose them. When they walked through the door, I treated them like they were a celebrity who'd shown up for an extremely rare appearance, like a prisoner returning home after a long sentence. I had a reputation in my gossipy dyke community as being an unusually attentive girlfriend, if a little crazy. But nobody knew why.

Fortunately, I tended to date sturdy girls, with a high survival rate, so all my worrying was thankfully wasted. I didn't mind being stuck in an endless dress rehearsal of mourning them, because after the performance I got to tumble into her arms, because I got to realize it wasn't real. I got to appreciate every cell of her, safe in my bed, thankful for one more day. But maybe if I ever stopped worrying it would happen for real. Flawed logic, sure. I don't have a problem admitting that. I'm left-handed; we're ruled by the artistic, creative side of the brain. The logical side of my head went dusty from disuse a long time ago. Yes, I failed math in high school, and had there been a class called Common Sense I would not even have bothered to show up.

Lydia isn't like that. She is more of an in-the-moment kind of lady than a worst-case-scenario one like me. Sitting and listening to her weep, having her body shudder against mine, I realized that it had never occurred to her, even once, that maybe I'd die before she did. That she'd stand awkwardly holding the heavy end of an inside joke for the rest of her life, searching for somewhere to rest it. She probably thought that she'd lose me after a gigantic fight or a natural friend-drifting, a broken lease or a huge insult. She thought she'd be the one in control, that she'd be the one saying, "Get the fuck out! I never want to see you again!" And now fate was the one screaming at her, slamming the door as she wailed in my arms. Fate was the cruel warden; she could curse in its face, she could yell and scream, she could fill out a billion yards of paperwork, but there was no undoing it. And so we lay there, clinging to each other, waiting for something to drag us apart.

After a little while, Lydia's phone rang. She wiped her snotty face on my bedspread and answered it. "Yeah? Yeah? Okay. Yeah. I'll be there."

"Who was that?" I asked, eying my contaminated bedspread warily.

"Laurel. Her and Danni and Ponyboy are going out dancing on the northside." She looked at me and started weeping again. I reached out to hug her, but she dodged me. She cried loudly into her hands for a few minutes, and then straightened herself out and said, "I am going to go out! And get really drunk! And find a cute girl! And fuck her! And then never speak to her again!" Her voice got very high-pitched at the end of her sentences, hanging on each exclamation point.

Then she got up and hurried out of my room, not bothering to shut my door. I heard her door slam and some more sobs, then a silence, and then she rushed past the door in a rather fetching outfit. I heard the front door slam, and then the house was quiet again. I tried to get back to sleep, but for some reason, I just couldn't.

CHAPTER 7

Over the course of the next few days, I became what is officially known as a Bad Housemate. I didn't do my dishes. *Fuck it, I'll be dead soon.* I did not jiggle the goddamn handle on the goddamn toilet bowl. I couldn't hear the water running from my position on the mattress, so I didn't care. I tied up the phone line for hours, on the phone with the welfare people, the hospital people, various doctors, the sweet lady at 1-800-1CANCER who listened to me cry and told me this long story about how she'd almost died but now she was just as good as new!

She told me to think of cancer as this really unfunny prankster. It was just a bad child who hadn't had enough discipline, running wild in my body throwing dirt-bombs, starting food fights, and just being a little hellion. The doctors were taking away my uterus, its favorite toy, and punishing it. Maybe it wasn't too late. She outsmarted her prankster; she'd laughed in its face, she'd gotten revenge. Maybe I could too.

This shaky metaphor made me feel a little better. Before, cancer had been an invading army razing my village. There was no way I could defeat it. But I could definitely outsmart a junior high student, no matter how much they raged against me. I used to work in group homes; I knew all about restraints and safety holds and coercion. I knew ways to calm people down when they were too angry and anger people when they were too calm.

My housemates were definitely way too calm. After I made my big announcement, we had a tense 24 hours, and then things returned to almost-normal. Normal, but with a shaky edge. Xandria invited me to drink at the train tracks with her and some boys, which she'd never done before. She had kind of a scared look in her eye when she asked me, which was also unusual. I wanted to punch her in the face, which I'd also never wanted to do before. Couldn't she see the bags under my eyes that were big enough to tuck surprises in? Where did she think I was going to get the energy to tromp around the gravelly train tracks, let alone drink beer, let alone tell stories?

When Lydia said we should all take a roadtrip to visit Teta at the subsistence farm next summer, I gritted my teeth and nodded at her. The thought of getting in the car and watching the scenery roll by for thousands of miles exhausted me. Not to mention, pumping gas, driving, hugging Teta and talking to all of her new Canadian friends. Didn't anyone see that I couldn't leave the damn house? Couldn't anyone see how sick I was? Didn't anyone remember that I was having major surgery in a few weeks? I knew they were just being nice, trying to act like everything was fine. I knew they didn't want to exclude me. For that reason, I didn't rage to their faces. I smiled and nodded and said, *sure, next year,* with all the assurance of those lucky assholes who had a next year guaranteed, and then I went up to my mattress and cried and cried until I was too exhausted to move anymore, which didn't take much. And then I would nap and get up the energy to cry some more and exhaust myself again.

I was almost too wiped out from all the emoting I'd done with the cancer lady to put the cordless phone back on its base, but I needed the phone charged for my own selfish reasons. Round 2 of Emotion-o-thon, after a nap. Nobody was downstairs, and I was glad that I wouldn't have to even try to be nice. I was glad that nobody was standing between me and my precious, precious nap.

Except it didn't matter, because I couldn't sleep. I laid on my mattress and thought about Myron. Myron was older than me; we'd met working at Wal-Mart when I was in high school. He was the only other queer person that I knew in my town. He was thirty-five and I was seventeen and we used to do drugs together on the weekends and he'd regale me with tales of living in the East Village, "back when it was cool!

Before the yuppies took over the place," he'd sniff. I'd never been to the East Village, or anywhere in New York City yet, but I ate his stories up like manna. I was starving back then. Myron had a wild couple of years and got AIDS somehow, and he had to move back to my shitty town in New Hampshire and live with his devout fundamentalist mom and work in the Wal-Mart pharmacy.

And he got really sick a few months before I left. He had to quit his job and go into the hospital. I visited him whenever I didn't have anything better to do, when I felt like I could handle it. Usually I didn't visit. I never asked him how he was doing, because I thought it would be a rude question somehow. Instead I nattered on and on about how I was going to go to college and how I was nervous but scared and who was sleeping with who at Wal-Mart and what bitchy thing which manager said.

Now I know how much Myron, sitting in his hospital bed, must have hated me. He was usually a charming faggot, so he never yelled at me like he should have. Maybe he didn't have the strength. But now that I'm laying in bed, now that my own life has been derailed while everyone else just keeps on chugging along, I think of how I was, and I hate myself.

I could be wrong, but Myron's dead now, so I can't ask him. When he told me he'd die soon, I choked. I gasped. But I didn't cry. I didn't see how it would help him to see my face turn all red and undignified. I just looked at him, breathing through my nose. Our hands were on different edges of the rough, ugly hospital blanket. I felt the texture. I memorized it.

Now I know that he wanted me to cry. I know he wanted me to reach across the bed and hold him and smear his face with my tears and let him know that I would miss him. Instead, I excused myself, went to the bathroom and cried all alone. Always the fucking tough-ass, while this amazing friend of mine sat in his hospital room by himself, waiting for the end of his life.

And I miss Myron, I miss his stories and the way he could sass out customers and get away with it. I miss going to Taco Hut with him high as a kite and freaking out the employees with inappropriate conversations at top volume. I wish I had told him that, but instead I wiped my eyes, stepped out of the bathroom, walked down the hall to his room, and said, "What are you talking about, Myron? You'll be fine. Of course you'll be fine."

At the time, I thought the look he gave me was mean. Now I'm glad that he didn't smack me for being so stupid. While I was getting drunk and smoking weed with other friends later in the afternoon, I told them about this, trying to make it into a witty anecdote. *That's Myron, being a bitch right up until the end. You've gotta admire him for that, I guess.* I saw him maybe once after that, before he slipped into a coma and died. And when he died I was sort of sad, I guess. Is that what people are going to think about me? Are they going to be sort of sad? Is that it, after all these years of screaming and fighting and fucking and writing?

I am going to be sad about leaving behind the following things: my friends, my bike, seeing bus drivers pull their empty bus to the side of the road to read a book or a paper for a few minutes, delicious smoothies on a hot no-air-conditioning summer day, drunken first kisses, steamy cups of coffee in the morning, being up all night writing, that minute when my typewriter keys sounded like a hail of gunfire because I was typing so fast, biking around listening to music from peoples' car stereos through their open windows, going swimming naked, good conversations that sparked, blue-sky autumn days, fresh vegetables, apple-cinnamon muffins right from the oven, hot sex, hilarious graffiti on the ladies' room wall at the library, talking to weirdoes, kittens, oranges, and every single thing I took for granted. All I can do right now is hope that these things are going to miss me too. I just hope that nobody is going to pretend that I'm going to be fine when I'm sitting in my hospital bed, and hope that I have the strength to tell them to fuck off if they do.

Eventually I gave up on sleeping and dragged myself downstairs. Tabitha was stirring a pot on the stove when I entered the kitchen. "Oh hey!" she said. "I stole this book from Barbs & Novels called Eat to Beat Cancer, and I made you some miso soup!" she crowed proudly. Two steaming bowls were laid out on the counter, and she was hunting through the dish-mound for some spoons. Something about her standing there, all dirty, her face red from the steam, made me feel calm for the first time in weeks.

"Tabitha, that is so sweet, especially after I was such a raging asshole the other day."

"Well, for real, dude," she said, her face getting earnest in a way that made me mildly uncomfortable. I get a little nervous having mushy conversations with all of my clothes on. "I mean, you're a really awesome person, and I want you to be okay."

"Aw, shit, man—" was all I could get out before Tabitha started crying. Seeing butch ladies and tough straight dudes cry is always so intense. It's not pretty at all. Her face got all contorted and turned bright red, and she emitted a series of bark-like cries. I reached out to touch her, but she shrugged me away. After a few minutes, in which I stood awkwardly and she shuddered, she straightened up, found a spoon, and washed it.

"Sorry," she said, not meeting my eyes.

"No, I'm sorry. I'm sorry that my tumors made you cry," I said. "They fucking suck. They aren't good for anything."

"My book said that this miso soup has been used as a cancer preventative for thousands of years," Tabitha said.

"Well, it's a little late for that," I said wryly.

"I'm glad you can, like, still make jokes and stuff. I'm glad that part isn't gone."

And I wanted to say something sharp-tongued, but I reeled myself in, and kept my thoughts to myself. Didn't she see, I mean couldn't she *understand,* that I was taking care of other people even now, when I should have been worrying about myself? That I couldn't stop? But then I thought, *shut up, you stupid bitch. This teenage girl—who, four months ago, was a total fucking stranger—just risked arrest to get you a book and spent money she probably doesn't have on a fresh tub of miso to try to save your sorry goddamn ass in the only way she knows how. And you want to tell her you need to be taken care of? You are being taken care of, you fucking asshole. So shut up and drink your soup.*

"I'm going to keep talking, as long as you keep feeding me," I said.

"Okay," she said, and we shared a look, and everything we didn't say fogged up the air, wrapped around me like a blanket. Then I raised the spoon to my lips and drank. It was delicious. Absolutely fucking delicious.

PART FOUR: LYDIA

CHAPTER 1

The doorbell rang. "I'm not getting it," I said.

"Not it!" Tabitha yelled. "I'm doing dishes!"

Violet sighed, in a pained way. "You can get it," I said. "You practically live here, anyway."

Violet stomped down the hall and opened the door. I heard a man's voice, some mumbling, then two pairs of feet walking back towards the kitchen. "Um, Lydia?" Violet said. "Maybe you can handle this..."

"Yes?" I sighed, like I'm at work and another bureaucrat's dumping more files on my desk. The man was middle-aged, white and nervous. He was wearing a dark blue windbreaker and pants that could only be described as slacks. He had a graying straw-like mustache and a nervous smile. He looked around the kitchen skittishly, like what he had to say was fluttering around somewhere and he just had to catch it.

"I'm, um, Henry McGillicuddy. Jasmine's dad?" he ventured shyly.

"Oh." I said. "Hi." I did not want to acknowledge him too warmly, because that would mean I condoned the sin of omission that he'd inflicted upon Jasmine. It would mean that I smiled upon everything he let go. Sebastian, my badass-genius-union-organizer brother, was fond of shouting, *Bad things happen when good people do nothing!* He usually said this when someone was buying something he didn't approve of, from a company that busted unions or exploited children or had a CEO who gave money to evil causes. Even though I agreed I still usually rolled my eyes at him, because really, don't they all. But the thought counted, as thoughts often do, and it burned itself onto me in the third degree. The shape of the scar, not letting me forget. Forgetting was so easy for some people.

I smiled at Jasmine's dad the same way I smiled at my more annoying clients. Professional, yet hard. A smile that said, *You need to earn my respect. And trust me, my respect is a highly valued commodity. My respect bounces off walls and shines windows with its sheer greatness.*

"I'm Lydia Morales. I'm one of Jasmine's best friends." I said, and took his hand in a firm handshake. He shrank back slightly, but still said it was nice to meet me.

"Yo, how's Jasmine doing?" Tabitha interrupted. "I saw her three days ago; she was looking good. Still talking, you know? Nothing can shut her up."

"She's...um....she's hanging in there," her dad said. "I haven't seen Jasmine in awhile, so it was...it was...quite a shock to see her now." He gave us a tense smile.

I gave him a tense smile back. I haven't been to see Jasmine since she went into the hospital, over a week ago. Some best friend, right? She'd called me a few times from her bedside phone, and I picked up, not recognizing the number. She sounded a little weaker, a little less sure of herself. But we still had shockingly normal conversations. She didn't really want to talk about her uterus that had been taken away, or whatever the hell she was going through. She wanted to talk about which nurses were hot and the stupid shit she saw on the TV bolted to the wall. And I listened and talked and laughed as though everything was fine, and then when we were through I hung up the phone and wailed. I cried and punched and gnashed and then wailed some more. I couldn't imagine what would happen if I really saw her.

She was supposed to come home two days ago, but she'd gotten a staph infection, so they were keeping her for another week. The placating part of myself that had been hammered in during social work school said: *It's just a staph infection! People get them all the time. She's in the hospital; they're monitoring it; everything is going to be just fine! Just fine! Just fine!* But the psychic part of me, the real part of me, the one I trust and honor more than any school or doctor or god, said *She's going to die. She's going to die. You'd better go see her while you still can. She's going to die.*

I got as far as the lobby last Thursday. Driving home from work, I thought I'd surprise her with a spring onion plucked from a crack in the parking lot. I parked my car and headed towards the main building, stepping over some spiky-lettered graffiti saying "DUMP ON US? WE'LL DUMP ON YOU." The mechanical doors made a little *whirr* as they parted, ushering me inside. I smelled the horrible disinfectant smell, saw the tacky art on the walls, and couldn't go on.

I rushed to a plastic-y upholstered chair and started sobbing loudly. It was the most unfortunate shade of mauve I had ever seen and that just made me cry harder. It was so *unfair.* So fucking unfair. Not that Jasmine was dying; people die all the time. But unfair that someone who appreciated color had to stay in a hospital—let alone live in a world—where this shade of mauve existed; where it was considered acceptable for the sick to sit in. Where it was deemed acceptable for the healthy people who loved them to see this, this hideous piece of chair, this ghastly thing that was supposed to be soft and comforting to those deep in grief. It was so off the mark from "soft" and "comforting" as to be insulting. I wailed into my hands until I couldn't breathe anymore. Just as I thought a wave was passing over me, I'd get a glimpse of that horrible chair and just start crying again. An infinite loop of tears. Can't stop. Won't stop.

And even though I hate Jasmine's dad for at least a dozen reasons, I love him for the bags under his eyes and the slight shake in his hands. I love him because he knows just like I know. He's the only other one who can see it, taste it, and feel it. The not-even-worth-it attempts at a smile. The sentences he trips on.

Everyone else is hiding behind a delicate, expensive floral arrangement I like to call "denial." Tabitha and Xandria and Violet and Ponyboy and Tatyana and every other person in this fucking city who doesn't care about Jasmine half as much as I do are all plying each other with reports about how she's strong, how she's tough, how she looks better today than she did yesterday. When they don't see the gigantic tower of obviousness. How her *uterus is gone.* How her *body is attacking itself.*

Jasmine's dad looked so blustery and gray and lost. He said, "She asked me to get some things of hers. Some books, and some clothes—here, I wrote this list out—I thought maybe one of you could help me find them?"

I craned my neck upwards and looked him in the eye. "Do you want to see her room?" I asked. He nodded his assent and I led him up the creaky staircase. I wanted to take his hand, but didn't. He was looking around at everything, too polite to say anything but clearly overwhelmed. I tried to see this familiar bedroom through a stranger's eyes: the dirty clothes strewn everywhere, the painting of two naked girls kissing hung on the wall. One of them is Jasmine; the painting was a present done by an old girlfriend. The ex is a mediocre artist, so the resemblance is less than stunning, but anyone with half a brain can tell that it's her. He let out a slight gasp at the picture and then just frowned all around the room. I almost said *this is your daughter's life. Deal with it,* but I was stopped by those gigantic bags under his eyes. If I said one more thing, he was going to break down, and I didn't think I could handle that.

Instead I said, "What does she need?" I dutifully handed him a few books off the overflowing bookshelf, a few ratty t-shirts, a few period-stained boxer briefs. He winced at the latter but didn't say anything, just kept looking around the room, drinking everything in. Once I ran out of things to hand over, I joined him in the staring. We stood like that for the longest time, way past the point where it was uncomfortable. I just couldn't think of anything to say. I finally came up with the brilliant one-liner: "She painted it this color."

"What?" he said, startled, as if I'd woken him.

"This used to be white. It used to be really boring. But she fixed that."

"Oh," he said, as if he didn't approve.

"Jasmine is a really cool person," I said. "She's been my....good friend for a long time."

"She's a good girl," he said. "A very good girl. Haven't seen much of her since she left college, but she's my daughter. She could always have come home. Always could have come home," and with that repetition, I realized he was mildly drunk. *Oh Mr. McGillicuddy, you middle manager disguised as a party animal!* I thought sarcastically. He sighed a ragged sigh. "This whole...situation...it's been rough."

"Yeah, I know."

"I don't know what I'm going to do...." He let the end of the sentence hit the floor, and we both listened to it roll away from us. He stiffened up. "I have to go back to the hospital. It was very nice meeting you, Miss Rodriguez." He shook my hand like he was my priest.

"Yeah," I said. We stood there, both of us. The sun had begun setting since he arrived, and the darkness was creeping in. A cockroach skittered across the floor. I suppressed a scream, and stepped on it. Mr. McGillicuddy shuddered and my face got hot from embarrassment. "We don't usually have bugs," I lied. "I don't know where these came from."

"Jasmine always was a mess," he said.

"Yeah, tell me about it." I said. "It makes me crazy. All these girls make me crazy." We looked at each other a second too long. I wanted to say *I know.* Instead I said, "Tell Jasmine I'll see her soon."

"Yes," he said. "Yes, I will." We both walked out of her room, and I shut the door behind me and walked downstairs calmly, as though nothing had happened.

CHAPTER 2

"Dude," Xandria said to Tabitha, "I just saw the craziest thing! I was out riding my bike and I saw that they're putting in a yoga studio on Fifth & Fitzgerald. At the old corner store that went out of business last year!"

"Dude," Tabitha said to Xandria, "that sucks so much. Now there's going to be *yuppies* moving into this neighborhood, cuz yoga studios, like, make them feel safer."

"I know," Xandria said, "I saw some, just the other day. This woman was walking this fancy dog down the street, and her hair was, like, perfectly done, and when she saw me she totally winced."

"Haha," said Tabitha, "gross."

They were in the kitchen and I was sitting on the loveseat in the living room. I was filing my nails, reading Assata by Assata Shakur, and trying, unsuccessfully, to forget my life. "What do you expect?" I yelled towards the kitchen. "When a bunch of white people start moving into a ghetto-ass neighborhood because it's cheap and there's nice houses, more white people follow. You guys are like cockroaches." There was a moment's delay before their reply. That moment said, *nobody asked you.* Oh well.

" Uh...Hey, it's not my fault," Xandria said.

"Yeah, I hate yuppies," Tabitha chimed in.

"It doesn't matter. *They* love seeing your little white face, cuz it's one less black face for them to avoid eye contact with," I sneered.

"You're not black!" Xandria said accusingly, stomping into the room and wiping her hands on her dirty overalls.

"So? So fucking what? I'm brown! Do you think white yuppies like seeing me?"

Xandria glared at me, and said, "Who looks more like a yuppie right now?" We stopped the screaming match for a second, almost involuntarily, and took a look, even though we didn't really have to. I'd just gotten home from work and I was wearing a ruffled light blue-and-white blouse and a darker blue skirt, which I liked because it made my ass look good but not *too* good, because I don't want to give my male co-workers a reason to keep on living. I was wearing white, control-top pantyhose and a pair of low-heeled business-casual pumps were sitting by my side. The outfit was accented by a string of fake pearls from the dollar store, for fuck's sake. Xandria was wearing her usual black overalls with the occasional patch sewn on with dental floss, with a holey red-and-yellow striped sweater on underneath. Her white-girl dreads looked like giant blonde cat-shits hanging from her head, and I stifled a giggle at that mental image. And I'd gotten used to the tattoo on her face, but I looked at it anyway. I didn't answer her question, because I didn't have to.

"None of those people wanna look at me!" Xandria continued. "I'm a scumfuck and I have this thing on my face. You've got a job just like they do, sitting in an office, collecting a paycheck. So who's making the yuppies feel more welcome?"

Oh, I wanted to kill her. "You people think you can just come in wherever you feel like it and then just do whatever you want! It's not my fucking fault if you sit on your ass all day. Nobody made you get that tattoo, so don't go bitching at me about how yuppies don't like you."

"I'm not bitching! I don't want them to like me!" Xandria yelled. "I don't want to have some sort of fucking job where I make other people rich! I don't wanna shower every day! I don't—"

"Yeah, because that's *totally* what I'm doing!" I yelled right back in her stupid face, cutting her off. "I'm sorry my job taking teens out of their shitty abusive homes and finding them better ones is so offensive to you! I'm sorry I'm saving people's lives, and I'm *really fucking sorry* that I'm not going to yes you to death so you can feel better about the fucked-up shit that you're doing." Sarcasm is, to me, like a good cup of coffee. It makes my eyes glow and my heart beat faster.

"Whatever," Xandria said, stomping up the stairs, "I'm not even going to bother arguing with you. There's no point," and I was happy, because that meant that I'd won. That sentence is nectar; it's ambrosia to my ears. I tried to get back to my book. But even though I'd made her mad enough that she went away and stopped bothering me, I was shaking with rage, read the same sentence about ten times without comprehending its meaning.

I can smell a rich kid from a mile away. I don't care how dirty they are or how many garbage cans they'd eaten from. Xandria had perfect posture, perfect diction when she wanted to. When she didn't want it, she could just cast it aside for mumbles and curses. I had to work to make my voice sound bland and non-threatening. My voice wore a business suit, not the comfortable-yet-stylish frock of the Spanglish I spoke with my mom and brothers and sister and Jasmine and my other good friends, what I slipped into when I was really safe with someone. When I was uncomfortable or angry or just at work, my voice got slower, grayer, more cutting. The business suit latched itself on and turned into a straitjacket.

And Xandria doesn't know that my soul has a hot-pink fauxhawk. But I grew up poor and I hated it, and everyone I know with hot-pink hair either has a trust fund or else they're stuck at some stupid coffee shop or record store forever. And I'm not falling into that trap. My hair is black, like it was the day I was born, and I wear it in a flip. Short, sassy, yet still business-casual enough to get health insurance. A nod to both the ironic world of 1960s airline stewardesses and the dykes who secretly loved them.

A nod to compulsory femininity, at playing hopscotch with the rules while still keeping your toe firmly in the boundary, so you don't fall off the edge. My hair now has got almost nothing to do with who I am inside, but it's close enough so that I don't feel like dying. My face is too round for a fauxhawk anyway.

I put a stray bus schedule in my book as a bookmark, grabbed my purse off the coffee table (where it was teetering on a pile of old newspapers, magazines with the covers ripped off, black plastic bags with napkins and disposable cutlery, and a whole bunch of other crap), and went outside to the porch to have a cigarette.

We have a trash-picked couch on the porch. It's a little moldy, and damp from yesterday morning's rain, but if I sat on the steps the bums would be able to see up my skirt. Bums always seem to have something to say about vaginas, and it's rarely witty or insightful. It's rarely something that makes you feel good about yourself, or the rest of humanity. So I chose to perch on the dirty porch couch. I worried about parasites crawling from the couch into my underwear and nesting in my vag, but it's a whole lot better than the peanut gallery. A whole lot better than thinking about Jasmine and what's going on with her, or about anything else that's going on in my stupid life. It's still too cold out to really be wearing a short skirt, but the chilly air on my legs feels kind of good. Distraction is everything.

About halfway through my cigarette, a dude wandered down the street. I didn't mean to catch his eye, but I did. Sometimes I can't help but look at peoples' faces. "Ey, mami," he wheezed, "lemme have a cigarette." He didn't look much crazier than most of the other dudes in my neighborhood, except for his hair, which stuck out and up at a bizarre angle, like his brain was sending out waves of intense electricity. Yet I knew somehow, before he even spoke, that he was crazy. I knew in the same way that just about every woman in the city, in any city, can tell. That instinct that makes me feel like prey. That instinct that's saved my ass, probably more times than I know, but that I hate anyway, because it reminds me that women have been hunted for so many generations that it's just natural for us to have something larger than ourselves teaching us how to survive. He bounded up the porch steps and stood in front of me. I pulled a cig from my pack and handed it over. He lit it up and then flopped down on a torn-up folding chair across from me. "You from around here?"

"Nah, I just moved here a few years ago. I grew up on the east side of the city."

"The east side?"

"Yeah, across the Taneyville River. Over in Woolslayer."

"Hmph," the guy said. "Woolslayer, huh? That's pretty nice."

"It's okay, except for that chlorine plant. Stinks up the air."

He lit my cigarette and blew the smoke out through his nostrils. "It's a lot nicer than here. I been in this neighborhood my whole goddamn life. I ain't never left," he wheezed.

"That's cool," I said, noncommittally.

"Cool? Cool! This neighborhood ain't cool! This is the worst place in the world. All the most fucked-up shit happens here every day. You don't know the shit I seen. You don't know it, mami." He said all of this to my breasts, so I pulled my hoodie zipper up as far as it could go.

Some people think that if you can string a sentence together, if you look halfway decent, you must have a super-easy life. And I'm a social worker; I know how bad my life could get. Even now, when everything is shit, when I can't eat anything because my throat is swollen from too much crying, when work is killing me, and I haven't gotten laid in over a month, and when there's two whiny white girls all up in my house bitching about gentrification like they have nothing to do with it, and Jasmine's, you know, *dying,* and some dude I don't even know is vaguely insulting me while appreciating my breasts even though they aren't on display for him; even now, I know how much worse everything has the potential to be.

"I've seen a lot of fucked-up shit too," I said.

He snorted loudly and continued smoking my cigarette. "What do you know," he grumbled, "what do you know?"

This guy was making me grit my teeth. I know a whole fucking lot, but I felt like enlightening him on this fact would be pointless. So I reached for my purse and he tensed up. "You think I'm gonna rob you, huh?" he shouted, inhaling the cigarette smoke sharply, like it was offending him.

"No," I said, "I'm thirsty." I reached into my purse and got out my tiny hot pink water bottle. I unscrewed the lid and took a long drink, half of which spilled down my chest, soaking through my hoodie and pooling in my cleavage. Classy. I took another puff of my cigarette, for something to do.

"Thirsty?!" he yelled. "Thirsty?!?"

"Um, yeah," I said. "It's, like, a natural response. Like, everyone needs water."

"I don't need water!" the guy crowed. "Back when I was in the Army, I was stranded out in the desert for seven days! And I didn't have no water! But I survived! You wanna know how I survived?"

"How?" I asked, in my most disinterested voice. I was *so* ready for him to leave.

The crazy guy took one last drag off my cigarette, and then stomped on it dramatically. He looked around and leaned in conspiratorially. "There was a...a female there." He looked around furiously again, and then said the last part in a stage whisper: "And I ate her pussy!" And then he leapt up with a dramatic flourish and ran off the porch as if I was going to come after him with a club for daring to say such things. He sped down Asterisk Street like a bat out of hell.

Like I said, people always have something to say about vaginas, and it's rarely witty or clever. I gave this guy bonus points for at least somewhat surprising me, but negative points for insulting my intelligence and smoking one of my cigarettes. I lit another one, and pondered who was more annoying: the yuppies building the yoga studio, the white girls who complained about it, or the crazy dude who talked about pussy like it was something put on this earth for his use, and his use only. I decided that I couldn't stand any of them, and smoked quickly, shivering in the cold. When I was done, I put my cigarette butt in the giant, festering coffee can we used as an ashtray and went back inside to finish my book in the privacy of my bedroom, which I have officially declared a crazy-free zone. Obviously, no place that I occupy is really a crazy-free zone, but I don't count myself in that census anymore.

CHAPTER 3

A few days later, it was a Sunday afternoon, and a very stereotypical one at that. Gray, boring, and nothing seemed quite right. Reading was pointless, I couldn't stand any of my friends, I didn't have anything to knit. Perhaps a good wank would distract me, but I was stuck on obsessing about how dirty my sex toys were. They had all been washed off beforehand, a quick rinse under the bathroom tap, but there's only so much that washing can do. Every so often, it's a good idea to sterilize the whole arsenal, you know? Who knew what germs were hanging out on Silicone Island, waiting to give my sex partners (or me) a nasty case of bacterial vaginosis? And so I boiled a cauldron of water in the kitchen, tapping my nails on the counter, with my pink polka-dotted sex-toy satchel next to me. When the water started steaming, I unceremoniously dumped the whole gang into the pot. A few droplets of water splashed my forearms, but I hardly felt the burn.

This house annoys the hell out of me, usually. Sometimes I almost forget that I have money now, that I get a paycheck every other week that's in the quadruple digits, and I don't have to put up with this shit anymore just because I'm broke. All the messes and drama, the hurt feelings, the leftovers eaten without permission. But I stay, and part of the reason why is because here I am free to do whatever the hell I want, all the time. Stand on the kitchen table and scream, fling a dumpstered cream pie at the wall or into Tabitha's face, and sterilize my sex toys in the middle of the kitchen, in the middle of the day.

The big blue cock was poking its head out over the water, and I flicked it down with the tip of my finger. The smaller burnished-gold-colored one was safely underwater, and my hot pink butt plug floated lazily. I stirred them with the tongs and thought sadly about how Jasmine referred to this whole process as "making dildo soup." She'd bound in when I was doing this and yell something like, "Making dildo soup for me, Mabel! Oh, you're so sweet!" It's weird, how much little things can hurt. I felt an ache as if she were already gone, like it was impossible for her to ever joke about my sex-toy-cleaning habits ever again.

The first night I realized Jasmine was going to die, I wailed in her face, but it didn't make me feel any better. Then I went out with my old friends Laurel and Ponyboy and danced my ass off; shook my cleavage all up in strangers' faces, drank whiskey sour after whiskey sour, but I still didn't feel any better. I wound up fucking Ponyboy, just to have something to do besides going to my bed alone and crying some more.

Ponyboy is a gorgeous boy-dyke. Gender-neutral pronouns. Utilizer of the hanky code. Skinny ass that they know how to shake. They're always after me, but I usually like to keep them at bay. They're too awkward for me to fall in love with, too apologetic, too scared, too different from the picture I have in my mind from the Person I Want. I'm thinking more like a tall brown woman with long wild black hair who can make longshoremen cry with her bad attitude and who can make academics wince with her perfectly pointy analyses. Not Ponyboy, pale and college-educated-in-a-stoned-way and smiling lazily, with a paragraphs-long gender identity, with insignificant thighs and a flat ass hidden under corduroys from the little-boy section at the thrift store. Not another skinny white girlboy who doesn't quite feel like home to me. Please, please, not another one.

But, politics be damned, I went for Pony that night because I knew they were an easy lay and I needed something to be easy. It was pretty hot climbing into their bunk bed, drunk and sweaty from dancing all night, pinching their nipple underneath layers and layers of t-shirts and binders.

Pretty hot making out underneath them, their thigh grinding against my clit and my hand tangled in the greasy curls on their head, as if I yanked hard enough I could drag them off into the land of Sex. Almost hot enough to distract me. Almost.

We rolled around as much as we could on the twin-sized bunk bed. Having sex on the top bunk, even really vanilla sex, feels a little more exciting because it seems like, at any second, you and your lover could tumble off the edge and land in a tangled heap on the carpet. And imagine if someone was in the bunk below? Whoa. That would be hot. But the only thing in the lower bunk was Pony's bass guitar, slumbering peacefully. And despite their multi-colored hanky collection, Pony's just about as vanilla as anyone can be. But that's okay, because fucking on top of this rickety frame was just about all the excitement I could take right now.

I wrenched my mouth away from our hot kiss and stuck it at the base of their neck. My teeth latched on and I gave them the angriest roaring tiger of a hickey. I love giving hickeys to the people I sleep with, something that will make them blush at work the next morning, something that will make their playful co-workers go, *Ooh, you got laid!* and their un-playful co-workers shake their heads in mute disapproval. Something small and dark and in-your-face, just like me, to remember me by. I loved bumping into them around town, seeing it fade from the neck, gradually. Various stages of healing: purple, puke-green, yellowy.

While I was sucking on their neck, they let out a guttural growl, shifting their body so their knee was no longer in my crotch. Pony pushed my dress up and ran their hand along my bare thigh, pausing for a moment at my damp undergarments. "Is this okay?" I responded an enthusiastic *yes* and they pushed my undies aside and running their finger just inside me, looking for my clit. It's right where it usually is. Their finger circled around it and my breathing got faster.

It felt so damn good that I pulled Pony's hair even harder. They wriggled down my body so they could push their face between my thighs and lap away. I thrashed around and yelped and moaned for who knows how long. When someone's got a talented tongue and it's in the vicinity of my clit, clocks melt, explode, go backwards. Time doesn't matter at all anymore.

At a particularly delicious moment, they stopped and took off their pants and boxers. Pony flipped over and put their knees next to my ears and slowly lowered their wet cunt close to my face. I knew from previous sex encounters that Pony didn't take their shirt off during sex, but was totally fine with any below-the-belt action unless they asked me to stop. I'm always fine with that sort of thing. I breathed in the smell for a second and then went to town on their clit. Pony gasped when my tongue made contact, and then put their face back into my cunt, grinding up against me, hips bucking. I reached around and slipped a finger into their wet open cunt. They gasped and didn't stop fucking my face. We stayed like that for approximately an eon, or maybe a minute. I fucked them and they fucked me until they came, crumpled on top of me and lying still for a moment, breathing.

Then they re-arranged themselves back down by my cunt, licking me until my thighs shook, like we were riding a city bus through a gravelly parking lot. They pulled away a few seconds before I came, watching me squirm, then shoved a few fingers deep inside me, while pulling the collar of my low-cut dress down to release my right nipple. Pony flicked the tiny barbell there with their tongue, not breaking rhythm with their hand, which was fucking me roughly. I came in roommate-unfriendly waves, screaming like I was being murdered, my face and right hand still slick from their pussy. They winced at how loud I was being, but didn't stop fucking me, Thank Goddess.

After I was done, Ponyboy dropped their half-naked body on top of mine and held me through the aftershocks. Warm and cozy, almost like we were partners instead of weird sexually tense friends. So warm and cozy that I started crying again.

"What's wrong?" they asked.

"Jasmine," I sobbed. "She's going to...she's going to...she's going... to...die," I choked out.

Ponyboy was Jasmine's friend before I was. They'd been at our house a lot over the last few days; they knew what was going on. "Shh," they said, smoothing my hair like a mom in a cough syrup commercial. "You don't know that," she said. "Even the doctors don't know that. We just have to wait and see."

I pulled away and looked at them with a look of utter horror. "Fuck you," I spat, and smacked them right across the face. They looked at me like a stepped-on puppy, and I realized that I'd gone too far. But I don't know how to take things back and I don't like saying I'm sorry. So there was nothing else to do besides leap out of their bed, not even bothering with the bunk bed ladder. Landing on the floor super-hard, I tried to pretend that it didn't hurt. I found my shoes and my bag somehow and ran out the door and into my car, where I cried and I cried and I cried some more, as the sun rose, until it was time to go to work looking like hell and feeling like shit.

Things have been kinda tense with me and Pony ever since then. They don't call me anymore and only meet my eyes halfway whenever we bump into each other. Their hickey was immediately covered up with a bandanna around their neck. I don't know how to tell them that Jasmine and I know each other like two little babies sucking on the same umbilical cord do. That when one side starts to fade, the other side feels it acutely. The other one does everything she can to make it stop. Even when she knows there's no stopping it. I don't know how to tell Pony that I slapped them because I was jealous that they didn't know, jealous that they lived in that comfortable ignorance, and I wanted to smack them out of it. And I'm sorry, I really am, but I don't know how to tell them.

And so I stir my sex toys in their boiling bath, nobody to use them on, thinking about all of those hundreds and hundreds of days laying around the house with Jasmine, bored and silly, all the stupid times we'd had; wishing so badly that she would back, walk through the door and say something, anything.

Instead, Tabitha came tromping into the kitchen. She peered into the pot to see what I was making, flinched a little, but also kind of chuckled too. That's why I don't leave this dump. My fancier friends are always looking for roommates and I know some of them live in cutely decorated, clean apartments, but I also know that they would get whiny about boiling sex toys in the kitchen during daylight hours. I'd have to sneak around like a drug addict. Making dildo soup in the middle of the night while my roommates slumbered doesn't sound like any kind of a life that I'm interested in living.

"I'm going to go and see Jasmine later on today," she said. "Do you wanna come?"

"Um..." I said. I stirred the cauldron, even though dildo soup doesn't really require a lot of stirring.

"She really wants to see you. It's really, like, hurting her that you haven't come yet," said Tabitha, looking at me like she was scared that I would whack her. I guess everyone is scared of that, these days. But I'd never whack Tabitha, no matter what.

"Yeah..." I said, looking off to the side. "Yeah, I guess I'll come. I don't know. When were you going to go?"

"In, like, an hour, I guess."

I looked out the window. It was starting to rain. I wondered if Tabitha would be asking me to go if I didn't have a car. "Yeah, I'll come."

"Um...would you mind driving?" Of course.

"Yeah," I said dismissively. I turned to the cauldron, lifting it off the burner. The blue flame wavered but didn't go out. Cautiously, I poured the water out at an angle that wouldn't cause my dildos to come tumbling out like playful puppies, bouncing their newly sterilized heads on all the dirty dishes. "I'll let you know when I'm ready to go, okay?" She retreated to some other room and I stood above the cauldron, the steam making my glasses useless, waiting for my clique of sex toys to cool down enough so I could pick them up without singeing my hands. I stood there, for minutes and minutes and minutes, waiting.

CHAPTER 4

I pulled into a parking spot that seemed incomprehensibly far from the hospital entrance. All those cars, all those people. The rain was coming down in sheets as I killed the engine. Tabitha unbuckled her seat belt and moved towards the door handle.

"Wait," I said. "I need another cigarette."

"Dude, you just had one!" Tabitha protested.

"Well, *dude,* I need another one," I snapped. I pulled one from my purse and pressed the lighter in my dashboard. My throat ached and my lungs said, *No, don't!* But I needed to buy some more time. The lighter popped out and I pressed my cigarette to its sweet glow. Tabitha drummed her fingernails impatiently on the door handle, clutching it like we were going to spring from the car at any moment. I cracked the window to let some of the smoke out, and rain poured all over my left knee. We said nothing. I could see that she was sorry she'd asked me, that she wished she were riding her bike in the freezing rain, instead of stuck in the car with me. "I'm just feeling kind of, you know, tense," I sighed. "You used to be a smoker too, right? You know how it is."

"Yeah," she said. "But Jasmine is still Jasmine. I was really scared the first time I went to see her, too, but it's really not that bad. It's not as scary as I thought it would be."

I took a puff and exhaled it sharply. *Quit being such a baby,* I told myself, and crushed the cigarette in the ashtray. "Let's go," I said, flicking my seat belt off like it was a sexual harasser. Without waiting for Tabitha, I slammed the door and started stalking across the parking lot, as confidently as if I'd actually known where I was going.

She caught up with me and said, "You're going the wrong way. It's the west entrance," and gently took my elbow as though I were a wandering senior citizen; steered me in another direction like an expert. When we crossed the threshold I wanted to turn back, but Tabitha kept sauntering in that general direction, and I knew I couldn't just stop, knew that I would be lost in the hospital forever without her. We navigated through a maze of elevators and escalators and endless rows of white and beige tiles. Finally we reached a room that looked like all the other rooms, save the word "McGillicuddy, J." written on a dry-erase board on the door in distracted nurse-handwriting. Tabitha strode up to it and gave it a tenuous knock.

"Yes?" came a voice from within, and we walked in. "Oh my god!" Jasmine shrieked. Her shriek had lost approximately 40% of its previous luster. I wished I hadn't noticed. "Mabel, I ain't seen ya since I had all my original teeth! And I've had dentures for years and years now," she crowed.

I couldn't think of anything in response, so I blurted out the first thing that came to mind. "I love you too, Herbert," I said; and there was a genuinely awkward moment where I realized I'd said the wrong thing, completely. I reached out to hug her and she leaned forward to hug me. But once she was in my arms, all I wanted to do was run away. Gone was the familiar Jasmine-scent of vegan BO mingled with Dr. Bronner's peppermint soap; in its wake was a completely harsh disinfectant smell. I pulled back after an appropriate time. She looked so tired. She greeted Tabitha and I bit my lip.

"So, like, how's it going?" Tabitha ventured.

"Oh, y'know," Jasmine said. "I'm in the fucking hospital, so it sucks. All last week I had this really fun roommate named Wanda Farmer who makes, like, the grandest gestures I've ever seen. I miss her. When she checked out she made me sign her hospital rulebook, like it was the program for a Broadway freakin' show or something. And I asked her why, and she said, 'Because *you're* the real star, honey!' so that was, like, cool, and then I..." I stopped listening and glanced around the room. A rumpled old-man jacket slouching on a chair suggested that Henry McGillicuddy had been around recently. A half-inflated balloon urged Jasmine to get well soon. Tacked to the bulletin board was a piece of paper with, "I'M NOT DONE YET!" in Jasmine's distinctive handwriting. My eyes stung.

"So, what's it like having good old Henry McGillicuddy in town?" I asked, working really hard to keep my voice from wavering.

"It's weird because it's not weird. You know? We watch Jeopardy! together. We gossip about our family. He sneaks soup in to me so I don't have to eat this gross-ass hospital food. And normally he'd, like, be criticizing my tattoos and my hair and my whole life, but now that he's all worried about me he leaves me alone. So that's nice."

We all looked at each other for about a minute. Then Jasmine said, "I'm starting chemo on Wednesday. They decided there's no time to waste."

"How long will you be on it?" Tabitha asked.

"I dunno, until the tumor dies. Or until I do, I guess," Jasmine said uncomfortably, and we all looked around. I am not a simpery girl. I've never shied away from eye contact. But I couldn't do it, not this time. The view out the hospital window was gray and endless.

After a few moments of awkward silence, Jasmine turned to me suddenly, a little of the old fire in her voice again. "Yes or no?"

"Yes or no what?" I asked.

"Just answer the goddamn question," she said, and I felt a surge of love flooding through my heart, un-dam-able, unstoppable. "Yes!" I crowed, and she smiled back. I knew I'd answered correctly. With great effort, she rolled onto her side, placed her feet on the floor, grabbed her IV pole with one hand, held her hospital gown closed with the other hand, and padded in the direction of the bathroom.

"Did you need my advice on whether or not to take a shit?" I said snidely.

"Oh shut up. And bring me those scissors on the desk," she answered back, just as snidely, but with a huge smile on her face.

In the harsh fluorescence of the bathroom, she looked at herself in the mirror resignedly. Then she took the scissors from my hand, held them up to her head, and began to snip at the tangled mass on her head. "I'm not gonna wait for the chemo to steal my hair," she said triumphantly. "I'm stealing it myself." Snip, snip, snip. Little flickers of hair dotted the gray formica sink. Tabitha and I watched her, not saying anything. Jasmine had always had short hair, but I couldn't imagine her bald. Her eyes would be so huge in her face. All I could think while watching her, while watching her scalp emerge like a photograph in a bath of developer, was *I'm not ready for this*—like it matters at all what I am ready for.

"I wasn't really sure if I had the gumption to do it"—her hair was almost all gone now—"but the way you said *yes,* Lydia, it was so infectious." She turned to me and smiled, a nearly-bald stranger with tufts sticking from her shockingly white scalp.

"You jackass," I said, as kindly as I could, "it's all uneven. Here, let me," and I trimmed like she was some exotic rare hedge. Warmth radiated from her scalp, and I was afraid to touch it but wasn't sure exactly why.

"Aww, Mabel," she purred, "you're such a good hairdresser."

"Hairdresser?" I said, in my best old man voice, "I'm a gardener! Oh, we have such a crazy out-of-control shrub here. It needs to get trimmed back. And I'm just the guy to do it."

"Why are you Herbert? I thought you were Mabel," she giggled.

"You think you always get to be Herbert just 'cause you're butcher than me? I wanna be Herbert sometimes too!"

"'bert in a skirt," said Jasmine, and we both giggled at the stupid rhyme. With that, I finished cutting the last wisp of hair. "There, all done."

She looked in the mirror and didn't laugh so much. "Well," she said, "I guess this is what I look like now." No one knew what to say to that.

"Sorry, but I'm tired, you guys," she finally sighed. "I think I need to take a little nap." She held out her arm and I helped her to her bed.

She held onto my hand for a little too long when she was saying goodbye to me. Or maybe I was the one who didn't let go. But once we finally disentangled, I nearly ran out the door. All I could think about was getting outside so I could have another cigarette. That's what I told myself, anyway.

Chapter 5

Another Monday at the office and stupid Brad from down the hallway was trying to impress me again. "Look at me, Lydia!" he crowed. He started dancing another flamenco dance, using staple removers as castanets. I barely looked up from my stack of paperwork. He was in the hallway, directly in front of my cubicle, and I almost wished that I had a client sitting in the waiting room, rolling their eyes and cursing my name. Then I could go into the conference room with them and shut the door and not have to see his skinny khaki-clad white-boy ass insulting me without even knowing that he's insulting me. It is mildly impressive to see someone wield those staple removers as if they were instruments of great beauty. But the mild impressiveness is overshadowed by the large waves of annoyingness.

I wanted to say, "I'm Puerto Rican; we don't do that." I wanted to say, "Get the fuck out of my cubicle, I don't want to see you right now." But being a brown girl in a mostly white office; I'm on my best behavior. Usually, anyway. Sometimes I just can't help myself. But whenever I say what's really on my mind, I get labeled as that brown bitch. I know that if I were wasting paid time like he is right now, they'd say I was lazy. But he can do it and he's just wacky and fun-loving.

"Your mother must be very proud of you, Brad," I said in a just-bitchy-enough tone of voice.

"She is!" he yelled, and then danced down the hallway, where he almost crashed into Stella, who was carrying two cups of coffee. She swerved to avoid him and splattered a few drops of coffee on the industrial gray carpeting. Stella is a middle-aged black translady who's been working here forever, seen it all, and genuinely does not give a fuck anymore. She gave Brad a look that could turn glass back into sand, and then said, "Lydia,

I need you in my office," and I followed her around the corner. She closed the door with her power-suited butt so as not to spill any more coffee.

Stella is the only goddamn person here I can stand, most of the time. She's been here long enough to be a bureaucrat, but she didn't toss her sense of humanity down the garbage disposal like the rest of them. She loves me because I'm queer and I'm brown and I'm not afraid to call bullshit. And so, even though Stella is my direct supervisor, she brings me coffee sometimes and I stop whatever rote tasks I'm doing. And she closes the door to her office and we talk some serious, *serious* shit. If anyone ever pokes their head in to ask what we're doing, she spits out a long list of jargon with such a professional air, such a no-nonsense lilt, that they eventually go away just to make her stop talking. Then Stella quietly critiques their outfit in a way that makes me squeal with delight. Sometimes she doesn't even need to say anything. She arches her eyebrow in such a way that I need to shift in my seat so I don't pee my charcoal-gray biz-cas pants laughing. That woman knows how to wield a fucking eyebrow.

"These people," I grouse. "Did you see that shit?"

"He's just a little boy who needs attention," Stella sniffed, and her intonation alone made me feel better. Today Stella was all business, asking me questions about my clients and the cases I'm handling, the progress I'm making. I was not in the mood to talk business. I wanted Stella to tell me about her life, before it's all gone. I wanted her to tell me how the queers in this city used to stick together, back when the stakes were higher. I wanted her to tell me wild stories about the sex parties she used to go to back when she was a gay man, the ones the cops were scared to break up. But she just wanted to talk about the damn clients. I looked into her eyes as she was talking. They looked tired and sad. *Me too,* I wanted to say. *Me fucking too, Stella. Let's talk about it. Let's touch each other. Not like* that. *Like sisters. Like friends.* Of course, I couldn't come out and say this, even to cool supervisors like Stella, so I just sat in my chair and listened.

"Where did you get that blazer?" I asked her. "It really brings out your eyes. You're a foxy lady, Stella," I purred.

"I got it at Starbucks," she said dismissively. "Now, what are you doing about Melissa Antoine? She's going to get kicked out of that emergency shelter this week; she's already been there way too long."

"I've been making phone calls all morning. Nobody wants to take her because she has a history of assaultive behavior and she's burned her bridges pretty much everywhere. They only want the charming street kids who don't have any problems, I guess." I sighed, angry at the whole system, at the impossibility of helping. Stella returned my sigh. She knew, all too well. "How did you get a blazer at Starbucks?" I asked.

"This bitch wouldn't quit staring at me and so I grabbed it off her chair and walked out while she was in the bathroom." Stella's eyes glowed and I couldn't tell if she was bullshitting me or not. "That's one thing I remember from when I was just a little drag queen—act like you own it and people will think you own it. I strutted right up there and walked out so confident that nobody said anything. Nobody was staring then; they just saw a career woman who knows how to *work it!*" We laughed. "What Melissa Antoine needs is to admit that she's a giant dyke. Her life will be so much better once she snacks at the clam bar, you know what I'm saying?" Stella likes to make blanket statements that are just this side of eye-roll worthy. Like, obviously this girl's life is going to suck forever. She has the saddest life story. They all do, and a little pussy-eating is not going to fix any of it.

At the same time, I could totally see Stella's point. I didn't repress my queerness for very long; maybe a few Catholic junior-high years. And I'm sure my mother will tell you that I was a better daughter back then, but I will tell you that I was an uptight pain in the ass until I realized why I liked Denise Romermayer's uniform better than the other girls': because it was a little too tight and showcased her breasts just so. And I turned the focus of my life from whining pointlessly and stressing over algebra to finding a pair of Denise Romermayer-esque breasts to squeeze, and I was a much happier girl for it. I was even happier when my older sister got me a copy of Our Bodies, Ourselves for my thirteenth birthday and I read about how you could masturbate by letting the stream from the bathtub faucet lap at your clit, and I came home after school every day and let Denise Romermayer's tongue, in the earthly form of a running stream of water, make me come in waves and waves. This did wonders for me as a person. Yup, everything got a lot better once I realized I liked the ladies. Even my hair. This college lesbian I met buying pride rings at the mall told me that girls don't go for girls with super-high hairsprayed bangs. What can I say; it was the 90s and I just did my hair like my wildest, loudest cousin without really thinking about it.

"Yeah, maybe Melissa is a dyke," I said noncommittally, jolting back from the bizarre path my brain had taken me on. "But until they start breaking ground for Miss Finster's Finishing School For Big Mean Future Dykes, we have to put her somewhere. We can't put her in the gay home if she's not out, so..."

"Have you even asked her if she'd be interested in the gay home? No, you're just making your little assumptions, Miss Lydia. Why don't you get her on the phone this afternoon and ask if she wants to go? You can at least get her on the waiting list."

"Because I don't want her screaming at me that I'm a dyke bitch who's trying to convert her."

"Oh, please. Look at you, scared of a seventeen-year-old. Is this the same Lydia Morales who stood up to the director of Human Services and, in perfectly polite, business-appropriate language, told him that he was a self-involved motherfucker who was guaranteeing our kids' failure, when he cut the budget for that program that paid for college textbooks for foster kids? While all these other assholes here thought the same thing but were too busy quaking in their ugly-ass pumps to say a damn word? You're not scared of *shit,* and you know it, and I know it too.

"Now, if only I didn't have a very important lunch with a very important foundation, I would be able to hold your sweet little hand while you tell Melissa all about Pride for Youth! And how she doesn't *have* to be a big old bulldyke like her cute little caseworker Lydia is in order to go there! And you can just see what she says, darling. You can see if she wants to go there and meet the girl she's going to gay-marry. And if she says a damn thing out of line, you know what to do. And if you talk to her in person and she tries to punch you, you can just call Bobo and she'll haul her out."

Bobo was the white butch dyke security guard. She was the mulleted type who dreamed of taking her girlfriend on an Olivia cruise, so we didn't have any real solidarity going on. She never returned my *what's up* nods until some fit-throwing client called me a dyke in the hallway. Now we nod sometimes in that way that queers have, of communicating that we see each other. Bobo reminds me of the kind of lady who could be a prison guard, but like she had a semi-change of heart and decided to hustle around wayward teens instead.

"Oh, okay, Stella," I sighed, picking up a pile of paperwork and shuffling it around aimlessly. I don't really care about Melissa Anton and her budding sexuality and her meanness. I don't care about any of these teens or their problems right now as much as I care about myself and my stupid-ass problems.

That used to be one of the best things about this ridiculous job: the perspective. When I first started, I felt like a brand-new person. No longer did I get all bent out of shape about a friend saying something stupid; or someone borrowing something that I want to wear; or meeting some girl that I wanted to fuck who had a boyfriend who I could just *tell* didn't go down on her. It was hard to care too much about any of those things when I spent all day, every day, hearing the horror stories and fighting back against the parents and schools and bureaucracies that created the horror stories. Figuring out ways to beat them; the joy when I won something for my client, when they started to claw their way out of a shitty life.

But you know what? Now I have real fucking problems too. And I don't have a caseworker to call people for me and figure out what the hell I'm going to do. I have a Xeroxed list tacked to my bulletin board with the addresses and phone numbers of every organization in this city who cares about their fellow humans at all, and I have no idea who to call. And if I did call them, what would I say? My best friend is dying and I slapped someone and nobody gets it? No. There are no organizations that can help me.

Instead, I called the emergency shelter where Melissa Antoine was staying. I'd only met with her a few times, and she was snarly and monosyllabic. She didn't trust me. Why should she? The person who picked up the phone at the shelter said that Melissa was at school for the day. Duh. Why do I even bother? I gave her my office phone number in my perfect sing-song professional voice, making sure to enunciate each number so she wouldn't write it down wrong. Otherwise, I might miss that special, magical phone call with Melissa on the other end, surly, snapping, "What the fuck do you want?"

I said to the message-taker to tell Melissa it's important, it's regarding her placement, and if she doesn't return my call bad things are going to happen. I don't care, I don't care, I don't really care if she never calls me back. I don't care if my office phone never rings again, if I quit my job and move into a cardboard box and bump into the kids I used to help, asking people for spare change downtown. I sipped at the coffee Stella had brought me, but it had grown cold.

CHAPTER 6

I came home to find Tabitha and Xandria sitting on the porch, smoking cigarettes. Tabitha looked pissed off and Xandria looked like she normally did, which was pissed off. I knew something was wrong. Of course, my heart leapt in my throat. *Jasmine.* "What happened?" I yelled, trying to keep the rising panic out of my voice.

"The fucking landlord left a fucking message on the fucking machine."

"Oh," I said, my pulse rate returning to normal. "So?"

"He's selling the house. He says we have sixty days to vacate." Xandria punctuated this sentence by reaching into the greasy paper bag on her lap, pulling out an enormous French fry, and putting the whole thing in her mouth.

"What?!?" I yelled. "He can't do that!" As I said it, I knew he could. People do it all the time. But that doesn't mean I can't yell about it.

"Sure he can," Xandria said, "I'm sure with all the yuppies moving in here he's going to get a whole swimming pool full of money, while we're out on the fucking street." She glared at me a little extra-hard at the word *yuppies.*

I gritted my teeth. I wanted to yell at Xandria but I didn't want to let the landlord divide us against each other just yet. I sat down on the porch couch, hard. Xandria chewed intently and the smell from the bag wafted towards me. A French fry sounded nice. Some salt and grease. Like I said, it's all about distractions.

I let a cigarette hang from my lips in a daze, as I reached across the couch for the greasy bag. I was in such a daze that I jumped, startled, when Tabitha came at me with a lighter. I sucked in her flame and took a big puff, then exhaled. "HE CAN'T DO THIS TO US!" I screamed at the top of my lungs. A man snoozing on the abandoned-house porch across the street lifted his head in a confused way, then went back to his mid-afternoon whiskey dreams. Tabitha just stared ahead sadly. Xandria had pulled out her knife and was idly stabbing the armrest of our tattered porch couch. I continued with my cigarette and my fistful of French fries, fuming. I was already making lists in my head about what I could do to stop this from happening. I could call Larry who works at Tenant's Rights, we went to social work school together. We could file a complaint against this stupid slumlord who apparently was tired of his little cash cow in the ghetto and wanted to sell it and embark on a new phase in his life. I even briefly wondered if I'd qualify for a loan to buy this fucking thing out from under him. For a second, it seemed kind of cool. I could grow old here and never have to worry about moving anymore. I could fill the place with housemates that I liked and quit throwing my money away lining my landlord's stupid pockets.

But then I looked at the giant gaping hole to the right of me, the hole in the porch where the wooden slats we walked on had rotted out. Six feet long, and nearly two feet wide. I shuddered, thinking of calling contractor after contractor trying to not get ripped off, and failing miserably. I thought about the ripply first-floor ceiling, the endlessly running toilet that froze sometimes in the winter, and everything else that would surely stop working once it was mine. No. No fucking way was I going to get crushed under the weight of this un-rehabilitable house, with its un-rehabilitable housemates.

"There's gotta be something we can do," Tabitha said. "Like, maybe we can call the news crew or something..."

"Yeah, I'm sure that all the suburban moms would feel really bad for us. Maybe they'd send us some chicken soup in the mail," Xandria said bitterly.

"It would leak all over our mailbox. So fuck that," I said. "But Xandria's right. The news thinks that it's good that this neighborhood is getting fixed up. Us having to move isn't really news. Lots of people are probably moving."

"But I can't just leave this house! I don't have anywhere to go!" Tabitha wailed.

"You could move in with Violet," I said.

"But Violet's *fancy.* Her housemates talk about *clothes,"* Tabitha shuddered. "And they don't compost! And aren't you always saying how stupid it is for couples to live together?"

"You and Violet are U-Haul dykes anyway. You might as well admit it. And she's got that big, nice, comfy bed. And you've got, like, two boxes worth of stuff..."

"Listen to you!" Xandria yelled. "You're totally ready to just give Tabitha away! You don't even want to fight for the house! Doesn't it mean anything to you?"

"What the hell are we supposed to do? Chain ourselves to the front door so the realtors don't get in? Take our landlord hostage until he agrees to let us stay in the house forever? There's no point in fighting it."

"You didn't answer her question," Tabitha said.

"Of course it means something to me. I've been here for three years. I had a lot of fun times here," I said, a little quieter than usual. My usage of the word *had* instead of *have* struck me. It was an official mile-marker: End of the Good Times. In this house, anyway. We all sat there, quietly. There was nothing else to say.

"Dude, what am I gonna *do?"* Tabitha whined.

"Dude, what am *I* gonna do?" Xandria growled.

I know exactly what I'm gonna do. I'm gonna get a cute little apartment, just like I've fantasized about doing so many times before. Maybe I'll move to the Flotilla neighborhood. It's closer to work and there's a whole bunch of dykes living there. Brown dykes, even. Sounds like a dream. I don't have to live on this dumpy block anymore. I have a credit card and I can make the minimum monthly payments. I'll get a set of beautiful, matching dishes and they'll only be dirty because I used them. The only sex noises I will listen to will be caused by or coming from me. The whole place will be decorated really fucking well. My mom will be happy that she raised such a hip and stylish daughter. Potential life partners will be so wowed when I drag them home that first time they won't ever want to leave. I'll have girls, boys and everyone in between fighting over who gets to take up designated shotgun in my queen-sized bed with the red velveteen comforter that's the softest thing in the whole world.

It'll be so great. So great that I put my head in my hands and wept. I heard Xandria light another cigarette and felt Tabitha's tentative little hand on my back, rubbing my left shoulder blade, stopping at the first roll of fat on my back. I was alternately comforted and irritated by her hand there. "*Fuck,*" I said.

"Yup," Xandria agreed, and we sat there, watching the sun sink beneath the stubby apartment buildings, beneath the corner store, beneath the rent-a-center, beneath the check cashing place, with the vision of people who've been told their world will be taken away soon. I saw every corner, every brick, every refraction of light from all the smashed 40oz bottles on the sidewalk. The same block that I'd seen hundreds of times. Thousands of times. The block that had become so familiar I barely noticed it anymore, like my own hands. We just watched it until it got dark and the streetlights came on. Eventually, tired of the darkness, we shuffled inside.

CHAPTER 7

Thank God Laurel called me that night. She's one of the few non-housemate friends who's still talking to me at this point. Dyke communities are basically junior high and everyone's mad at me because Pony is mad at me. This sort of community and solidarity is great when people are on your side. The only time you call it petty and immature is when it's directed against you. But, I've been through enough queer drama to know that eventually someone else will create a scandal so huge that everyone will forget that I ever slapped Ponyboy.

That doesn't mean it doesn't hurt when people who hugged you last week avoid making eye contact this week. Still makes you wonder if you're, like, completely expendable or if everyone you know is just really stupid. It seems unlikely that *everyone* is stupid, and therefore the little monster on your shoulder gets to say, "See, see, it really is you," and then you feel like *shit,* and it's never gonna change until you leave town and even then it won't really change because a) all dykes, all scenes, are pretty much the same everywhere and b) who the fuck are you kidding, you ain't ever leaving this city. Not alive, anyway.

So. Friend of the Year Award goes to Laurel because she stepped above the drama and invited me to a party at Fort Square!, a house full of older, quieter anarchists. Mostly straight, so the chances are good that nobody in attendance hates me. So, sure, I'd go. I needed to get out of this doomed house.

I put on my party hoodie, but before I did that I sprayed a little perfume in my cleavage just because it seemed like a funny thing to do. Like I still had hope or something. I doubted anyone would be burying their face in my tits tonight, but you never know. Then I clambered onto my bike and pointed it in the direction of Laurel's house. My bike usually sits pouty and unused in the backyard but I thought tonight would be a good night to give it a spin and remind it of its purpose in life. My bike is an old-school red cruiser. It's got as much personality as it does rust so I try to avoid doing anything heavy-duty with it. Just little stupid trips, to parties. I know when I ride home bombed at three a.m. I won't be able to go too fast and that will be a blessing.

I squeaked and shrieked all the way to Laurel's house. She lives in a third-floor apartment on the edge of my neighborhood. Hardwood floors and a quiet roommate she barely knows. They're both queer and like philosophy and don't eat each other's expensive organic cereal; that's enough for Laurel. She's not really happy, but nobody is. Her last name and first initial was written in gorgeous handwriting on a cutesy piece of crafty cardstock next to the buzzer. I leaned on it and she buzzed me in.

Laurel. Six-foot tall redhead. Her very presence spells *trouble*, which just happens to be my favorite word. When I tromped up the stairs she was trying to sausage into some ridiculous ruffled outfit. I sat on the edge of her bed and looked through the pile of clothes on it, making comments on the relative cuteness or not-cuteness of each piece. She sang to me and I clapped when she was done. We debated making some more coffee because we were both exhausted, but decided against it. Drinking coffee before booze always makes me so sick. So instead we rolled on down to the beer distributor and each got a brightly colored 40 of cheap malt liquor with some sort of energy beverage mixed inside, guaranteed to make us both completely insane, and then walked the rest of the way to Fort Square! We talked about lots of things, but I didn't tell her that we were getting evicted. Just wasn't in the mood to bring the evening down. Besides, talking can sometimes make things real, and I wasn't ready to have this be real. Not yet.

Fort Square! lives up to its name, but sometimes it can be fun in a low-key way. When we got there the front porch was full to bursting and nobody was inside. Typical. We pushed our way through the porch to investigate, anyway. There was a bearded manarchist playing some old-yet-important punk record. A few other manarchists sipped their 40s in tune with the verses and yelled the chorus, fists in the air. Laurel's always good for a shared eye-roll. Now was one of those times.

Laurel's upper arm is strong and soft, and I clung to it as she led me through the narrow house to the kitchen. Kitchens are good places to hang out when the music is kinda crappy and you don't really know anyone. Kitchens are good places to crack open your malt liquor, clink it with your companion's, and wait for something good to happen.

I've been drinking a little more than usual lately. I think it's fine. It's not like I'm turning into Xandria or anything. Just loosening the worry that I'm carrying in my lungs and shoulders and heart as of late. Drinking's the easiest and quickest and most effective way. Not the best way, not the smartest way, but I know I've gotta be mediocre sometimes. Drinking is also excellent for dealing with boring parties and loosening sexual inhibitions. So, I'd like to thank the beer distributor for being there when I need them and to the fine makers of this beverage, Panther's Piss or whatever the fuck it's called, for contributing oh so much to the quality of my life.

The scene in the kitchen was a little more relaxed, a little more accessible. I distributed my hi's to acquaintances and participated in the usual party chit-chat. Halfway through my first twenty ounces Laurel had somehow found the gayest man possible and together they had staged a coup over the stereo. They put on the pop station that all the younger, dorkier clients at work love and Laurel was busy dancing all up on this guy's willing butt. What else could I do but take a few heroically huge sips and join them? All those formerly fist-pumping dudes are sullen in the corner now, arms folded, staring daggers or laughing condescendingly.

I stood in front of our new buddy, facing Laurel (who's really going to town on his fine posterior), so he's the gayboy meat in our nutritious queer sandwich. He giggled coyly at me and I reached up towards his cliché bleached-unnaturally-blonde-and-spiky hair and pretended that one of his gel-spikes had pricked my finger, making a face like I was in sharp unnecessary pain. He giggled some more and I couldn't help but giggle back because we are just the gayest thing in the whole wide world. Those punks can talk about whatever they wanna talk about on the porch. We're fine right here.

Eventually the stereo was strong-armed away from us, but by then we were too drunk and giddy to care. We went outside to the porch and collapsed in a silly heap. I pulled my cigarettes from my stockings and a lighter from my cleavage and lit up. My new best friend Brent just collapsed in a fit of laughter and said, "I *loooove* her!" His enthusiasm seemed so out of place on this stern porch, and I wondered how he wound up here. How did any of us wind up here? Questions to ponder on a front porch where you aren't *un*welcome but aren't exactly welcome either.

Brent went inside to fetch us some cheap beer because we're dangerously, dangerously low and tonight is just getting started. While he's away I listened to an intense debate about the merits vs. dangers of eating roadkill. I bit my lip and tried to circle-breathe like I learned in some tantric skill-sharing class I took two girlfriends ago. Perhaps I can get to some elevated state where things like anarcho-primitivists ignoring germs and best friends dying of cancer and evictions and bad parties just don't happen. Breathe in. Out. In. Out. I'm trying to nourish myself with this bad city air, with these bad vibes.

But that wasn't enough to stop me from blurting, "Eww! Don't you know that shit can kill you? You're not supposed to be eating meat that's been lying there!"

The intrepid roadkill eater turned his head slightly towards me, regarded me for a second, and then turned back as if I were not even worth acknowledging. Thank gawd Brent was headed back towards me with another beer. I took it and turned to Laurel. "Let's get the fuck out of here.

I hate these people!" I was so drunk already and it was barely midnight, but big deal. Of course, the alcohol loosened my already tenuous grip on my volume control, and everyone on the porch could hear what I just said. At my passionate declaration that I hated them, some of the roadkill fans turned to me to give me extra-pointed glares. "Where the hell am I gonna take you?" said Laurel. "Because, you know…"

"…all our friends hate me?" I said, and then collapsed into a round of bitter giggles. It probably sounded more like a garbage truck than a sound of true mirth, but whatever. I'm not trying to win a laughing pageant. The roadkill guru finally deigned to speak to me. "People hate *you?*" he sneered. "*Whoa.* I wonder why." This drew a large round of giggles from the peanut gallery. And it gave me license to open my mouth.

"Oh," I yelled, "I'm soooooooo concerned about what a bottom feeder like you thinks! I'm sure you're an excellent judge of character, motherfucker! Why don't you fry some tire-flavored squirrel and, like, shut the fuck up!" Before anyone could react I grabbed Brent's arm. "You have a car, right? You're sober enough to drive, right?" He nodded. "Let's go!" I heard someone laughing raucously at what I'd just said. It was Laurel, of course. Everyone else was looking at me in a state of shock.

I hopped off the porch and started walking until I realized I had no idea where I was going, because I'd never seen Brent's car. I should have guessed that it had the little blue and yellow equals sign plastered on the rearview mirror, a quiet nod at the gays. We shuffled into the car before we realized we had nowhere to go. There was talk of going to the all-night diner across town, and talk of going to the incredibly cheesy gay bar that was a little closer. Brent's car smelled like disinfected pot, with a strong fake-cherry scent. I sat in the backseat and laughed to myself. I was just happy to be out of the house. Out of that house, out of my house, out of any one of the houses. I just don't care anymore. Let me sit forever in the overly-clean car of this person I barely know, obviously a parental knockoff, a quiet sensible car that belongs in the suburbs, that has no idea how it wound up on this current block, in its current predicament. Oh, sentence me to a lifetime of non-sexual backseats, of sitting and letting somebody else drive, somebody else make the decision. I accept, I agree, I surrender. I'm done.

EPILOGUE: TWO MONTHS LATER

Tabitha was scrubbing the bathtub for the first and last time. She had never been motivated to clean it before, wasn't really the bath-taking type, hardly noticed if there was a little ring around the tub, or if the toilet was discolored and rusty, or if there were toothpaste splatters on the sink. But now the Security Deposit and the prospect of losing it loomed above her. It was the Landlord, that mysterious name at a suburban address, ruining everything by stepping back into the picture. It was, finally, the Last Day of the House.

Tabitha shook another cloud of corner-store cleaning toxins out of the shaker can, held her breath for a second so the scary poison dust wouldn't settle into her lungs, and looked around her. Already, the house felt like a historic battlefield: empty, but with palpable ghosts all around. Moving all of her shit out had been bad enough. Somehow, the one bag that Tabitha had brought when she moved to this city had sprouted into a whole closetful of stuff. She had thought that she pared her belongings down to the bare minimum a person could have while still maintaining a tiny bit of sentimentality.

But it didn't all fit into her army bag, milk crate, old suitcase and saggy cardboard box. She had packed those days ago, and there was still so much of her life seeping over the edges. Where did all of this come from? She couldn't recall going shopping, couldn't recall getting any presents, besides the copper-colored dildo and harness from Violet. That was more for Violet's benefit than hers, so it hardly counted as a present, and it was safely stored at Violet's anyway. But all this stuff! No matter how much she packed, it seemed as if she'd just begun. She looked around at her room, the walls bare again, just like they had been when she first arrived, and thought *I should be better at leaving places by now.*

But she'd somehow gotten it all done, and last night, Violet had borrowed her roommate's car and together they had shoved all of Tabitha's belongings into the trunk and backseat. The usual moving mishaps occurred: Tabitha stepped on Violet's foot and Violet got pouty; Violet threw a box into the trunk too hard and there was the unmistakable *crunch* of something breaking, and for a moment it seemed as if the little car didn't have enough room for all of Tabitha's things. Violet's house wasn't far and they could always make two trips, but it seemed like a bad omen somehow.

Tabitha decided to forfeit her place at the front seat to a few boxes, and just ride her bike over to Violet's…no, *their* house to help unpack. She rode furiously, hoping to somehow beat Violet, in that car weighted down by all of her earthly possessions. But of course Violet arrived first, at that place that couldn't yet be called home. And they'd hauled all the boxes upstairs, piled them in a pile that seemed so large and impossible to deal with, and Violet's room seemed so small now. Tabitha had slept there hundreds of times before, but now it was strange, now she thought of her little room on Asterisk Street and wished she were there, even if it meant that she was alone. But when Violet pulled her close, and whispered into the space between her shoulder and her neck *I'm glad you're here with me,* Tabitha relaxed and fell asleep inside of a confused happiness.

And in the morning she got up and rode back to her old house, because they only had one day left to make it clean enough to maybe get some of their money back. The house was never going to be clean, it couldn't possibly be clean enough, it was pointless to even try, but they were going to try and keep trying and try some more, because they didn't know what else to do, because if they weren't cleaning they might be crying, and they couldn't cry now, not when there was so much work left to be done.

The paper towel seemed impossibly heavy. The scrubbing motions felt unbelievably futile. Nothing was ever going to get any better. This tub was never going to be clean enough. How could she know how clean the landlord wanted the tub to be when she'd never even seen his face?

She wiped the tub again and then threw the dirty paper towels into an overflowing black trash bag in the hallway. Stepping over it, she walked past the oversized closet that used to be Xandria's room. Xandria had taken off last week. Hadn't said goodbye to anyone or even said she was leaving. One day her room was full of winejugs and t-shirts, the next day it had nothing but a key, gleaming and silent in the middle of the floor. Tabitha walked into her room. It was no longer the place where she'd first read so many books full of ideas that blew her mind wide open, first fit her entire fist into Violet's cunt as Violet writhed and moaned beneath her, first learned what it was like to wake up safe and happy. Now her room was little more than an unfinished to-do list: Carry mattress down stairs, throw out. Sweep floor yet again. Recycle old stack of newspapers. Paint over graffiti. Say good-bye.

But she couldn't do any of these things, not yet, so she shuffled past Lydia's room, now just a collection of neatly-stacked boxes and a pile of unsorted things on the floor. The door was open, Lydia's back to it, and she was leaning out the window, singing along with her stereo in a powerful and sad way. By the way her head was thrown back, Tabitha knew Lydia thought she was alone in the house, and there was something about the mournful lilt to Lydia's voice that was mesmerizing.

Lydia sat on her floor and sang along with the stereo. She was all cried-out and useless, packing boxes in a daze. She'd signed a lease on a tiny, cozy one-bedroom apartment in a cute little building with hardwood floors and accordion heaters; a gardening-and-dogs faggot couple on the bottom floor, an acrylics-and-plastic-toys wild-eyed artist lady above her. Now there was nothing left to do but be on autopilot.

Somehow, packing boxes was more fun when she pretended that she was a robot. *Just 5 more boxes, and then I can plug myself into the power source!* She laughed despite herself. She had the usual moment of wondering whether or not she was crazy, and then the self-reassurance that if she actually were crazy, she probably wouldn't know it. Pack, pack, pack, in time with the music, only stopping when a song really hit her and she just had to sing.

The rain started pounding down outside the window, and Lydia hated the rain, hated being damp and cold, but something else compelled her to open the window as wide as she could and lean out, dangerously, precariously. The rain soaked Lydia's hair, it fogged up her glasses, and it ran in rivulets down her neck. But something about it made her feel awake and alive, like all the droplets had some sort of electricity. She sang along with her stereo, out to the whole neighborhood: *In my dreams you're alive and you're crying/and your mouth moves with mine, soft and sweet...* It was just then that her glasses slid off the bridge of her nose and crashed to the sidewalk below. "SHIT!" she yelled, breaking the reverie, and scrambled out into the hallway, past a confused-looking Tabitha who was hanging out in the hallway for no apparent reason, and down the stairs, out the door in barefeet.

She scooped up her glasses; they were untraumatized by their leap. Now that she was outside, she couldn't help but twirl around a little bit in the rain, it just felt so good. She spun and spun until she was dizzy, and it wasn't until a car slowed and some man inside said, *Damn, girl, you want a ride?* that she realized the white vintage lace slip she'd been wearing had become rain-soaked and translucent. The moment thoroughly ruined, she stomped inside.

The mail was scattered all over the floor, under the mail slot. She'd been in too much of a hurry to pick it up before, but now she bent over and grabbed it, rifled through for the final time. It seemed strange, like mail being delivered to an empty lot, like the postman should know about their lives were being uprooted and return all their mail to its senders. A store circular, a community-college catalog addressed to some unknown person, and a letter addressed "To the Asterisk Street Ladies," in familiar handwriting with an unfamiliar return address.

It was from Jasmine. Jasmine, whose room had been standing empty for a long time now. Whose endless piles of crap Lydia had boxed and driven to the house of an aunt in the suburbs who was letting Jasmine stay in the guest room while she was recovering from chemo. She'd wanted to come back home, but two weeks into the treatment it had become obvious that that wasn't going to happen. She endlessly tied up the house's only bathroom with her gagging and retching and barfing, and everyone knew that she was going through hell so nobody wanted to say anything, but their distended bladders and sphincters were becoming a problem, rushing into the foul-smelling, scary-energy bathroom between vomiting rounds.

And then there was the simple fact that Jasmine was so different now, so sick and so scared-looking, not able to eat or talk really, perched in her room like a vulture. It made them all uncomfortable, especially her. So one Saturday, Lydia's car was loaded up, pulling a U-Haul trailer behind it, with a shaky Jasmine up front, gripping the front door handle like she was going to jump out of the car at any second. And they hadn't heard from her since. Sometimes Tabitha called Jasmine's aunt to get status reports, so they knew that she was still alive, but very sick, and didn't want visitors. But here it was, an actual communiqué! Lydia's hands shook a little. She opened the envelope like she was taking off someone's underwear for the first time, and hungrily read:

hi guys,

i'm sorry, i know you're not guys. ladies. women. whatever gender you identify as. i miss you all, and i wish i could be there with you to help get the house ready. i am sorry if you had to clean up any of my messes. it's been weird being out here in the suburbs. i'm glad my aunt ranette is letting me stay here, cuz i'd be totally fucked if she didn't, but it's so weird being inside a normal-people house again. everything is so quiet. and clean. and disinfected. & it's what i need right now, it's just the way it is. i guess i never appreciated our house enough when i had it (well, i did, but i didn't, you know?). & now it's gone, or it will be, soon enough.

don't repaint the walls white until you have to. don't be too grossed out when you scrape the dried tomato bits off the walls and scrub the rotten pear splatters off the ceilings. own it. remember it. love it. it's the most beautiful rot, because it's ours. i know it looks disgusting in the morning, but remember that night when it happened? that's the important part.

i don't even have to tell you. you know all this. it's hard for me to talk these days, i really have to be in the mood and the mood usually strikes in the middle of the night when nobody's around. but i can write when i'm feeling better. pretty sick most of the time. feel like shit. TV has never been so informative or necessary. right on my level. nobody in that little glowy box looks like me, or like any of you, or like anyone i love really. it makes me sad, but i don't have the energy for anything else right now. i want you to write me and tell me how you're doing.

i wish i could be there. i really do. i want to stand with you all at that final moment, when the door is locked for the last time, deadbolts turned, & then you all take your keys and throw them through the mail slot just like the landlord asked you to. right before you let go of the keys, you will all look at each other like, "well, what now?" & when you open the mail slot, the sun will be setting towards the back of the house, & you'll see the light shining through the crack. it will be so, so bright, & it'll make your heart hurt for a second (yes, even resident badass Xandria and badass-in-training Tabitha and seen-it-

all-social-worker Lydia, do not think you are exempt) because you want to be inside with it, but now you're outside, and as the key clinks to the floor you will realize that you've lost your chance to get back inside, forever. & the light will begin to look terrible, & you'll all have to hug quickly and then leave. rip that band-aid off. i know it sounds stupid, but i want to stand there with all of you when you hear that clink. i want to be there, with all of you, when it ends.

xo, jasmine

AUTHOR'S NOTE #1

If you didn't know, "Food Not Bon-Bons" is a jokey reference to Food Not Bombs, a long-running group with chapters all over the country that makes food for hungry, usually homeless folks using food that grocery stores have thrown away (not from dumpstering, which is illegal in most cities/states). i changed the name because they're a notoriously paranoid bunch (although i guess i'm blowing up their spot here), plus the name made me giggle to myself throughout the long hours of writing. Intrigued? Look them up!

AUTHOR'S NOTE #2

Thanks to everyone who donated to the IndieGoGo campaign to help make this book happen. Were it not for all of you, this book would not exist in its physical form.

Extra-special thanks to those who dug a little deeper and contributed above and beyond:

Erin Bruckner
John & Patricia Bruckner
Jackie Capewell
Jill Capewell
Etta Cetera
Dr. Helgo Eberwein
Cara Levine
Sequoyah
Mike Thompson
LizBot Walsh
as well as a few kind souls who have chosen to remain anonymous.

Thank you.

GRATITUDE

Thanks first and foremost to my punkhouse comrades from 2001-2007, especially the residents and hangers-on of La Concha & Cobra Command. You've taught me so much. Extra special thanks goes to Sharon. Were it not for her overflowing compost pile and fierce belief in my writing, this novel would not exist. Also extra-special thanks goes out to Axi Nue, the high-voltage thug of brilliance, for a spark that lasts decades & the awareness that we have to make shit happen, *now*.

Thanks to my editors/encouragers. It truly does take a village to raise a novel, and they raised it from a bratty four-paged story to a real live book: Arthur Larsen, Brenda DeMartini-Squires, Emily Jacobson, Fran Padilla, Jill Capewell, Lara Hauer, Maxine D'aubin Costa, Merrill Feitell, Monica Avery and Oliver Haimson. Ray helped with the title. Cassie J. Snider, Karen Lillis, Maranda Elizabeth and Sassafras Lowrey provided invaluable self-publishing advice and encouragement. The craft nighters Amanda, Amy, Ben, Heather, O'Ryan and Stephanie were an attentive and respectful early audience, and every single person who showed up at this novel's first reading at Fleeting Pages (RIP) in Pittsburgh truly made my heart overflow, and helped me believe that I could really do this.

Thanks to my mom, Jackie Young Capewell, for getting me hooked on books at an early age and partially inspiring this book with one of her wacky statements. Thanks to my dad, Richard Capewell, for showing me the power of a good story told well. Thanks to my brother and sister, Tom & Jill Capewell, for being hilarious and creative and always believing in me. Thanks to my chosen siblings Erin Bruckner, Eric Gloeckner and Kastoory Kazi for twenty years of good times. Thanks to the Thompson family for your support and your embrace of the wackier side of life. Thanks to everyone else in my chosen and blood family. You know who you are.

Thanks to all of my friends near and far—too many to list, but you know I love you. Thanks to Adam for being the sweetest vegan cupcake that ever was, and for getting me a copy of InDesign so I could lay this book out. Thanks to Ari (and MRR) for teaching me how to use InDesign. Thanks to clients for keeping me humble, making me laugh & teaching me about resilience; thanks to my co-workers for getting it. Thanks to everyone fighting the good fight, especially the ones against prisons and apathy. Thanks to zine and blog readers. And of course, dear reader, thanks to you.

ABOUT THE AUTHOR

Ocean Capewell was born in Queens and raised on Long Island, NY. She learned how to edit at SUNY Purchase, and became a nicer and more community-minded person in Pittsburgh, PA. She has been writing ever since she could hold a pen, and has been publishing zines since 1996, most recently under the semi-popular High On Burning Photographs title. Ocean now lives in the San Francisco Bay Area. She is a (unlicensed) social worker by trade, and currently works in the crisis residential mental health field. She is also a prison abolitionist, and has been involved in prisoner support work since 2001. She is writing a memoir called The Wrong Universe, about the boundaries of gender and what happens when we transgress them.

Ocean is (generally) better about responding to postal mail than e-mail. You can write to her and send her (non-creepy) stuff at: P.O. Box 22274, Oakland, CA 94607. (Incarcerated people--I love and support you, but I can't afford to send free copies of this book; and I can't take on another fulltime penpal. Sorry. But I'd love to hear what you think of this book; you're more than welcome to drop me a line!)

Ocean also blogs about this book and the process of creating it at http://www.mostbeautifulrot.com.